BOOK ONE

# HUNTING
# MONSTERS

## ALLEN CURRIER

Solstice Publishing - www.solsticepublishing.com

# Hunting Monsters

## By

## Allen Currier

For Luther James Gaffney, a man who taught me that being a father has nothing to do with biology. The greatest man I'll ever know.

# Chapter One

Their heads had been severed. The wife's terrified features, pale and ghoulish, taunted him from the body of her husband. The son-of-a-bitch had switched their heads. Detective Steve Belcher leaned in and examined the crude stitching on the couple's necks. He rubbed his finger across the stitches, and it slid between the dried scabbed skin and tissue. He jerked back in disgust, and the head fell over, restrained only by the stitching stretched over the loose skin. He reached over and pushed the head back in place. Fear ran through him, and a cold sweat covered his forehead as he imagined the horror they'd faced.

Their dried out eyes had already begun to shrivel in their sockets. A pale white glaze was forming over the pupils, nearly obscuring the blue color. The built up gasses in the bloated bodies' decaying organs permeated the air so thickly the stench filled his nostrils and mouth.

He gagged and almost vomited. He swallowed hard. The skin on the bodies had dried and shriveled to the point of cracking and revealed the tissue underneath.

In his twenty-five years on the force, he hadn't felt this level of fear mixed with hatred erupting in him. He didn't know what kind of sick bastard had done this, but he would find out.

He left the bodies and continued around the rest of the house. No matter where he looked, no clues seemed to be left behind. Everything was too clean. The pictures on the walls of family, the decorated place mats on the dining room table, showed how the couple cared for the house. The numerous windows wore only a top valance, exposing the crime scene to the many on-lookers in the neighborhood.

To have two bodies desexualized in such a manner and have no mess told him it hadn't happened here. He needed to look elsewhere, but where, he didn't know.

The coroner reached up and closed the eyes of the victims, completing her work. Doctor Fisher, dressed in her blue pants suit and white coat, stood up and removed her gloves. She turned to the detective. "This is a new one for the books," she said. She had been with the Sheriff's Department for as long as Steve. Her short brown hair, covered by the hairnet she wore, just covered her ears.

"Yeah, just what I needed this morning," Detective Belcher said. "Do you have any ideas?"

"None at all, and I'm not sure where to start, either," she said. "Let's get them back to the lab so I can find some answers," she told the men waiting to bag the bodies for transport. She picked up her bag, ready to leave the scene.

***

Steve watched the local news reporter, Lacy James. She stood on the street in front of the crime scene, fingers pressed to her ear. Her long blonde hair moved with the breeze. Only five feet tall, she was petite and fit. She got the lead on the best stories to report.

"The police have told us two people were found murdered in the house behind me, a husband and wife of thirty years. At this time, the police will not speculate on any motive or suspects. We will keep you up to date as soon as we know more. This is Lacy James reporting live, back to you in the studio."

She ended the cutaway. "Load up the van," she said to the cameraman. "Let's go."

The gurneys, with the two body bags to be loaded in the awaiting van, were wheeled out. Lacy stared into the forming crowd and met Steve's gaze as the detective left the house. Dressed in his oldest suit and nineteen eighties wingtip shoes, he probably looked like something out of an old movie to her. Every day the mirror told him his silver-streaked hair and exhausted face revealed the stress of too many years working long hours. His dark blue piercing eyes looked right through suspects, but they didn't faze Lacy, and she ran to catch him.

"Detective, is there anything you can tell us? What happened in the house?"

"Not now, Lacy, you'll have to wait for the press conference like everyone else."

"Can you at least tell us their names?" she said with contempt in her voice.

He got in his car and drove away. At the station, Detective Belcher reviewed the photos of the scene, pinning them up on a cork board in his office. The place needed a good cleaning. Desks and chairs were covered with folders containing unsolved cases. They'd piled up over the years. Most of the cases were petty theft or drug related. The stifling pile of paperwork would leave most looking for another kind of work, and it even kept him bogged down.

Belcher, however, loved his job. From the first time, as a child, when he'd watched old cop movies and television shows, all he dreamed of was being a cop. Hatred of the perpetrator pulsed through him.

He studied the pictures on the board. No blood pools, no splatter, no drops, no footprints in blood. Nothing to show anything had gone on in the house at all, except two bodies sitting in recliners, posed to watch the television, wearing each other's heads.

Who'd done this and how? He picked up his pad and pencil, his preferred way of recording his thoughts. First, find out who the couple had been in normal life he wrote down. One thing he'd learned over the years, in the light, no one appeared the same. Someone had a real ax to grind due to the innate depravity of the crime. But who? Family... Friend... Co-worker... Lover... Where would all this lead?

"Good morning," Steve said and slapped Tom on the back as he walked into the room. Tom, a young, cocky college grad who was first in his class was the "all books and no street smarts" kind of cop, trying to make his name by being smarter than anyone else. He completely personified the opposite of Steve. Standing only five foot eight, with dark black hair and blue eyes, his build confirmed that many hours were spent in the gym to stay fit. He dressed as if he was headed to a photo shoot for GQ magazine. He looked sharp from head to toe in the latest fashion styles for the young detective on the rise.

Jerry, who sat next to Tom, was Steve's second in command. He'd come to the department straight out of the military. Standing six foot four inches, and slim built, he looked like a cardboard cut out from a recruitment poster.

Four other uniformed officers rounded out the core group of the task force charged with discovering what had occurred in that quiet, little house. The worst the neighborhood had seen were broken windows and a few mail boxes smashed on Friday nights after the local football games.

They were compiling the details of the case when the mayor walked into the room. His overpriced suit and Italian shoes screamed old family money. Sheriff Lester, who was a friend of the mayor, and carried himself like an old west lawman, came with him. He was calm and collected most of the time, but this tall man could get riled up if he needed to. With gray hair and a wrinkled, weather worn face, he wore the badge with an enormous amount of pride. Both longtime friends and supporters of Steve, he smiled seeing their friendly faces.

"Good morning, gentlemen. What do we have, Steve?" the mayor said in a tone indicating he was in charge.

"Not much, Mayor. Two dead bodies and no clues

yet," Steve said. "But it's early in the case. We're still waiting on the results from the crime lab." They'd found no hard evidence, but Steve hoped something would turn up on the bodies.

"Well, keep me in the loop on this one. Carl and Nancy Peterson had been around since my family moved here forty years ago. We grew up together. Anything you need, let me know," the mayor said.

"Thanks, Mayor," Sheriff Lester said. "Steve, let's you and I handle the press conference and keep the part about the mutilation behind closed doors for now. No leaks to the press, unless approved by the mayor or me. Understood?" he asked. "You guys know when this hits the wire service we're going to be overrun with reporters from every television and newspaper in the state. So let's make sure where and when we talk about this case. We don't need this turning into more of a circus than it has to be."

"Jerry, dig into the Peterson's and find out anything you can, go to his employer, and see what you can find," Steve said. "Tom, look into the couple's finances, see if there's anything there. Locate the daughter and see what she can tell us. The rest of you go back to the scene and see if there's anything we missed, interview the entire neighborhood and find whatever you can."

\*\*\*

Steve met his team at 16:00 in the squad room. The officers had returned from canvassing the neighborhood. Everyone sat down.

Steve turned to Detective Tom Jenson. "Did you discover anything about the couple's history, Tom?"

"Not really. They paid their bills on time, no change in bank transfers, their house is almost paid for, and both their cars are free and clear."

"What did you find, Carol?" Steve asked the medical examiner.

Carol shook her head. "Not much," Carol said. "Besides their heads being cut off and sewn back on each other's bodies with fishing line, there's nothing, no trace evidence. I sent blood to the lab, but it'll be forty eight hours before I hear anything."

The mayor, walking in from the hallway said, "I'll call the mayor in Columbus and see if we can't expedite the results. What else do we have?"

Steve turned to Jerry. "What did you find at the plant?"

"Well," he straightened up in his chair, "it would appear Carl was well liked. The only thing I got was from a janitor called Old Bob," he said with a smirk. "There was this one feller who got in a spat with Carl some twenty years ago, but Old Bob can't remember his name and didn't know what it was about. The CEO is looking into the records to see if there's anything to this. Other than that, it looks like a dead end."

"What about the neighbors?" Steve asked.

"None of the neighbors heard anything. Carl and Nancy were well liked in the community," Officer Brown said.

"What about the daughter?" Steve asked.

"Terry Peterson, single, works in LA as a clothing store manager. She's on a flight coming in tonight at 19:30," Tom replied.

Silence fell over the room. Steve looked up from his empty coffee cup and stared at the pictures on the board. The naked bodies of Carl and Nancy mutilated in such a manner and not one clue to go on.

"Come in," Steve said answering the knock at the door.

"Sorry to interrupt" the clerk said, "but there's a mob of reporters outside the front door."

The mayor and Steve exchanged a look. "Steve, give them what we have, except the head thing. No one needs that in their dreams tonight," the mayor told Steve.

"Okay," Steve said, "but in the meantime, Jerry, check

with the State Police and the FBI to see if they have any open cases of this nature around the country. Might be someone else out there who can help us," Steve said.

\*\*\*

Steve walked outside to where the reporters waited. He was inundated by a flood of flashing cameras and shouted questions. "Calm down now," he said over the hubbub. The crowd quieted. "Both Carl and Nancy Peterson were found deceased, as you already know. We still have no information on how they were killed, why this was done, or who the killer is. We are asking for anyone with information about this, or anyone who thinks they might have seen something, to please contact the police department. No questions, sorry." He turned and walked inside with the barrage of questions and shouts pursuing him through the door.

# Chapter Two

"They can't find me now," the hunter said to himself as he drove away from town.

"I have killed the monsters and sealed them in hell forever," he proclaimed. He looked in the rearview mirror of the van to see if he was being followed. "The monsters will follow you and trap you if you're not watchful," he reminded himself, the monsters running free in his thoughts, always ready to surround and attack him.

He drove out through the woods to the only place he felt safe. His hideaway where the monsters couldn't come. The safety of the wisdom of the Old One ringing in his ears, *"Hang this talisman in the window, it will drive away the evil spirits."* "I'll make my own talisman, my own to ward off the evil that haunts me day and night."

He worked through the night to cover every inch of his surroundings.

"Now I can rest," he said as he lay down to sleep. The hunt was over and he was again victorious.

But sleep didn't come. Again the monsters invaded his dreams. They chased and snarled after him. He could feel their hot breath on his face. He ran to hide but not before being trapped in the hot sting of their claws that ripped his flesh.

"Why do you hunt me?" he cried and covered the wounds. "I wish I was dead and the pain would stop." He said it over and over as he lay hiding in pain after another attack from his tormentors.

Many times he's tried to run. Run and never stop. No one would care. But he can't get away; they always find him and drag him back to the nest of monsters that sting with every touch. He heard the bone chilling shrieks from the lair of the most vicious of all beasts as he stood in fear of their arrival.

"If only I was bigger and had some way to fight the dragons."

Again he failed, thrown into the dungeon, into the lair of the monsters. Never to be safe, he whimpered and cries in the corner.

"Help me, someone please help me."

Awakened again by the monsters howls, and with tears running down his cheeks, his face turned cold and lifeless. "They're still out there. They'll hunt me again. I must find them before they find me."

Again he left the safety that he knows. He set traps that only he could see.

"If they come for me, I'll know. They'll feel the pain." He gathered his tools and climbed into the van. "Your monsters will not find me. I will hunt them all. Soon they'll all be gone and then I'll rest," he yelled.

Looking into the rearview mirror he said, "I know where they are, you can't hide them from me, I am the hunter. They'll never see me coming." He drove back into the night.

All night he drove. "No time to waste," he told himself. The monsters can move from lair to lair. They'll try to fool you. The words of the Old Monster rang in his memory. "They're nomads, no home for too long. They must move and hide or their secrets will be revealed."

He remembered the teachings from before. The pain of the lessons marked on his flesh.

"Learn to follow them, not to be seen. Not even to be heard. The monsters can smell you; always know where to approach from."

His thoughts run wild from past hunts. Every lesson learned burned into his memory.

"You can't stop me," he yelled out, hearing the monsters coming again. "No matter where you hide I'll find you, you'll all die."

He drove into the night, far away from his home. "There's your nest," he said to himself pulling up a gravel road, he drives by as he sees the monsters leaving the den.

"Must not be seen," he told himself and drove past the lair of the beasts. "Now I must find a place to hide, must learn about these monsters. This won't be an easy hunt. These are the biggest monsters I have hunted yet. I am the hunter, I cannot fail, and I must take their power. All the monsters must die," he said and he drove away.

Night falls on the hunter as he watched from where he hide, safe in the woods. The woods never hurt him. They protect him and hide him from the monsters.

"They come," he said when he saw them arrive back at the lair. "They're unaware of me." He covered his scent with leaves from the trees he rubbed on his skin.

"They won't smell me, either." He'd learned the trick from the old one. "*Cover your scent, always use the smells and sounds around you. Become the land, or tree, or river. You must blend in to hunt the prey.*"

He watched the monster enter the lair, he waited and learned every move. The sounds, the lights going on and off, recording each movement in his mind.

"You must remember what the prey is like. There is no book to write in, only the book in your head." He remembered as the old one slapped him on the back of his head and knocked him to the ground.

"Get up," the old one yelled. "Maybe you're not worth teaching." The old one's words cut deep.

"But I am, I am the hunter," he told himself. "You'll see who the hunter is. I'll kill all your monsters. I'll take all the power," the hunter said to himself and slid back into the darkness of the woods.

# Chapter Three

Detective Tom Jensen stood outside the terminal gate at the airport waiting for Terry Peterson to arrive. Holding a sign written in black letters with her name, he pondered what he, being new to this position, was going to say in this situation. With palms sweating, he noticed the young woman headed toward him. With long, red hair and green eyes, the very shapely woman, wore a knee-length black dress that clung to her curves. In any other circumstance, he'd have a completely different conversation with her. She spotted him and raised her hand to wave. A sad smile graced her face.

"Hello," she said, "I'm Terry."

He reached out to shake her hand. "I'm Detective Tom Jensen with the County Sheriff's office." Picking up her suitcase, he continued, "Sorry for your loss, Mrs. Peterson. I have a car to take you anywhere you want to go."

"It's Miss, but please call me Terry. Thank you for meeting me. Is there anymore news about my parents?" she asked. Sorrow clouded her eyes and sat heavily on her face.

"Not yet," he said. "But the case is still very new."

"I would like to go and see them, if I may," she said.

They walked through the airport out to his waiting car. Tom opened the door to the passenger side, and Terry lowered herself onto the seat. Her skirt slid up her thigh and revealed her tanned, firm skin. For a moment, Tom's eyes fixed on the image being burned into his memory.

He regained his composure and shut the car door. Opening the back door, he set her suitcase on the seat before getting in the driver's side. Thoughts of this beautiful woman raced through his mind. He struggled with controlling himself.

"Can I go and see them?" she asked again.

"I'll call ahead and tell them we're coming. It might be too late tonight. It's after 8:00 p.m., and most likely everyone has gone home." Tom picked up his cell phone and dialed the number to the station.

"Sheriff's office," a voice answered.

"This is Detective Jensen."

"Hi Tom," the evening shift dispatcher answered.

"Is there anyone still in the morgue tonight?" Tom asked while glancing over at Terry who watched him.

"Nope, all locked up and closed. Just the night patrol leaving for their shift. Is there something you need?"

"No, we'll see you in the morning. Thanks," Tom said. Tom turned to Terry's discouraged face. "I booked you a room at the motel in town. I'll take you there now. Do you need anything before we get there?" Trying to hide the attraction he felt and still show concern for her wasn't easy.

"No," she said. "I ate on the flight, but I would like to see my parent's house before we go. Is that okay?"

"I'm afraid not." More of the light drained from her face at his response. "It's still a crime scene. We'll talk to the sheriff tomorrow and find out when you can get in." Tom pulled into the only motel in town. Operated by a widowed man in his seventies, it had been in the town since 1923. A little old, but well-taken care of over the years, Jake's family had owned it the entire time. Tom stopped the car and jumped out. He tried to get around to open the door for Terry who had already done so.

"I got it," she said, "not used to having doors opened for me." She smirked.

Tom grabbed her bag from the backseat, and they walked to the motel office.

Jake, the owner, opened the door. "I've been waiting up on you. Sorry about your folks, Terry. Known them a lot of years, they was good people."

"Thanks, Jake," she replied.

"Got your room all ready. Anything you need, you let me know, okay?" Jake said with a kind fatherly smile giving her a comforting hug. He retrieved a key to the room and led them down the hall. He opened the door, reached in, and turned on the light. "Is this okay?"

"It'll be fine," she said, mustering up a smile.

"Well, here's your bag, and I'll pick you up in the morning around 8:00 a.m. Okay?" Tom asked.

"That would be great, and thanks for everything." She reached out and touched his hand.

"No problem. I'll see you tomorrow. Try to get some sleep. Good night," Tom said.

"'Night," Jake said and turned to leave.

"Good night."

Tom stood by the door and heard her quiet sobs coming from inside the old hotel room. Reality had hit her. She must have realized that the town she had grown up in, and her parent's house, would never be the home she remembered again.

***

Tom woke up, jumped out of bed, and having seen the time, ran to the shower. In a rush of soap and water, he hurried to get ready, anticipating where he'd be going this morning.

"What are you thinking?" he said to himself. "She doesn't need you panting over her like a dog while this is going on, just back it down."

He returned to the shower, allowing the ice cold water to tame the raging heat in his body.

Tom, dressed in his best suit and spit-shined shoes, stood in front of the mirror to admire himself.

"You're ready," he said and left his apartment. He pulled up to the front of the motel and went inside.

"Morning, Tom," Jake said lightheartedly when he

waked through the doors.

"Morning, Jake. Have you seen her this morning?" Tom asked.

"Nope, I just got down here myself. I can call the room if you like; better make sure she's up." He picked up the phone.

"Terry, this is Jake. Are you up?"

Terry's voice came through the phone as slight vibrations, but Tom couldn't understand what she said.

"Well, Tom is down here to get you," Jake said. Another buzz of Terry's words came to Tom.

"Sure thing, Terry. "Jake turned to Tom after he hung up the phone. "She's going to need a few minutes. You know how females are about getting ready." He smiled. "I got some coffee going if you want a cup."

"That would be great." Tom sat down while Jake brought the coffee and the morning news report switched to live coverage outside the police station.

"This is Lacy James outside the police station where there is still no further information on yesterday's killing of Carl and Nancy Peterson. The two were found dead in their home at around 08:30 yesterday morning. The detectives told us there were still no leads in this baffling case. For now, that's all we have. We'll keep you informed as developments arise. This is Lacy James reporting from the police station."

"Sorry I took so long, Detective," Terry said from behind him.

Tom turned and Terry walked towards him. Tom stood to greet her and almost spilled the coffee in his lap.

"No... Oops... No problem," he said with a sheepish grin and tried to collect himself. "Ready to go?"

"Yes," she said. A smile lurked in her voice.

Tom, feeling the playful mood, relaxed and escorted Terry out to the car.

***

Steve and Jerry were going over the details of the case with Sheriff Lester when Tom arrived in the squad room.

"We have a few names from the plastics plant we can run down, but it doesn't look promising," Jerry said and grabbed a cup from the coffee stand.

"That pot is from yesterday," Steve said. "And it's pretty bad."

Jerry grabbed the pot and left the room with it anyway. Tom smiled and shook his head.

Tom, with Terry in tow, said, "Sheriff Lester, this is Terry Peterson."

Sheriff Lester stood up, shook her hand, and said, "Sorry for your loss, Ma'am. Your folks were good people. Let me assure you we're doing everything we can to find out what happened."

"Thank you," Terry replied.

"This is our lead detective, Steve Belcher. He's heading up the investigation."

Steve rose and shook her hand. "My condolences, Ma'am."

"Thank you, but please call me Terry. Can I see my parents?" she asked.

Steve, startled by the straight-forward question, stuttered to respond.

"Why don't you sit and talk with Steve for a while, and I'll go and check with our medical examiner and see when would be a good time," Sheriff Lester interjected. He hooked his thumbs in his utility belt then jerked them out again.

"Thank you," she replied.

"Please, sit down." Steve gestured to the chair across from him.

Tom stepped over and rolled the wheeled, cloth covered desk chair out for her. She smiled and sat down.

"I know this is a hard time for you, but we need to ask

you some questions about your folks, if that's okay?"

"Okay," she replied. She twisted her hands together in her lap and bit her lip.

"Is there anything you can tell us about their past? Was there someone who ever threatened your folks?" he asked.

"Not that I know of," she replied with a shake of her head.

"Were there any problems in their marriage, like money trouble? Someone else in the middle? I don't want to be too crude, but I have to ask," he said.

"No, they didn't have any money troubles, and they bickered like most older couples, but nothing else that I'm aware of."

"When was the last time you talked to them?"

"Wednesday or Thursday of last week. We talked at least once a week. They seemed fine, and we talked for about an hour," she said staring past him for a moment as if recalling the conversation. "Who'd do this?" She started to break down, taking quick breaths.

Tom reached for a box of tissues from behind him.

"I don't know," Steve said. Tom handed her the box of tissues. "But I'm going to find out."

Watching the victim's daughter cry bolstered Tom's determination to help solve the case even more. Steve looked at Tom.

"Go see what the hold up is with Carol."

***

In autopsy, Carol pulled Carl back onto the table. Tom didn't know what had held up Sheriff Lester but he arrived after Tom.

"Morning, Carol," Sheriff Lester broke the cold silence in the drab room.

"Morning, Sheriff," she replied. "Morning, Tom."

"Taking a second look?" Sheriff Lester asked.

"Yeah, I want to see if there's anything I overlooked that could help."

"Well, how about we hold off on that and let Terry come in and say goodbye to her folks," Sheriff Lester said solemnly. "Are they okay to view?"

"Yes, I have them cleaned up. I won't uncover the neck or chest areas," she said pulling back the cold white sheet to show Sheriff Lester the horrific sight. "Their heads chopped off, it had to be one swift *blow* from a large blade. Look how clean the cut is."

Sheriff Lester looked on in disgust. Tom made himself look and swallowed, refusing to put his hand to his throat.

"Never seen anything like this, have you?" she asked.

"No, and I don't want to again," Sheriff Lester said in a grim tone. "Get them ready. Tom, can you bring her down in about half an hour? And make sure we don't give her nightmares, okay?" he added before he left the room.

Carol replaced the head in its proper position on the body and repositioned the sheet so only the head was visible. She moved over to the holding cooler door and pulled out the gurney that Nancy's cold, pale body resided on. She moved it into the room and placed it beside Carl. She prepared the body in the same manner so the two of them together appeared almost peaceful.

Tom left, dreading how Terry was going to react. They weren't his parents and he felt queasy.

***

Steve was consoling Terry when Sheriff Lester and Tom entered the room.

"Are you okay?" Sheriff Lester asked.

Terry wiped the tears from her eyes, gave a nod, and tried to compose herself. "Can I see them now?"

"Yes," Sheriff Lester said.

She stood up and met him at the door. He stepped aside and gestured for her to go down the hallway first in a gentlemanly fashion. Sheriff Lester turned to Steve.

"Find this freak," he said before he followed Terry

down the hall.

Steve stood and flipped over the board with the pictures of the crime scene he had turned around to keep Terry from seeing it. He walked back and forth glaring at the photos. Fresh anger built, and he muttered, "Who are you?"

Jerry entered the room with a fresh pot of coffee and poured a cup. Grabbing the stack of folders he'd retrieved from the plastics plant earlier, he sat down at the table to read the files.

"What do you have, Jerry?" Steve asked.

"Not sure yet, picked these up this morning from Carl's plant and am getting my first look at them."

"Tom, help look into them. We have to find this guy, or I'm never going to sleep again," he said. "I'm going downstairs."

Jerry grabbed the stack and left the room with Tom following him. At his desk, Tom picked up a file. He'd been researching the couple's finances the day before. "There's nothing here. From all indications they were the perfect American couple," he said in defeat.

"Here," Jerry handed him two of the files, "look into these two and I'll look into the others."

"What's this?" he asked.

"Employee files from Carl's plant. They think one of these guys may have had it out for Carl twenty five years ago," Jerry said. "It's a long shot, but let's see what we can find on any of them."

"Okay." Tom opened the first file and began to type and read at the same time.

"How can you do that?" Jerry asked.

"I learned it at the prom." Tom lashed back.

Jerry laughed and walked to his desk to read through the files in his hand.

# Chapter Four

Steve caught up with Terry and Sheriff Lester at the autopsy room doors. He opened the door, and Terry stopped in silence at the entrance, afraid to enter.

"Are you sure you're ready for this?" he asked.

Reaching up to wipe another tear from her eye, she nodded and stepped inside.

The room was cold and well lit, typical for a room where bodies were dissected like frogs in a science class. The lifeless bodies of her parents lay peacefully in the middle of the room.

Carol stood on the side of the room almost unnoticed. Terry walked toward the bodies, both draped in cold white sheets.

"Can I see them?" she asked. Tears rolled down her face unchecked.

Steve nodded to Carol who moved over and pulled back the sheets enough to see their faces. Terry gasped and wept harder. She reached out to touch the face of her father and looked to the face of her mother.

"Did they suffer?" she asked, breaking through the tears.

"I don't think so." Carol said.

"How did they die?" Terry asked without taking her gaze from her parents.

"We're not sure yet," she said.

Terry looked at Carol. "Please find out what happened to my parents." She turned and fled the room.

Terry re-entered the squad room where Jerry and Tom worked at their desks tracking down people from the files.

When Terry walked in, Tom jumped to his feet causing files to slide over his desk. Sadness filled the room.

"Can I get you anything?" Sheriff Lester asked.

"No, thank you. When can I go to the house?" She wiped away more of the pain.

"Well, we're still—"

"It's okay, Sheriff," Steve said. "We have all we need for now."

"Steve, will you have someone take her home?" Sheriff Lester said. It was more of an order than a question.

"I'll do it myself," Steve said with a nod.

Tom frowned and let out a sigh before he sat down and returned to work.

"Thank you for everything," she said. "You too, Tom. I really appreciate everything you've done." She reached out to shake his hand.

Tom jumped out of his chair, dropping the file he'd been looking at. It missed the desk and landed on the floor. Papers scattered.

"You're most welcome, and if you need anything, let me know." He shook her hand, trying to hide his embarrassment.

Tom knelt down to retrieve the scattered papers from the floor.

"Smooth move, Don Juan," Jerry said.

Laughter erupted in the squad room. Tom sheepishly returned to his desk.

Steve escorted Terry to the parking lot where he opened the door to his not so late model dark green four door car that most people called the tug boat.

"Not paying you much?" she said, getting into the front seat.

Steve walked around to the driver's side and said, "I like the old ones. They're more reliable and easier to fix. Besides, there's more than meets the eye." Turning the key, the powerful sound of the four hundred horse engine roared. He looked over and smirked. "Some of the old ones still run the best."

"What do you do in LA?" he asked, keeping the conversation light.

"When did they find them?" she asked instead of answering his question. "I've seen the news reports that they found them Monday morning. Is this true?"

"Yes," he replied. "No one had heard from them all weekend from the reports, but we think it occurred sometime late Saturday or early Sunday."

"You mean killed," she said sternly, correcting him.

"Sorry," he said with a slight shrug.

"No, I'm sorry. I know it's not your fault," she said. She looked down at her hands then out the car window.

"No need," he said. "I can't imagine how you feel, and I'll do anything I can to find who did this." His hands tightened on the wheel with his resolve.

"Thank you."

They turned down the street where she used to live, and an eerie feeling engulfed the car.

It was the same street she grew up on but had forever changed. The neighbors working in their yards were a familiar scene, one she'd known all of her life. Now, all of them seemed to be staring at her traveling down the long street leading to the family home.

Husbands and wives working over rose bushes stopped, looked, and turned their heads, slowly following the passing car. She had to see the whispers and hidden points from fingers realizing who was in the car. Holding the position of Chief Detective and being well liked in the town, Steve's car would be noticed anywhere. So they all knew why the car traveled down this street where the worst crime in the town's history had transpired.

They reached the driveway of the two-story, Cape Cod house. The yard and flowers were all kept like most on the street. The white paint on the house, new this year, made it stand out on the street like a bright beacon. The glass front door was still the same from her childhood.

"They put that door in just before my first day of school," she said with a sniffle. "It's like they're still standing there waiting for me like they did then. Like they did when I left for California."

Steve stopped the car, but she didn't move.

She turned to Steve. "Take me away. I don't want to see this."

He put the car in reverse without saying a word. He backed out of the driveway and returned up the street.

She looked out the window of the slow moving car, the same neighbors who had watched them arrive still stood in the same places. Their eyes fixed on the moving spectacle they all knew had to be the daughter of the slain couple down the street.

In silence, they turned the corner. Steve kept the silence, not knowing where to go, but only that the silence compelled him to keep the car moving away.

He stopped at a red light.

She turned to him. "Can you take me to rent a car? It looks like I'll be here a while. There's a lot I have to take care of." She turned in silence and looked back out the window of the car.

Steve drove away, headed for the only place to rent a car in the town, at the airport.

Steve arrived at the airport car rental and waited for Terry to complete her business inside. While he sat in the car, his mind replayed the pictures of the couple and the shocking sight he found walking into their house. In his twenty five years of law enforcement, he'd never had a case rattle him. Some he hadn't solved, but nothing that kept him up at night. Watching people pass, entering and exiting the airport, he wondered, "Is it you? Or you?"

"All set."

He jumped and turned to see Terry standing next to the

car.

"Okay," he said. "You know it's about lunchtime, why don't you let me take you to lunch? It would be my pleasure."

"Okay. I'll follow you." She turned and walked to the rental car, a new mid-size type Steve would have referred to as a *chick car*.

He turned the key, gunned the engine and got her attention. She turned and smiled at him.

"I'll try not to lose you in that Tonka toy," he said over the roar of the big engine.

\*\*\*

In the squad room, Tom had tracked down the information on the people in the files given to him earlier in the day. Peter Smiley, age forty three married with three kids living in Utah. The other was George Becker, dead two years of a heart attack in Arkansas, both dead ends.

Closing the file he informed Jerry of what he'd found.

"Well, that's that," Tom said, "How's your search going?"

"Well, the first one, Jeremy Rogers is in the National Guard and has been overseas for the last twelve months, and the other one, Wallace Holt, left the company in 1984, nothing in his file explaining why. He lived in Columbus until 1988, and he didn't show up in Cincinnati until 1992. He didn't appear in Youngstown until 1995. He showed up in Lancaster, Ohio in 2001; then he dropped off the planet. Nothing on his record in any police agency, so I'm still looking to see where he'll show up next," Jerry said.

"Let's check with the IRS to see if he's worked in the last nine years, give me his social," Tom said.

Jerry read the numbers and Tom put them in the computer search. "We should get his DMV photo so we can see who we're looking at."

"Already pulling it up," Tom said. A picture of

Wallace Holt at age thirty nine, taken at the Lancaster, Ohio DMV, popped up. Six foot two inches and two hundred forty pounds, blond hair, blue eyes.

"Well, he hasn't had a license since then."

"It's not a license, just an ID card," Tom said.

"What?" Jerry said and stood up. "Let's get with Steve and run down to Lancaster and see if we can find something out."

"He's still out with Terry at the victim's house. Also, Mr. Holt has no work reported since 2001. His last job was at a hardware store down there," Tom said.

"Before we waste time running down there, let's call the Lancaster police and see if they have anything on him, but I'm getting hungry. Let's go to lunch, playboy." Jerry sent another jab Tom's way.

* * *

The best place to eat in town, a little diner most people from bigger cities wouldn't even notice and, if they did, wouldn't enter, was called *Gretta's*. All the locals knew it and at lunch time it was the place to be for the best home cooking and the juiciest gossip: from who was sleeping with whom, to where the best sweet corn was grown in the county.

Jerry and Tom pulled up to see Steve and Terry walk in the front door. Tom noticed Terry and stopped.

"Down, boy, don't want to scare off the nice lady, do we?" Jerry said with sarcasm.

Tom slyly flipped the bird at Jerry. As Tom was fifteen years younger, Jerry liked to torment him like the younger brother he'd never had growing up. They had immense respect for each other's particular talents, Tom being the computerized, book smart, can do anything with a mouse, rookie detective and Jerry being the rock hard and nose to the grindstone, high and tight haircut and starched uniform detective you would want taking the lead if you had to enter a dark house full of bad guys pointing guns at you.

"Hey, Steve, Miss Peterson, want to join us for lunch?" Tom asked.

"Don't mind if we do," Steve said. He looked over at Terry before joining them. Steve reached the two men first and in a low tone said, "That's if junior here can manage not to dump anything on Miss Peterson." Steve and Jerry snickered.

"After you," Jerry said and held the door for Terry to lead the way into the diner. She nodded and entered the restaurant.

A sign read, "Seat yourself," and under that it listed the Tuesday special of Meatloaf and sweet corn.

"Hey, boys." Wanda called out over the crowd. The waitress had been there for most of her life.

"Have a seat," she said. "And who's this pretty thing with you?"

"I'm Terry Peterson," Terry said.

"Oh my God, child, I'm so sorry. Are you okay? It was so shocking to hear about your momma and daddy."

"How about some water to start, Wanda," Steve interrupted.

"I'm okay," Terry answered.

"I'll bring that right out. Did y'all see the special?" she asked.

"I think I'd like a menu, if that's okay," Tom said.

"Be right back." Wanda whirled away. Steve turned to Terry. "Sorry about that."

"Don't be. I grew up here, remember. It's going to happen sooner or later," she said with a smile.

Wanda returned with the four glasses of water squeezed between her stubby fingers and the menus stuck up under her arm. She set the glasses on the table and started to hand out the menus.

Tom reached for the glasses of water to pass them out until Jerry stopped him.

"I'd rather not wear it." He smirked, grabbing the glasses and handing them out. The group chuckled, and Tom frowned.

"Don't worry, kid," Wanda said, "you'll stop being the new guy someday. Now, do you need a few minutes, or are you ready to order?"

"Meatloaf, meatloaf, meatloaf," the three men stated in order of rank.

"And you, little lady?" she asked.

"I'll have a salad with some Italian dressing and that'll be all," Terry said.

Turning away, and laughing in her loud and boisterous manner, Wanda said, "Not gonna get any meat on them bones eating that way."

"Just how I remembered her," Terry said.

*\*\**

Having eaten their lunch, and having avoided all conversation concerning the events at hand, Steve asked, "Terry, you want to follow us back to the station?"

"No," she said. "I think I better start getting things arranged. I guess I need to go see Stanley."

"Okay," Steve said. Everyone in town knew the funeral director.

"Would you like someone to go with you?" Tom asked hopefully.

"No, this is something I need to do, and you guys need to get back to work and not babysit me," she said with a smirk.

"It's no problem. Call us later at the station." Tom handed her one of his cards. "Here's my card, with my cell number, if you need anything."

"I'll go with you, Terry." Steve said. "I have a few details I need to look into anyway."

"Whose turn in the barrel?" Wanda asked, bringing the bill to the table.

"Let me get that," Terry insisted.

"Not a chance!" Jerry said and reached for the bill.

"Well, thank you," she said with a smile. "I guess I can't put this off any longer. I'll see you guys later."

The men stood up as Terry rose. She and Steve headed for the door. Tom's gaze fixed on Terry.

Jerry slapped the bill in his hand into Tom's chest breaking his glazed stare.

"Here, Rookie, pay the bill and get your mind back in the game."

Jerry laughed and walked away leaving Tom standing there with Wanda holding out her hand and grinning.

"Aren't you ever gonna learn?" she said with a smirk.

Tom reached for his wallet watching the others walk out the door.

***

Jerry and Sheriff Lester sat in Steve's office discussing the case. Tom sat with them, feeling like he would have been more help to Terry.

"What kind of force would someone need to do this?" Jerry asked.

Overhearing Jerry as she entered the room, Carol said, "A lot. I just got off the phone with a colleague of mine who's coming out to go over the bodies with me. Doctor Peter Miller is a PHD in forensic science at the State Medical University. I've called in some help on this one."

"Call whoever you need," Sheriff Lester said.

"Well, another dead end," Tom said. "It seems the last of the four, Mr. Wallace Holt, died in a one-car crash in 2001 when his car went off the road and down a ravine. The car caught fire and started a blaze in the woods, according to the Lancaster police," Tom said.

"So we're back to square one. Any news from the state police or wire services on any other killings like this?" Jerry asked Tom.

"Nothing, not even a case that looks similar."

"This can't be a random killing." Tom said with his frustration showing.

"There's evidence of drugs in both victims," Carol added. "GHB in trace amounts, not enough to kill them, but enough to render them easy to control."

"Tom, go back to the house and check for any prescriptions they might have had. Jerry, look into some of the local drug dealer contacts we have and see if anyone is selling GHB. We're going to have to get lucky on this," Sheriff Lester said. He rubbed his hand over his chin.

"I'll go give a report to the mayor. You let me know if anything turns up," Sheriff Lester said.

Jerry nodded, never taking his gaze from the board of gruesome pictures.

# Chapter Five

Steve and Terry pulled up to the front of the local funeral home and found Stanley out front shaking hands and greeting people there for a showing.

She parked the car on the street, and sat there for a moment.

"Maybe I should've made an appointment," she told Steve.

Stanley Jackson owned the funeral parlor. It had been in the family for fifty years. A meek and quiet man she'd gone to school with, but never really knew. He seemed to be on the outside of everything, always keeping to himself. Partly because of the family business, he and the whole family were a little creepy. Dealing with dead people the entire time made normal people uneasy.

She shut off the car and opened the door. Taking her purse, she and Steve left the car and walked slowly up the sidewalk.

Stanley, dressed in his black funeral suit and black tie, stood solemnly, portraying the guardian of the gates to the afterlife. A sad feeling overcame Steve as he watched Terry. In the back of his mind, he knew someday the inevitable would happen and would have to enlist the services of an undertaker, but it felt too soon.

As she approached the steps, Stanley's face changed.

"Terry," he said quietly.

"Hi, Stanley, I guess you knew I would be by," she said sadly.

"Sadly, yes," he said and looked at Steve. "Hello, Steve, Let's go into my office." He gestured toward the house and led them past the line of family and friends there to say goodbye to a loved one.

Walking by the doorway, she passed the open casket of an old man.

"Mr. Pearson," Stanley explained, "Died last Friday, at ninety two years old, in the nursing home."

With no response, they followed him into the office. He offered her a black, leather covered chair and moved around to the leather captain's chair behind the desk. Steve stood behind her.

In a voice that had been rehearsed down through generations, he said, "I am truly sorry for your loss, Terry. This came way before it's time." The tone of his voice, practiced to sooth the emotions of the mourner of a lost family member, washed over them.

"Now, your parents came in some time ago and have already taken care of all of the arrangements in case of their death. They wanted to make it easy on you in this time of sorrow," he said in his rehearsed manner. "All we need from you is to find out if there is anyone you want to do the invocation and eulogy. Do you have someone in mind?"

"No," she said.

"We can call the minister of the local church, whom we usually fall back on, if it's okay with you."

"That would be fine."

"Now, unless you want to upgrade the casket package your parents picked out..." He paused glancing at Terry. "I know this is hard, but we need to discuss this."

"What they decided on will be fine," Terry said cutting off his sales pitch in mid-sentence.

"Then all we need is for the coroner to release your parent's remains and we can set a date."

"That should be later today," Steve said.

"How many showings would you like to have?" Stanley asked.

"Just one," she said. "You can give me a call at the

motel in town if there's anything else you need." Terry rose to leave the room and reached out to shake his hand. "Thank you for all your help." She forced a smile.

"If there's anything else we can help you with, please let us know," Stanley said. Terry turned and left with Steve close behind her.

This time, she didn't stop to look at anything or anyone. Steve could tell she was trying to hold back a wave of emotions as she rushed for the car. Upon reaching it, she slid into the driver's side, grabbed her seatbelt in a hurry, and started the car.

She drove away and only made it a few blocks before the tears ran uncontrollably down her face. She pulled the car over in a shopping center and stopped. She covered her face with her hands. Steve sat silently as she sobbed. Not sure what he could say to help.

"Sorry," she said trying to compose herself. "I guess I need to take you back so you can catch this bastard."

A glare of hatred shone in her eyes as she turned and drove away.

***

Tom pulled up to the front of the victims' house. The crime scene tape was still in place. He climbed out of the car and stood adjusting his pants and coat, staring at the front door. Uneasy, since it was his first crime scene in his short tenure being a detective, he slowly walked up to the front porch and bent under the tape. Reaching up, he pulled the tape from the door and took the keys from his pocket and dropped them on the floor. He reached down to pick them up and a stray cat sprang from under the porch glider. Tom startled and jumped back.

"Get a grip, you pussy," he muttered to himself. He inserted the key and entered the house. The stairs lead up to the right at the entrance to the parlor. The two story house appeared well kept, like the outside. Nothing out of place, it was like walking into a museum.

Tom slowly walked through the entryway into the living room, where there was a void left from the chairs and area rug that had been removed and taken to the crime lab.

He walked to the kitchen where dishes were still in the sink and a pan of dried spaghetti sauce on the stove.

He searched the cabinets for any medications, but found nothing. He walked back through the living room, gaze focused on the void.

Slowly, he climbed up the stairs to check the couple's bathroom. The bathroom, decorated in bright flowers and every possible accessory, had everything in place, right down to the matching flowered trash can.

Opening the medicine cabinet, he found everything in place. Burn cream, antacid tabs, toothpaste, shaving gel, but no narcotics. Closing the bathroom door, he heard the front door close. Already unsettled by the surroundings, his adenine pumped up even higher.

He pulled out his 9 millimeter. Slowly, he crept back to the stairway and peered around the corner. This was the first time he'd pulled his weapon on the job. He started to sweat, his heart pounding in his chest. Silently, he made his way down the stairs.

At the base of the stairs, he leaned around the corner to see the shadow of someone standing in the living room. The hammering of his heart thundered in his ears. He moved to the entrance way and slowly moved into the living room.

"You almost got shot!" he said lowering his weapon.

Terry stood in the void in the center of the room, unfazed by Tom's presence.

"Is this where it happened?" she asked calmly.

"We don't think so," Tom said.

"I saw your car outside. I need to get some clothes for the funeral parlor," she stated in an unemotional voice. "Is that okay?" She turned before he answered and started up the stairs to her parent's room.

He climbed the stairs and entered the couple's room to find her rifling through the closet.

"Where is it?" she said as she looked back through the clothes. "There it is." She pulled out a full length blue flower print dress. "She always loved this dress." Holding it gently, moving to the other end of the closet, she reached in and pulled out her father's navy blue suit. "This way they'll match." Laying them on the bed, she returned to the closet and retrieved their shoes. Moving around the room, randomly selecting items, she didn't seem to notice Tom standing in the doorway wondering what he should do. *I should stay quiet,* he thought.

Continuing her task, she grabbed a black suit bag from the closet and packed her parents' belongings in it. When she closed the bag Tom stepped into the room.

"You need help with that?" he offered holding his hand out.

"No thanks," she said. "What are you doing here?"

"Looking to see if we missed any clues," he said.

"And did you find anything?"

"Just you and a black cat trying to give me a heart attack," he said with a smirk.

"Sorry," she said with a forced smile.

"Let me carry that out for you," he insisted. He carried it to her car and placed it in the back seat.

"Thank you," she said.

"Do you have any plans for dinner?" he asked kindly. "I hate to see you alone."

"That would be great," she replied with a slight smile.

"I'll pick you up at the motel at 07:00 p.m., okay?"

"Great, see you then." She climbed in the car.

Tom stood on the driveway while she backed out and drove away. Walking back to the door to lock up, a smile spread across his face. He nodded his head as if he'd achieved an unbelievable task.

\*\*\*

At the hotel, Terry was getting ready for the funeral. She stood in front of the mirror and told herself, "Just hold it together for a few more hours."

She put on her makeup to hide her week-long puffy eyes. She heard a knock on the door and opened it to find Tom standing in his department dress uniform. Spit shined, from head to toe.

"Hey there," she said. "Don't you look good in uniform?" She tried to muster up a cheerful smile.

"Just here to serve, ma'am," he replied.

"Come on in, I'll be another moment," she started heading back to the bathroom to finish getting ready. She returned and inquired, "Look okay?"

"You look great," he responded after giving her sleek black, curve hugging dress, a look over.

\*\*\*

At the funeral home, the line of people stretched around the block. Tom pulled into a reserved spot and helped Terry out of the car. Stanley and Laura greeted them and escorted them to the side door and into the viewing area.

"It's early, but your folks had a lot of friends in this town," Stanley explained.

The local minister arrived and joined the group.

"Terry, this is Pastor Robbins, the one I told you about," Stanley said.

"My condolences for your loss." He offered his hand and took hers.

"Pastor Robbins, thank you for doing this, I know my parents didn't attend church on a regular basis."

"Don't think another thing about it; we're all still God's children, even if we don't visit home as often as we should." He smiled.

"We can start anytime you're ready, Terry," Stanley called to Terry where she sat with Pastor Robbins.

Terry nodded to Stanley and they opened the doors. The viewing lasted for hours, everyone from the mayor, to the people Carl worked with, to all the neighbors, and almost everyone in the little town paraded past the coffins to pay their respects to the Petersons.

"I didn't know they were so well liked," Terry confided to Tom with contempt. "I think they're only here to be seen at the funeral; you know how small towns are."

After the service, the couple was carried to their final resting place in the center of the cemetery, and both were slid into the concrete lined mausoleum, cold and alone.

"Mom always said, *'don't put me in the ground',*" Terry muttered to herself.

The ceremony ended and the crowd cleared. Terry and Tom were the only ones left at the site. Terry reached up one last time to touch the name plates for both her mother and father to say goodbye.

She turned to Tom, who stood almost at attention, a guard on duty standing his post.

"I'm ready now," she said calmly.

The two turned and walked back to the car. Tom opened the door to let her get in. She stopped and turned to him and placed her hand on his cheek. She leaned close to his ear and whispered, "Thank you."

She gently kissed him on the cheek. A tear ran down his face. She reached up and wiped it from his face and turned and got into the car. He returned to the driver's side of the car, and silently drove away.

# Chapter Six

"Now I have the power," the hunter told himself as he closed the door behind him. He climbed into the van and removed his gloves.

"Your monsters have failed again," he said looking into the rearview mirror.

"They'll never hurt me again." He drove away as silently as he came.

"You must move as quiet as the mist on a lake," the Old One told him. "Learn not to be heard, you must move through the trees as a whisper of the wind. Your prey must not know you're there." The Old One's words rang through the night as if he was still beside him.

The long trip back to the place where he felt safe is full of danger. "You must be alert," he remembered.

"Why do you haunt me?" His thoughts filled by the screams of the monsters only there to torment him at every waking moment.

Again he ran to hide, but they are everywhere. Finally, he reached home. Safe again, surrounded by his own talismans to keep him safe.

"You know you can't hide, they'll find you no matter where you go," he told himself in the mirror as he parked the van.

He walked inside and sat down, picking up his tools to make more charms to protect him. Furiously, he worked to make as many as he could. He hung them up all around him. No spot left open for the monsters to peer in and find him.

Finally, with no space left open, he settled down to

sleep. He rocked himself back and forth with his arms clasped around himself and chanted, "They can't find me here, they can't find me here." Then he finally drifted off to sleep.

"Please stop!" he cried out. Running from the monsters as they scarred his flesh with their claws. He ran through the woods and hid behind a tree.

"Shhhhh," he told himself.

"They'll hear you," he said to try to comfort himself.

"No," he screamed as they pull him from the trees.

The monsters carried him back to their lair, stinging his flesh with their claws and tearing his soul with their screams that scared him.

He awoke crying and reached to feel the scars on his back. He transformed from the scared, crying little boy into the hunter.

"Now, I'll take your power, I am the hunter, you will torment me no more."

He left the safety he knew once again.

"There are more monsters I have to find. Find and kill them all before they come for me."

"I must travel far for this hunt," he said as he looked in the rearview mirror.

"Your monsters have moved their lair again. I'll hunt them down and take their power. I'll find them all. I won't stop until they're all dead."

He grabbed his head. "Stop trying to trick me," he yelled.

He felt the pain of the lashes they placed on him and the pain inflicted by the monsters in his mind.

"Get back here, you piece of shit." The words of the monsters sting his thoughts.

Even as a small one, he fought the monsters. He can't remember a time that he didn't fight the evil monsters.

"When will they stop?" he cried.

"When I kill them all," the hunter said looking into the

lifeless eyes in the rearview mirror.

"The hunt has begun, with only one end. I will take their power. They will chase the little ones no more."

# Chapter Seven

A week had passed since Tom took Terry back to the motel after the funeral. Watching her walk away had depressed him.

He knew she had to go, but it didn't lessen his day dreaming. He sat in the quiet squad room, with things back to normal.

Jerry walked in with his normal greeting. "Morning, Tom."

"Morning," he said back in a somber tone.

"Still pining for the one who got away?" Jerry asked.

Steve entered the squad room and joined in the banter.

"You're not going to walk around all day with your lip on the ground are you?" he asked.

Tom didn't respond, he continued the work in front of him.

It seemed the town had turned back to normal after the week of turmoil, almost like the awful murders hadn't happened.

Sheriff Lester entered the room and called the group together. They entered the conference room and took their seats around the table.

Sheriff Lester discussed the cases at hand for the day. A knock at the door interrupted him. Jerry, being closest to the door, opened it.

The front desk receptionist stood on the other side. "Sorry," she said looking around the room. "Sheriff Lester, there's an emergency call for you."

Sheriff Lester left the room and vanished into his office where he picked up the phone. He left the door open and the squad room became whisper quiet while everyone pretended not to be listening in.

"Hello, Sheriff Lester," he announced into the phone.

Sitting down, his expression became wooden. He scribbled furiously on a notepad, taking down the information the caller was giving him.

"I'll get someone down there ASAP," he said and hung up the phone.

In the squad room, the quiet transformed into chaos with the sheriff's return.

Steve was the first to speak. "What's up, Sheriff?"

"It seems he's struck again. A father and son in Milford, Ohio were found this morning in the same shape as the Peterson's. Steve, you and Jerry get on the road." He held a slip of paper out to Steve.

"Here's the address, I'll call Carol and head her that way too. Sheriff Baker down there received our report and thinks we can help. I told him you'd be there in an hour."

Steve looked at Jerry who already stood anticipating their departure and they both headed for the door.

"What can I do, Sheriff?" Tom begged like a player trying to get in the football game.

"Stay close to the phone. They may need your help with computer searches."

"Will do," he responded and headed for his desk, disappointed that he was being left behind.

Sheriff Lester walked over to the board and turned it back over. The pictures of the Peterson's were still there.

"Here we go again," he muttered before leaving the room.

Steve and Jerry headed out of the station and ran into Carol on her way in. "Grab your bag, Doc," Steve told her.

"What's up?" she said surprised.

"Tell her on the way," Sheriff Lester said.

The three headed for Steve's car. He fired it up and laid

rubber tearing out of the parking lot.

"Want to let me get my belt on?" Carol blurted out, struggling to stay to one side of the car as Steve took the corner.

"He killed two more," Jerry told Carol.

"Where?" she asked still fumbling with her seatbelt.

"Milford, Sheriff Baker called and asked us to come down. We should be there in less than an hour," Jerry said.

Steve drove rapidly, not speaking as the other two discussed the issue. His thoughts focused on the pictures imprinted in his mind of the Peterson's.

"Slow down," Carol yelled. "It won't do us any good to get killed before we get there."

"Take it down a notch, Steve," Jerry told him.

"Sorry," Steve replied backing off the accelerator, but still driving faster than normal traffic. "I have got to get this guy."

Steve took a quick glance in the rearview mirror when Carol's phone rang. Carol fumbled for her phone, grabbing the door when Steve negotiated a curve. Answering it, she said, "This is Carol!"

Steve just missed the back end of another car changing lanes in an Indy race car move that could have taken the pole.

"Carol, you okay?" the voice coming out of the phone asked loud enough he could understand the words.

"Yes, on a death ride with Steve," she replied.

Jerry turned around and snickered at her comment.

"What's up?" Carol said into the phone.

"We just heard there was another killing, is it the same as last week?" the loud voice asked.

"Not sure, we're on our way down there ourselves. If we live," Carol said.

"So am I," the voice added, "see you there."

Carol hung up the phone. "Well the press already knows, that was Lacy James. It's going to be a circus."

They continued on their way, slipping in and out of the slow moving traffic.

***

Steve, Jerry and Carol arrived in Milford and snaked their way through town to a rural section of the county. The neighborhoods turned into farms and plots of land where the city dwellers had moved. Close enough to have some city, but far enough out to be private, where the neighbors weren't able to look in their windows from their windows.

They spotted the crowd of cars and police vehicles in the distance.

"Well, this must be the place," Jerry said.

Steve slowed down to a crawl to get through the mass of reporters and police surrounding to the scene.

A police officer, standing in the middle of the road, motioned Steve to stop. The officer walked up to the car where Steve had rolled down his window.

"You'll have to turn around, the road is going to be blocked for a while, Sir," the police officer informed him in a polite but commanding manner.

"We're from the Springfield County Sheriff's Department. Sheriff Baker asked us to come down," he told the officer and showed the officer his badge.

"Just wait here please, Sir." The officer grabbed his radio. "Patrol One to Sheriff Baker," he spoke into the mic clipped to the shoulder of his uniform.

"Go ahead," a voice answered.

"Sir, I have Detective Steve Belcher from the Springfield County Sheriff's Department here to see you."

"Let him through," the voice on the radio commanded.

"Go right ahead, Sir," the office told the group. He walked to the front of the car and removed the barrier blocking the road.

Steve slowly drove up the long gravel driveway to what appeared to be a peaceful home. A larger than normal brick ranch house with a three car garage, nice landscaping and flower gardens full of colorful blooms lining the driveway came into view.

"What a pretty place," Carol said when they arrived at the house.

They stopped the car and got out. A tall slender man, dressed in a business suit, with his badge hanging out of his breast pocket, walked out of the garage to where Steve had parked.

"I'm Sheriff Baker," he announced. "Detective Belcher?"

"Yes, Sir," Steve replied, "and this is Detective Stevenson and Doctor Carol Fisher, our County Coroner."

"Thanks for coming down so quickly," Sheriff Baker replied. "I believe we have the same problem you did last week. A Mr. Robert Wilson and his son Josh were found by the housekeeper this morning at 07:00 hours. No wife, she died of cancer three years ago. They were sitting in the family room, naked, with their heads removed and put onto each other's bodies." He looked at the house for a moment. He removed his sunglasses to reveal his dark brown eyes.

"I'm telling you, Detective; this is the damnedest thing I've ever seen." He led the team through the garage.

They walked into the house through a laundry room and into a pristine kitchen.

"We haven't moved the bodies yet because we wanted to see if it's the same as your case up there," Sheriff Baker said.

They walked into the family room where the ME from Milford leaned over the bodies.

"This is our ME, Doctor Martin Cline. Hey Doc, these are Detectives Belcher and Stevenson, and Doctor Fisher from the Springfield Sheriff's office." Sheriff Baker turned to the ME. "What you got, Doc?"

"From all appearances, about the same thing you found up in Springfield. But I'll know more once we get them back to the lab," he said. "Doctor Fisher, would you like to assist me in the autopsies since you've already done two in this matter, it might speed up the information for the detectives?"

"I'd be happy to, Doctor Cline."

"Call me Marty," he said.

"Carol," she replied.

"Okay boys, if you got all the pictures you need, let's get these two back to the house," Doctor Cline said. "You can ride with me, Carol, if you want to, and we can get started."

"That's fine," Carol said. "I'll see you guys later," Carol said to Steve and Jerry.

They looked over the room, the scene, just like the Petersons, chairs facing toward the television.

They looked around and found no sign of a struggle, no drag marks, and no blood of any kind, except what had seeped from the bodies of the two men onto the chairs. The distinct odor of death saturated the air.

Steve fought back the sick feeling in his stomach from the overpowering smell. The bloated bodies looked as if they could explode at any minute. The gruesome sight was one he would have expected to see in a wax museum, or a slasher film, but not in the homes of everyday people.

"What do we know about the deceased?" Steve asked Sheriff Baker.

"Well, not a lot yet," he replied.

"Can we talk to the housekeeper?" Steve asked.

"Yes, we already took her statement, but she's still here, out back. She didn't want to stay in the house. She's pretty shaken up," Sheriff Baker said.

Sheriff Baker led them out a sliding door that opened into the backyard and revealed an in-ground pool. At one end of the pool, they approached a table where the housekeeper and an officer sat.

The housekeeper, Glenda Fuller, still upset and crying,

looked up as the men approached.

"Mrs. Fuller, these detectives are from the Springfield Sheriff's Department, they would like to ask you a few questions, if that's okay?" Sheriff Baker asked.

"I'm Steve Belcher." He tried to seem friendly in order to calm her down. "How long have you been working for the Wilsons?"

"About three and a half years, just after his wife died," she answered.

"And when did you last see Mr. Wilson and his son?"

"Friday morning, when I came to work."

"What time was that?"

"Around 7:00 a.m., that's when I usually get here, just before they left for work around 7:30 a.m.

"Do you know of anyone who would want to hurt them?" Steve asked.

"No!"

"Thank you for your time, Mrs. Fuller, here's my card; please call me if you think of anything else. You can go home now; I'll have an officer escort you home."

Sheriff Baker nodded to an officer to assist her out.

"The family ran a small meat market called Wilson Meats, about twenty minutes from here. If you want, we can head over there while the guys finish up here," Baker suggested.

"Sounds good," Steve said.

The three men exited the back yard going around the side of the house where they watched the two deceased men get loaded into the coroner's van.

"Hell of a way to go," Jerry started watching them close the doors on the van.

"You can follow me if you can keep up in that old thing." He laughed and pointed at Steve's car.

"Don't you worry, Sheriff," Steve said. He and Jerry grinned and climbed into the vehicle.

They followed Sheriff Baker out, past all the reporters

who waited on the road and shouted questions.

Sheriff Baker stopped and stepped out of his car, stating in a loud voice, "You'll all be informed at a news conference this afternoon, I promise."

He got back in his car and drove away to the same cascade of unanswered questions he'd started with.

Following behind Sheriff Baker, Steve and Jerry spotted Lacy James standing at the edge of the crowd. She tried to wave them down, using her best pretty please face. Steve shook his head and refused to stop.

"That's not going to get you in good with her, you know." Jerry snickered.

Steve grinned, stepped on the gas, and roared after Sheriff Baker in a cloud of dust.

Steve drove the dusty gravel road like a race pro. He pulled out his phone and handed it to Jerry.

"Get Tom looking into the Wilson's background, by the time we get back I want to know every time those two took a dump. And have him call his new girlfriend and see if her parents knew the Wilsons."

A moment went by and Steve, fully frustrated, blurted out, "And tell him to find me a psychologist, someone who can tell what this freak is thinking."

"It's the same guy," Jerry told Sheriff Lester. "We're headed to their place of employment to check it out," Jerry said into the phone.

"Tom is going back through the file looking for anything we missed," Sheriff Lester's voice came through the phone's speaker.

"Tell him to start a background on a Mr. Robert Wilson at 1563 St. Rt. 420 in Milford, Ohio. Steve also wants him to call Terry Peterson and see if they knew each other."

"Got it," Sheriff Lester said.

"We'll be down here most of the day, we'll call you with any other updates," Jerry said before he hung up and grabbed for the dashboard to hold himself up as Steve slid sideways on the gravel road.

# Chapter Eight

After pulling into the parking lot of Wilson Meats, Steve parked the car beside Sheriff Baker's squad car. They walked across the parking lot filled with Wilson Meats delivery trucks.

On the dock, workers on forklifts moved whole skids of stacked boxes and people with two wheeled carts moved product.

Steve turned to Jerry. "Hell of a business, explains the house, huh?"

Jerry nodded in agreement.

"This has been in their family for about thirty years, first the dad owned it, Bob Senior, Robert Wilson's father. When he passed on, the son took over back in 1997," Sheriff Baker explained while walking up the steps to the dock.

He led the two men through the maze of workers on the dock into a large office space with a few desks in it. Filing cabinets and posters of livestock and calendars covered all of the open wall space.

At one of the desks, a man in a white hard hat and blood-stained white butcher's coat, sat. His butcher's coat formed around his upper body, betraying his size. He was a working man, the kind of guy who could pick up a whole side of beef and carry it over his shoulder.

The man stood up as they entered the room and revealed he was also very tall, six feet seven inches at least, he towered over the three men,

"Can I help you?"

"Good morning," Sheriff Baker said and pulled his

badge from his inside suit pocket. "I'm Sheriff Baker, and these are Detectives Belcher and Stevenson from the Springfield Sheriff's Department. And you are?"

"I'm Harry Matherson, the plant manager," he responded, walking around the desk and holding out his bear sized hand. The sleeve of his coat rode up his arm, proving it was hard to find a coat that would fit his rather large stature.

Jerry's gaze went to a tattoo on the man's forearm.

"101$^{st}$ Airborne?" Jerry asked.

A smile crossed the large man's face. "I thought you looked like a military man, you can spot one of us a mile away. Have a seat," he said walking back around the desk.

Harry sat down and took off his hard hat and threw it on the desk, revealing a shaved head that appeared to have been in a struggle or two in his life. He rubbed his hand over his head and leaned back in his chair.

"What can I do you for you, Sheriff?"

"When's the last time you saw the Wilsons?" Sheriff Baker asked.

"Around 16:30 Friday afternoon. They were the last ones here when I left for home," he answered. "They should be in anytime, they usually show up around noon or so on Mondays, what's the problem?" he asked concerned.

"They won't be in this morning," Sheriff Baker said. "I'm sorry to tell you they were found dead in their home this morning."

Harry sat straight up in his chair in disbelief. "What?" he stammered. "How?" His demeanor changed to one of confusion.

"We're working on finding out," Sheriff Baker said. "We're going to need access to your staff and their files, is there another family member we could talk to?"

"Both of them?" Harry asked in anguish.

"I'm afraid so. We need to speak to any family members there might be."

"Just Bob's mom living in Florida, I can get you her number," he said and pulled an old leather covered phone book out of a desk drawer.

"Is there anyone you can think of who could have done this?" Sheriff Baker asked. "Did the Wilsons have anybody threatening them?"

"Nothing I can think of, I mean, there's lots of people who didn't like him. He's tough to get along with, but no one I know of wanted to kill them." He handed the phone number to Sheriff Baker.

"We're going to need to talk to all of your employees," Sheriff Baker said. "For now, keep this quiet. I'll have detectives here this afternoon to start interviewing the employees."

"That's fine."

"Did Mr. Wilson have an attorney?" Sheriff Baker asked.

"Yes."

"You might want to call him, we're going to be looking through the files. Thanks for your time, we'll be in touch."

On the way back to their cars, Jerry looked at Steve.

"I sure hope it ain't that guy," he said shaking his head.

"Yeah, it would take a whole army to bring him in," Steve stated with a snicker in his voice.

The three men reached their vehicles and Steve turned around. He'd taken a back seat in the questioning of the plant manager due to Sheriff Baker's lead and not wanting to step on his toes. In his silence, he'd noticed every emotion and move Harry made. He'd also noticed the employees when they entered and left the property.

"Did you notice how no one even cared we're here? Look," Steve said, "they're going about their day as if we never came."

"What are you thinking?" Jerry asked.

"Our killer isn't here," he stated, convinced.

"Well, follow me back to the station, we can meet up with the boys from the scene and see what they've come up with," Sheriff Baker said.

Sheriff Baker and the two detectives climbed into their cars and slowly left the parking lot. Steve quietly followed Sheriff Baker, He'd been a police officer all of his life, but this time he felt puzzled, truly puzzled, for the first time. Being a very street savvy detective, he'd solved most of his cases with good old fashioned police work.

This one was different. They had a serial killer. He felt fear, not for himself, but for the next victims. He knew it wasn't over. He kept thinking to himself, *"Who's next and why is he doing this? Am I good enough to catch him?"* he wondered.

***

In Sheriff Baker's office, Steve, Jerry and Sheriff Baker greeted the detectives from the morning's crime scene.

"Let's meet in here," Sheriff Baker said leading them into a conference room.

They crowded around the table and Sheriff Baker closed the door. Steve and Jerry sat in the back of the room under the picture window.

The two detectives from the local sheriff's department sat across the table from them.

"Well, boys," Sheriff Baker said, "what do you think?" He looked at Steve and Jerry.

"It's our guy," Steve said.

"Great, a God damn serial killer," Sheriff Baker said. "Just what I needed today. It started in your back yard detective and now it's spilled into mine. I'll get with Sheriff Lester up there, my boys will do the leg work on the investigation down here." He turned to the other two at the table.

"You boys get to Wilson's Meats, talk to everyone there and see what you can dig up."

Someone knocked on the door of the conference room. Sheriff Baker answered the door to find Carol and Doctor Martin Cline on the other side.

"Come in," Sheriff Baker said, "What can you tell us, Doc?" He sat down at the head of the table.

Doctor Cline and Carol sat down across from the Detectives. Carol looked at Doctor Cline and nodded her head, letting him take the lead.

"Speak up," Sheriff Baker stated annoyed.

"It's the same killer," Carol said when Martin didn't speak.

"We did find some bruising on the son not apparent on any of the other bodies, and something a little strange in the appearance of the blood, but the lab will have to tell us what it is. Other than that, they're exactly the same. Not much more than we had before, I'm sorry to say."

"When the reports get back, we'll send you copies of all the autopsy results for the file," Doctor Cline said.

"Thanks for all your help," Steve said. "I guess it's time to get out of here and let you get back to work, Sheriff." he said reaching out his hand to shake Sheriff Baker's.

"I'm sure we'll be seeing each other a lot before this is over," he said.

"I think we'll get out of town before the news crews arrive for the news conference," Steve said.

"Too late," Sheriff Baker said. "Might as well join the show."

# Chapter Nine

Steve watched as the time approached for the news conference and all the reporters gathered in front of the doors. They vied for the perfect position to get the best shot.

Lacy James and her camera man, Tim, were no different. They stood to the left of the two glass doors leading into the building. It was about an hour before the conference, but no one wanted to be in the back row. They were like animals at a feeding trough—first come, first served. With all of them in their places, the hungry pack waited for the morsels of information Sheriff Baker was willing to hand out. All of them with questions they had worked on all day since the breaking news story began.

The moment drew closer and each time the door opened, the cameras came on and flashes of lights from the newspaper photographers blared, and questions blurted out of every mouth as if they were a nest of birds waiting for the return of the mother bird to feed them. But each time, it was someone leaving for the day with no comments to sustain their hunger. Without a meal, they quieted down into the nest and waited for the next sighting.

Sheriff Baker and Steve walked to where the group had been standing for over an hour. They shouted out their questions, and Sheriff Baker held up his hands and in his informative, but commanding manner, spoke.

"Good afternoon. As you all know, the murders of Mr. Robert Wilson and his son, twenty-four-year-old Josh Wilson, were discovered today. Their bodies were found in their home this morning by the housekeeper. We are working with all the resources we have to find out the details of their demise. For now, that's about all we know. The investigation is just getting started, and I'm sorry, but that is all we have at this time."

He turned and walked away. Lacy James bolted forward, pointing her microphone at him.

"Sheriff Baker, isn't it true you're working with the Springfield Sheriff's Department and this case is related to the double murder in town two weeks ago?"

The group of reporters quieted when Sheriff Baker turned back around.

"We have called the Springfield Sheriff's Department in case the two are related. But it's not confirmed at this time," he replied.

Not giving him time to escape, Lacy continued, "Isn't it also true, the bodies of all four victims were somehow mutilated?"

"That will be all!" Sheriff Baker said refusing to acknowledge the question.

This only made the nest of hungry birds chirp louder sensing a meal was somehow just out of their reach. Sheriff Baker and Steve retreated to the safety of the police station. Steve watched as Lacy turned to her cameraman, Tim.

"Okay, let's tape this and add it to the news footage for the 18:00 deadline.

Tim counted down. "In 5.. 4.. 3.. 2.. 1."

"This is Lacy James, reporting live in front of the Milford Sheriff's office where as you have just seen, he has confirmed another brutal double murder has been committed. He would not, however, confirm if the two incidents are related. The police are holding back details from the investigation at this time. But this reporter has learned two detectives from the Springfield Sheriff's Department, and the Springfield County ME were called to the scene and have spent most of the day going over the case. Although they declined comment, they were seen leaving the scene of the second killing. We will bring you updates as they arise. Live from Milford, this is Lacy James from ZKN news."

"And we're done," Tim said.

Steve, Jerry and Carol escaped out the back of the station.

"Well it's going to get crazy now." Steve said getting into the car for the ride home.

\*\*\*

The next morning at the station, the group sat around the conference table. On the board, a new row of pictures had been added to the row from the Peterson's murder, eerily the same in every aspect.

Steve sat in a daze and scanned the board, back and forth, a thousand questions running through his head and no answers for them.

Sheriff Lester walked in taking a sip of his morning coffee.

"Morning," Sheriff Lester said to Steve. Steve sat going over the details of the previous day with Jerry and Tom. "From what Sheriff Baker tells me we have a serial killer."

"I believe that's correct," Steve answered.

"What do we know for sure?" Sheriff Lester asked.

"Well, he or she, hell could be "them" for all we know at this point," Steve said, "have killed four people in what we believe to be the same fashion. No real leads from the first two. Sheriff Baker's group is running down all the leads from the second killings."

"What about the bodies?" he said turning to Carol.

"Same results we found in the Peterson's, except some small anomalies in their blood that the lab is working on. Should have the results in a few days," she explained.

"I've called the state police in on this. I'll arrange a meeting with them and Sheriff Baker. I'm also gonna call in the FBI on this one. Steve, I'll let you know when they'll be here. I want you and Jerry still running point on this." Sheriff Lester said. "Any word on the Peterson woman, Tom?" All eyes turned to Tom.

Tom squirmed as if he was caught with his hand in the cookie jar. "Not yet, I haven't reached her."

"Well, don't stop until you do. Okay, let's get to work," Sheriff Lester commanded. He got up from the table and left the room.

Jerry, not one to miss a chance at Tom, leaned over to him. "Trouble in paradise?" he said, nudging Tom's shoulder. He and Steve snickered.

***

Tom left several messages for Terry, but got no response from her. He sat down at his desk and picked up the phone. He dialed the number and his mind wandered back to the drive after her parent's funeral. He knew she had an afternoon flight back, leaving the cemetery she was headed for the airport. While he drove her back to the motel to collect her belongings, she didn't mutter a sound. Pulling into the lot, she'd turned to him.

"I want to thank you for everything you've done for me," she'd said kindly. "I'm sorry we had to meet like this. But I'm glad you were here."

She got out of the car and he rushed to help her. "Would you like me to go to the airport with you?" he'd asked hopefully.

"No, you've done more than I could ask. And I don't want to keep you from your work. I can make it on my own," she'd told him with a hint of a smile.

"Well, I might need to get in touch with you for some reason," he'd said in a desperate fashion trying to make the conversation last.

She'd reached into her purse and pulled out her business card. "Here's all my numbers, call me when you find something out about my parents." Then she'd turned and walked away, entering the motel.

In his mind, he stood there in the parking lot holding the car door trying to remember everything he could about her. The way her hair slowly swayed back and forth as she walked. The touch of her cheek, wet with tears as she gently kissed him at the cemetery. The first time he saw her walking down the corridor in the airport and the glow she had in her eyes. She'd walked away as if they'd never met.

The phone rang and his mind still lost in lustful memories was brought back to reality by the sound of her voice.

"Hello. Hello."

"Terry?" he stammered.

"Yes."

"This is Tom Jensen from the Springfield Sheriff's Department."

"Tom, how are you? Is there any word on my parents' killer?"

"Not really," he admitted. "But I do have a couple of questions I would like to ask, if you have the time?"

"Sure, now is good."

"The reason I've left you so many messages was that, I, uh, we need to know if you or your parents ever knew anyone by the name of Robert Wilson?" he said trying to cover up the stammer in his voice, still nervous talking to her.

"Not that I'm aware of. How many times did you call? My phone has been out of order the last few days."

"Just a couple," he answered, although the actual number was much higher. "Had your parents ever been to Milford?" he asked trying to keep his voice from cracking.

"No, I don't think so," she said. "What does this have to do with my parents?"

"Well, we're running down a few leads from another case that might be related," he told her trying not to tell her about the other killings. "Well," he said trying to keep her on the phone, "how are you doing?"

"You know, trying to get on with my life," she said with a sigh and his heart fell again. "Hey, Tom, I'm thinking about flying out there next week to see my parents' attorney for some papers I have to sign. Any chance you would like to have dinner, and I could repay your kindness?"

"That would be great!" he responded, trying to keep his seat.

"Great, I'll call you and let you know when I'm coming. See you then," she said and hung up the phone.

Hanging up the phone, he turned to see Steve and Jerry standing behind him with their arms crossed, shaking their heads.

"What?"

They both turned and walked away. Jerry turned to Steve. "You're going tell him 'bout the birds and bees aren't you?" They both snickered and walked sat at their desks.

Tom turned around and rustled the papers on his desk, trying to ignore the laughter behind him.

\*\*\*

"Morning, Junior," Jerry said walking into the room where Tom was setting up for the morning meeting. "I brought donuts for this morning's meeting, I thought you might need the energy after yesterday's call."

Tom stood and stared at Jerry. He wanted to tell him what the conversation had really been about, but wanted to wait to see him eat his words. Those chances came few and far between, and he wasn't going to waste one. He would wait until he could parade her around in front of them.

\*\*\*

The officers entered the room and Steve took his normal

seat alongside the board where all of the pictures hung.

Sheriff Lester entered with three strangers in tow. "This is Sergeant Brian Winslow, from the State Police, Special Agent Herb McIntyre, from the FBI, and Criminal Psychologist Melissa Harris, also from the FBI."

Sheriff Baker entered the room. "Sorry I'm late, got a little late start this morning."

"Thanks for coming everybody. I think we have a problem on our hands bigger than all of us. I've asked the State Police and the FBI to give us some insight, if they can, on what we're dealing with. Sheriff Baker and I have decided to run the investigation from here. Steve, we want you and Jerry to head up the task force on this. The rest of us are going to do anything we can to help. So Steve, you have the floor." Sheriff Lester said and sat down. Steve rose out of his chair.

"Well, first, thanks for coming and helping. Let's start with what we do know and maybe you can fill in some of the blanks. We have four victims, all killed in the same way, by decapitation. They're drugged, we don't know if it's before or after their abduction, they're drained of blood and their heads are sewn on each other's bodies. Their bodies are washed and returned to their homes and placed in front of their televisions, without so much as a hair to go on."

Steve flipped over the board and revealed the gruesome display of bodies.

Steve continued when no one interrupted with any questions. "At this point we have no suspects, no motive and not much else to go on. The latest two, the Wilsons, did show some small differences; the ME's from both counties are still working on those." He tapped his finger on the Wilson's picture. "The detectives from the Milford Sheriff's Department were given the task of tracking down all the leads from the Wilson's life to see if we have any crossovers with the first victims," he said and gladly sat in his chair.

"We can also reach the conclusion, if he or she is working alone, whoever it is, must be very strong. Having to carry and place the bodies back in their houses, without leaving any drag marks, would be no easy task. Have I left anything out?"

"Doctor Harris, is it?" Steve said addressing the FBI Criminal Psychologist. In her late forties with black hair streaked with grey, she was dressed in a black business suit and black flat shoes. "You're the FBI's expert on serial killers, can you shed some light on who we're looking for?"

"Well, from reading the case files sent to us, your subject is suffering from some kind of delusion, probably brought on by displaced anger. In his mind, it's bringing him to act against what he believes is the root of his delusion. Someone or something in his life that has caused his mental trauma." She reached up and pushed her glasses up from the end of her nose.

"He is well educated, deliberate in his actions. They are well planned and carried out to the smallest detail. He needs seclusion to complete his work, so we're looking for someone who takes his victims to remote locations to kill them and take his revenge." She pointed to the board, focusing Steve's attention on the gruesome sights. "He's not choosing his victims at random, there must be a pattern somewhere. He's not leaving any clues, but somewhere there is a clue to who this person is," she said as she searched the pictures, examining every detail of the scene. "I'm afraid there'll be more killings before we can find out who he is. He's not going to stop—he can't—not until he rids himself of the trauma feeding his delusions." She turned quickly from the board knocking a picture off that floated and landed on the floor at Steve's feet.

"So this wacko is gonna keep on killing until we stop him?" Steve asked in a frustrated tone of voice leaning over to pick up the picture of dead eyes that stared back at him.

"Yes, he will, I'm sorry to say." She held her hands out in front of her, palms up before she clasped them into fists and dropped her hands to her sides.

"But what about switching the heads?" Steve asked. As he held up the picture he had picked up from the floor.

"I have no idea, I haven't heard of anything like this before. Best guess, he is feeling that someone in his past betrayed him in some way," she said with another glance at the pictures on the board.

"In other words, you really don't have a clue," Steve said. "What can you do to help us?" Steve turned his question to Special Agent McIntyre.

"Knowing what we do now," Special Agent McIntyre said and got to his feet, his medium build and short brown hair could set a stereotype for FBI detectives on television. Square jawed with a tanned face, he spoke as if he was giving a lecture at the academy. "The FBI is already running down the leads we have. We don't know of any cases matching this type of mutilation." He tapped one of the pictures with a pencil. "But it might take a couple of days to get the information. From the case file, it looks like he's struck twice, two weeks apart. If he holds pattern, we have a week and a half to track this guy down. I'll advise my superiors, we need to offer all the resources we have to help in this investigation. This won't be a turf war," he said offering a reassuring nod to Sheriff Lester.

"Your department will take the lead, we can supply as many men as needed until this guy is caught," the agent concluded.

"I could use some help chasing down all the old employees from the Wilson Company," Sheriff Baker said. "There are around two hundred that we know of."

"You'll have the help tomorrow," McIntyre responded. "If you can send any lab samples to the FBI lab, we can make them a priority and get the results back quicker. I would like your permission for our ME to examine the bodies, just for another look, if that's okay."

"They can be here in the morning," Sheriff Baker said.

"Doctor Harris will be working out of the regional office with me. Keep us up to date on any information and any needs you may have, so we can assist," McIntyre said.

"The state police are also here to assist in any way we can. We can provide extra manpower anywhere needed," Sergeant Winslow offered.

"What do we do about the press? They're already all over this," Sheriff Lester asked.

"The only thing we really have to go on are the details of the mutilations—they have to remain within these walls. If the press gets wind of this, it'll be what the killer wants, he wants to see this on the news. It's part of his justification and gives him satisfaction," Doctor Harris said.

"But the press already knows we're hiding something," Steve said.

"The best we can do is, no comment. If we feed his delusion, it's been our experience his killing spree will escalate. We're on his time frame, sad to say. Unless we find a clue quick, all we can do is keep looking and hope he leaves us something," Sheriff Lester said.

"From here on out, all press reports will come from this office, understood?" Sheriff Lester ordered.

"Thanks for your help. I guess that's all we need for now, we have our work cut out for us." Sheriff Lester said and the group rose and filed out of the room.

Steve remained staring at the pictures on the board.

Jerry turned to Steve. "What do you see?"

"You don't believe all that mumbo jumbo crap do you? I think this guy is out for revenge and some people on this earth are born to kill. They don't all have to be crazy, like the doc says, some are just mean," Steve said.

"But the way this guy is doing it, it's nuts," Jerry said.

"You and the doc might be right, but I think all this

psycho stuff is bullshit," Steve said staring coldly at the pictures on the board.

\*\*\*

"Jerry, look, can you believe this," Steve said with contempt in his voice. They stood inside the glass front doors. Outside the police station, the news media had set up camp. With two sets of murders, reporters lurked around waiting for any information. Their hunger for information growing and speculation rising, they stood watching for any chance to hound the police. He gathered his thoughts and exited the front of the building.

Special agent McIntyre trailed behind Sheriff Lester, Sergeant Winslow and Sheriff Baker followed. No doubt none of them wanted to miss the photo opportunity. A case like this could propel all of their careers. Even Doctor Melissa Harris joined the group walking up to where the reporters had set up their cameras. When Sheriff Lester engaged the media, Steve and Jerry watched from inside the building.

"All of them looking for their fifteen minutes." He walked away from the spectacle.

# Chapter Ten

Steve, Jerry and Tom had been scrutinizing every scrap of paper coming in from the investigative task force. It trapped them under an endless load of paperwork. Statements from over two hundred employees from the Wilson Meats company, neighbors and friends of the family. The canvas of the surrounding businesses was also included in the mound engulfing the three detectives. In the squad room, the group of officers, from all the agencies, worked round the clock entering the information into computer databases trying to formulate a pattern that would lead them to the killer.

Steve looked around him. The room buzzed with people on phones and the sound of keys on keyboards being hit at rates that would seem they'd been transported back in time where secretarial pools were still the normal office sight. The scare of the serial killings had been covered on the network news. It was the major story leading every newscast. Fear gripped the town. Not knowing where the killer would strike next was the discussion on everyone's lips. And everyone wondered why had the killer started in this town?

"I'm about to go blind reading all of this," Tom said rubbing his eyes and stretching his arms over his head and yawning. The loud noise broke the silence between them.

Steve and Jerry looked up at the young detective who rose from his chair.

"I need to stretch my legs," Tom said.

"While you're up, grab us a fresh cup of coffee, Junior," Jerry said.

Tom grabbed up their coffee cups with a look of contempt on his face and headed toward the coffee pot.

"He's going to make somebody a good wife someday," Jerry said with a grin.

"Let me know if you need help with the big words," Tom said and set the coffee down in front of Jerry. Steve watched Jerry wondering if he'd take the bait. They all needed a break.

Jerry had gone into the Army right out of high school and had received all of his training in the military. Just an average student in school, he'd never really cared about learning. A typical jock, he had excelled in sports, but was lacking in book work. His career in the military had strengthened his work ethic at the cost of many hours on latrine duty. Part of the reason he had only made E5. He was, *jump in the fight and let the book guys figure out what happened.* His natural born street smarts had let him survive through his tours of duty, and in situations where that was the only thing that kept him alive.

Jerry stood up from his desk, apparently willing to let the bait go.

"I need a break, too. Tom, let's go check out some more of the leads I've been working on."

"What leads?" Steve asked looking up from the file he was working on.

Jerry stretched as if he was trying to reach the moon and replied, "Looking into the possibility of where the drugs came from. I still haven't talked to all our contacts yet."

"Okay," Steve answered. "But make sure the kid doesn't get lost out there."

"You got it, Boss, I won't lose him, maybe," Jerry said.

Steve looked up at the board, covered in photos and a map of the state. Two red pins stuck in the map marked the sites where the bodies were found. The distance between the two places was around seventy five miles.

"He traveled a long ways to do his work," Steve thought. He searched the map, wondering, like the pictures he had been staring at for days, if it would tell him where the killer hid. He followed the road markings with his eyes and noticed every turn of the intermingling colored lines making up the twisted intersections of little towns along the path.

"Where can you be?" he said to himself. "How did you get from this couple to the next?" The endless list of questions continued to plague his thoughts. Frustrated and tired from the long hours of peering into the endless pile of folders, he decided he needed a break as well.

Steve dropped the file in his hand on the desk and walked out of the room leaving the board full of unanswered questions looming over the room.

\*\*\*

Steve returned from a walk around the building. He'd stopped to get a cup of coffee from the local corner store. On his way back, he passed Sheriff Lester in the parking lot.

"How's it going, Steve?" Sheriff Lester called to him.

"Slow and tiring," he said.

"Yeah, the leg work on this one alone is going to be hundreds of man hours," Sheriff Lester said, sounding to Steve like the cost of the operation meant more to him than catching the killer.

Not caring about the price of catching criminals, Steve ignored the comment and the two walked back across the parking lot to the station.

"Run across anything yet?" Lester asked.

"Just more of the same dead ends, Jerry and Tom are out checking on a few things, but nothing solid yet," Steve said.

"I hope something comes up soon," Sheriff Lester said

as he walked in the front door, bending over not to hit his cowboy hat on the door jam.

Steve walked into the squad room where a young woman sat at one of the desks.

"May I help you?" he asked in a tone of voice that said, *Who are you and what are you doing here?*

Startled, she jumped up from the chair and dropped the case file she'd had in her lap on the floor. She picked up the file and introduced herself.

"I'm Julie Simms from the FBI forensics department. I'm here with Doctor Singer who is in examining the bodies," she explained. Her face turned red showing her embarrassment.

"Sorry, they said I could wait in here and go over the case file."

"It's okay," Steve said and tried not to laugh at her while she composed herself.

"I couldn't stay back there," she admitted with a nod of her head in the direction of the morgue and pulled back the long blonde hair from her eyes.

Steve smiled and said, "I can't take it much either, what do you think so far?"

"This is really weird," she said as more of a question than a statement. "I've read all of the files on serial killers from the FBI and this doesn't match anything I've seen before. With what I read in the autopsy reports, this guy is *out there.*"

"Is that your professional opinion?" he asked getting a smile to cross her face.

"Doctor Singer, this is the chief detective on the case, Steve Belcher," Carol said walking up behind Steve. "They're from the FBI crime lab to assist in the case."

"And I see you've met my assistant, Julie," he said.

"Yes," Steve said with a smile.

"Well, Doc," Steve said and sat down at the table, "any more light you can shed on this thing?"

"Not much more than Doctor Fisher. Going back over the bodies gave us a little more insight than before," he said. "Your killer is a hunter who knows how to drain the bodies of blood. Like I discussed with Doctor Fisher, they appear to have been hung to remove all the blood." He removed his glasses and rubbed his eyes. "As if they were a deer hanging in someone's shed after the hunt. The removal of the heads is the puzzling part."

"It's as if in one fast easy motion they were taken off with enough force to not leave any hesitation marks." He gestured, making a hand chop on the table. "It would have to be a very sharp, large bladed object, a sword or an ax of some kind. That's the kind of damage I'm seeing on the bodies. I can't be sure, but it's as close of guess as I can make. They're restrained in a position allowing this to happen. How, I don't know, but your killer wanted them alive when he did it. Otherwise the heart would have stopped and the blood would pool in some areas before they were hung up."

When she spoke, the other three in the room listened without interruption. The coldness of the crime had reached another level.

Steve looked up at the pictures on the board. Thoughts of how the killer could have done it, and whatever could drive him to such an act of violence, was a riddle he couldn't understand.

\*\*\*

Returning to the squad room, Jerry and Tom entered as Carol escorted Doctor Singer and Julie back out to the lobby. They passed the three walking down the hall and Jerry commented, "Tom, there's another chance for you." Jerry referred to Julie who was young and pretty, dressed in a nice pants suit showing off her features in a very attention getting manner.

"Give it a rest," Tom muttered and walked into the

conference room to continue work on the files.

Steve sat staring at the board of information, lost in the unbelievable story unfolding around him. The two detectives returned to their seats and began to pore over the files.

Steve turned to Jerry and asked, "Find anything?"

"No, nothing," Jerry said with an edge of frustration.

"Well, while you two were out screwing around, the FBI doc was here and gave us some more info."

While he caught them up on every gory detail of the report, Tom used his computer and started to enter the information in the profile he had been creating. When Steve explained that the victims had been hung up to drain their blood after their heads were removed, Jerry went pale.

Steve watched him as his eyes lost focus and he stared into space. Did the gory murders bring back images of the atrocities he'd witnessed in the war?

The mutilated bodies of the war dead and some captured noncombatants displayed by their killers took over Steve's thoughts. He'd seen too many news reports on the war Jerry had fought. If he felt the heat from the fires from the burned out homes on the news reports, how did Jerry live with it?

Jerry rubbed his eyes as if sweat burned his eyes from the heat, and the sand blowing through the air on those news stories.

"We had to cut them down," Jerry said, his gaze a blank stare. "The smell of the decayed and partially burned and rotted flesh hung in the heat with flies filling the air in a swarm around the stench. Cutting down a body as pieces of flesh fell off the bone, was the worst. You poor bastard, what did you do to deserve this?"

"Jerry, Jerry!" Steve repeated, shaking him and bringing him back to the conversation.

"Are you here?" Steve asked, he'd never seen Jerry so lost in the past. "Where were you?"

"Sorry, wandered for a minute," Jerry said wiping the sweat beaded up on his forehead and hands away.

"Maybe it's time to call it a day," Steve stated. "Go home and see that wife and kids of yours, you too, Tom, get out of here. That's an order."

"See you tomorrow," Jerry said.

\*\*\*

Steve still poured over the files long after the rest of the task force had left for home. He drank coffee and tried to stay sharp for the mind numbing task. The case gave him a reason to be away from home. Home reminded him of everything he'd lost. He looked over interview after interview from the Wilson employees and after a while they all read the same. No one saw or heard anything. It was almost as if someone had made copies of the statements and filled the folders with the same useless information to give him something to read. He turned back to the board and peered at the pictures again.

From the information Doctor Singer had given him earlier, he began to imagine them hung upside down, blood dripping from their lifeless bodies. The shadow of the sinister killer stood in the dark and held their heads in his hands like trophies from the hunt. The killer moved from the shadows and thrust them up to his face with the victim's eyes wide open and staring at him.

Steve jerked up from the table where he'd fallen asleep an hour before. The file's folded edged had formed a crease on his face. Things in the room came into focus, he blinked and realized it was a dream.

He relaxed back in his chair. Still shaken from the dream, he turned to the pictures on the board.

"I'll find you, you bastard," he muttered to himself. He got up and left the room.

"I need a drink." He walked down the hallway to leave the station.

# Chapter Eleven

Tom shuffled into the conference room. Monday mornings were hard enough, but this one meant another day of the group gathered around the pile of paperwork, looking for something none of them could define. Things had calmed down in the town and were somewhat back to normal once again. Tom smiled. Everyone looked so grim. But he had Terry's evening arrival on his mind. The anticipation lifted his mood despite the circumstances of his job.

"What's up, Junior? You look like you won the lottery," Jerry said to the smiling Tom who offered no response.

"He's hiding something, Steve."

Steve looked at Tom over the top of his glasses.

"Yeah, he's hiding something, you can tell by the guilty look on his face," Steve said. "Come on, kid, give it up, we're police officers, we *will* find out." He said the words in a joking but intimidating tone of voice.

"Can't a guy be happy in his work?" Tom said with a grin.

"No," Steve and Jerry said at the same time.

Tom smugly returned to the file in his hand. *They'll find out soon enough,* he thought.

"Good morning, guys," Carol said when she walked into the room wearing her lab coat and carrying a file in one hand and a cup of coffee in the other. "I got the results back from last week. Along with the GHB, they found traces of Coumadin, a blood thinner. They also found traces of quaternary ammonia on some of the tissue." She held up the file in her hand.

"Now the blood thinner we believe was used to thin the blood so it would drain easier, but the quaternary ammonia is used as a sterilizing compound in some food processing plants."

The three men sat up in their chairs, listening to the report.

"I can understand the blood thinner, but, why the sanitizer?" Steve questioned.

"Maybe to kill bacteria or remove any trace DNA he might have left behind," Carol answered.

"Jerry, call down to Wilson Meats and see is they use that *quat* stuff in their process anywhere. Tom, check out all the medical records for the deceased and find out if any one of them was on a blood thinner. Thanks, Carol," Steve said.

She nodded, and grabbed a cinnamon roll from the box on the table on her way out.

He hadn't found anything in the report on the Peterson's house, so Tom started looking through the medical records from the Wilsons.

"Nothing here," he reported to Steve quickly.

"Well, I knew it was a long shot. That stuff has to be a prescription drug, do a search and see if any has been stolen lately. We could get lucky."

Jerry picked up the file on Wilson Meats and dialed the phone. "Hello, this is detective Stevenson from the Springfield Sheriff's Office. Is Harry Matherson available? Sure, I'll hold."

"Jerry, ask them what concentrate they use and have on hand," Tom said.

"Yes, I'm still here. Can you tell me if you use quaternary ammonia in your operation? And if you do, can you tell me what concentrate you have on hand?" Jerry asked as he nodded to the others confirming the use in the operation. "Fifty parts per million and you can buy it just about anywhere. Thanks for your time. No, no information yet. Thanks we'll be in touch," Jerry said and hung up the phone.

"Well that narrows it down," Steve said sarcastically. "See what you can dig up anyway, it's a long shot, but it's all we have."

The group split up to follow their own leads as Sheriff Lester walked into the room. He moved to where Steve and Tom pored over the files.

"How's it going?" he asked.

"Still chasing my tail," Steve said.

"I've scheduled a conference at 10:00 a.m. with the FBI, and the State Police, to keep everyone in the loop. We'll do it in my office."

"We don't have much to tell them, this guy doesn't leave any trail to follow," Steve said.

"He will, they always make a mistake, and when he does, you'll be there to catch him," Sheriff Lester said in a reassuring tone. "See you at 10:00 a.m. and don't be late."

***

"Nothing on the quat," Jerry reported, "it appears you can get it from several hundred companies, online or most chemical distributors."

"No reports of any stolen Coumadin, it is however one of the most powerful blood thinners doctors prescribe after a stroke or heart surgery," Tom said.

Steve noticed the time. "Shit, I'm gonna be late," he said remembering he had to be at the sheriff's office for the conference. Jerry and Tom looked at each other as Steve bolted out the door.

Steve rushed into Sheriff Lester's office with the conference call already in progress. The door banged shut behind him. Everyone looked at him and his face grew warm.

"Sorry," he said. He crept across the room more softly.

Special Agent McIntyre was in the process of greeting and announcing everyone on his end of the call. Sheriff Baker and Sergeant Winslow from the state police smiled when he walked over to take an empty seat near them.

"Okay," Special agent McIntyre said. "Any new leads from your end Sheriff Lester?"

"Not really, we're going over all the reports we've received. I assume you've seen the reports from your ME and the toxicology from your lab?" Sheriff Lester asked.

"Yes, we have them in front of us." McIntyre said.

"Is there any more insight from the psychology reports?" Sheriff Lester asked.

"Nothing more than you already know. The only thing I can add is he must be watching them for some time to be able to move in and out and know how to get to them without being noticed. From the reports, the drugs are introduced through food or drink, so our killer could be working as a server at a restaurant or bar, or simply be a delivery man for a pizza shop. He's someone they trust to handle their food, that's for certain," Doctor Harris said.

"Okay," Sheriff Lester concluded, "we'll be in touch."

"That narrows it down to about a half a million people," Sheriff Baker commented with sarcasm. "I could have done a profile that good." He scratched his head. "Well, we'll have to keep looking through the files and hope something comes up before he kills someone else."

As the group left the room, Sheriff Lester turned to Steve. "Stick around for a second."

Steve sat down while Lester escorted the other men back to the lobby. He came back and closed the door.

"I got a call from Lacy James. She wants to have lunch today. She had a tone in her voice that made me uncomfortable," Lester said. He hooked his thumbs in his gun belt and rocked back on his heels.

"What did she want?" Steve asked.

"To speak off the record, she claims. I want you there

too," he told Steve. "I know how much you hate the press, but maybe she can help with this. We're running without any direction here. Let's go see what she wants and then you can go back to hating the press, okay?"

"You know I hate those blood suckers, but looks like I have no choice, so, I'd love to," Steve said with a frown and he returned to the conference room.

Steve entered the room to see the two detectives going through file after file.

As he sat down and began to work, Jerry asked, "Well, are you gonna fill us in?"

"Nothing to add, they're as lost as we are," he told them.

"I'm ready for some lunch," Jerry proclaimed. "You boys want to join me?" He rose from his seat and stretched tall enough to touch the ceiling in the room.

"I could eat," Tom said.

"What about you, Steve? You ready to get out of here for a while?" he asked.

"You guys go ahead. I get the pleasure of having lunch with Sheriff Lester," he said.

"Aren't you special," Jerry said with a sneer.

"Yeah," Steve said back in a condescending tone.

He would have rather eaten lunch with anyone on the planet than have lunch with someone from the press. He viewed them as no better than parasites. All they did was feed on the misfortune of others. Reporters put the worst parts of humanity on display. The real issue was that humanity was obsessed with the failure of others and couldn't get enough of it. That was what gave reporters a job in the first place. People needed tragedy in their lives. They weren't satisfied with a quiet existence. They had an innate need to know every last detail of someone else's life, right down to the hidden details everyone kept locked away, hoping no one would ever discover.

When Sheriff Lester came in and asked if he was ready

to go, Steve took off his glasses and threw them on the file he was reading. He rose from the chair, grabbed his suit coat from the back of the chair, and proceeded to follow Lester down the hall.

At Lester's car, before he got in, the sheriff looked over at Steve and said, "You could act a little more pleasant when we get there."

"Don't worry, I'll put a smile on my face."

Not one to hide his emotions, everyone always knew where he was coming from because he wore most of it on his face. He couldn't help it. Just as a bird had to fly, Steve had a never ending supply of cynicism. He had no problem using the "bull shit" card if he needed to.

As Lester drove to Gretta's Steve asked, "What's this all about?"

"Don't know. We're gonna go find that out," Lester said with a grin.

The restaurant was mostly empty as the midday rush had passed. There were only a few long lunchers hanging around to avoid going back to work.

Already seated at a table, Lacy waved to them as they entered.

"Lacy, you know Steve don't you?" Lester said. He pulled out a chair and sat down.

"Yes, how are you detective?" she said putting the menu down in front of her.

"I hope you don't mind, but I asked Steve to join us," Lester said.

"No, that's fine, I can get the story from both of you," she said.

"You see the special, boys?" Wanda blurted out in her usual flamboyant manner and held out the menus

"We'll just have the special," Lester said.

Wanda left with the order.

"What's this all about?" Lester asked as if he was conducting an interrogation.

"Well, Sheriff, I thought you should see the lead story for the evening news, and have a chance to comment before it hits the air," she said handing him what she'd written.

He took the sheet of paper from her and began to read. Reading it, the easy relaxed look on his face turned to one of a more intense nature. He stopped and handed the paper to Steve. Steve read the page, and his mood changed, not to one of surprise, but of concern. This was the only fact that hadn't been released, the signature of the killer.

"No one needs to know this," Lester said and slapped his hat down on the table.

"The public has a right to know the truth," Lacy said.

"They have no need to know this killer mutilated these people like this, not yet," Steve stated in a harsh manner while he tried to keep his voice from being overheard.

"We're still trying to find the freak." Steve took off his glasses and pinched the bridge of his nose. Anger made his face burn when he looked back at Lacy.

"Where did you get this from?" Concerned about the leak of information, he knew she and Carol had been close for years.

"There are a lot of people involved in the scope of this. Did you think it was going to be kept secret forever?" she said.

"You're just looking for your big story," Steve scoffed.

"Yes, I am. You would do the same thing in my place." she said.

The group quieted down when Wanda brought their food to the table.

"Make ours to go," Lester said. He picked up his hat and placed it back on his head.

Wanda turned away with the plates of food and Lacy continued, "Just wanted to see if you have anything to add."

"You don't have to do this yet," Steve said. "How about you wait a week and we'll let you in on everything we have. It's too early in this investigation for this to be released. It'll hinder us even further, and cause more senseless media gossip for us to deal with, and we don't have the time," Steve said. "Just think about what you're doing for once, instead of your ratings!" He stormed away from the table and out of the door. With his anger out of control, he paced outside the restaurant by the sheriff's car.

Lester joined him carrying the meals they'd ordered. "It's not going to do us any good to piss her off, so cool your jets."

"That blood sucking bitch is thinking nothing about the families, or how this could affect this case, she just wants ratings!" he said still in a fit of rage.

"There's nothing we can do about it now, let's go," Lester said and climbed in the car.

"She's right, you know, it was going to happen sooner or later. When we get back, let's get everyone together. The answer to questions from now on is, *no comment*. I don't care if they're asked what they had for lunch, the answer better be *no comment*."

"Where do you think she got the information?" Steve wondered out loud.

"It doesn't matter, could have come from a hundred people not under our control. The point is to stop anything else from leaking. I guess this guy is going to get his publicity after all," Lester said.

***

They arrived at the station and Steve gathered the group together. Both he and Lester had calmed down somewhat but were still distressed about the situation when they explained what had transpired. Everyone looked around the room trying to guess who'd informed the press.

"We're not looking for how it got out. We need to be careful who we're talking to and where. Understood?" Lester said in a commanding tone.

Back in the conference room the detectives took their seats. Tom spoke up, "Steve, can I talk to you for a second?"

"Sure," he said.

Tom left the room and moved down the hall. Steve followed him. Tom stopped outside of earshot of anyone else and turned to Steve.

"What's this all about?" Steve asked.

"I'd like to have the next couple of days off."

"What's up?" Steve said in a concerned voice.

Looking around to make sure no one could hear him, "Terry is coming in a couple of hours, and I'd like the time to help her out with a few things."

A smile spread across Steve's face replacing concern with surprise.

"And don't tell Jerry," he said holding his hands out palms up. "That's all I need is for him to find out about this. He'd be following us around in camouflage pants and taking pictures."

"Yeah, Jerry would have way too much fun with this," Steve said in agreement.

"Okay, I guess you deserve a couple days off, and I won't tell Jerry," he said laughing, "but keep your phone on in case we need you."

"Thanks, Steve, I will," Tom agreed.

The two men walked back into the squad room where Jerry still worked on the files. Steve walked around to his chair and tried to hide the grin on his face from the thought of their very own, "Ranger Jerry" dressed in camo and lurking through the town gathering information on Tom. A thought sprung into his mind.

"Jerry, did we ever cross check any of the employees for those with military backgrounds?" Steve blurted out. "This guy's been watching them for a while, able to abduct them in silence, return them, and disappear like a ghost. Who do you know who has that kind of capabilities?"

Jerry's face lit up.

"I'm on it," Jerry said.

"You need some help, Jerry?" Tom asked.

Before Jerry could answer, Steve spoke up. "I thought you had somewhere else to be?"

Tom took the hint. "Yes, I do," he answered. He grabbed his coat and headed for the door.

"Where you going?" Jerry questioned with a puzzled look on his face.

"Personal business," Tom said.

"None of the suspects have any military background," Jerry said.

"Check with the local VFW and see if there's anyone new hanging around," Steve said and sat back down with the display of violence again capturing his focus.

*** 

"Well, here we are," Tom told Terry as he pulled back up to the front of the motel.

"Thanks for helping me all week," Terry said with a smile.

Tom ran around the car as she waited for him to open her door.

"See, it's not so bad having a guy open doors for you, is it?" Tom grinned when her smile turn to a cute laugh.

"Do you really have to go home tomorrow?" he asked in a wistful voice. He walked her to the door of her room.

She turned to him and with a frown said, "Yes, I have a shop to run."

He leaned in to kiss her goodbye. She hesitated but moved forward to meet his lips with hers and the two shared a kiss. Their bodies pressed together and his arms wrapped around her to hold her close. He never wanted to let her go. She wrapped her arms around his body. The emotions that ran wild in his soul convinced him that she had to be feeling the same things he was. His soul touched hers and their kiss turned into a passionate embrace. When they parted, she looked into his eyes.

"I better be going," she said in a breathless tone.

"Let's keep in touch," he told her.

"Good night," she said and closed the door.

With a feeling of loss, Tom turned and walked slowly out of the hotel to his waiting car. Climbing in, he still felt the rush of blood pumping through his body. The heat of the kiss they'd shared was still hot on his lips.

He got back out of the car and returned to her room. He knocked on the door and as it opened he reveled in the smile on her face and the hunger in her eyes. They embraced again and he shut the door behind him.

Continuing the embrace, losing themselves in each other, they made their way to her bed. Slowly sitting down on the bed, she pulled away from him.

"Wait," she exclaimed, catching her breath. She picked up the remote control and turned on the television, and turned up the volume. "We don't want to wake up Jake do we?" she asked with a smile.

Standing in front of Tom she unbuttoned her blouse and pulled down one shoulder to reveal her black lace bra.

Tom fixated on her every motion. She slid the blouse over her head and the sound of the evening news came over the television.

"And we go live to Lacy James reporting the latest on the brutal serial killings, both here in Springfield and in Mason Ohio. Lacy?"

"Yes, Jim, as I reported earlier in the week, the police still won't confirm that the bodies of the four people brutally murdered had their heads removed and sewn onto each other's bodies."

The television went dead. Tom had picked up the remote and turned it off.

Her blank stare, while she covered herself with her

blouse, told the story of the shock she felt. Tom rushed to comfort her and knelt down in front of the chair and reached out for her and touched her hand. She turned to him.

"Why didn't you tell me?" she said with tears welling up in her hazel colored eyes.

The first tear dribbled down her cheek and Tom said softly, "We didn't think you needed to hear that. It's the only lead we had in the case and it wasn't supposed to be released."

With her tears flowing freely, he tried to comfort her, reaching out to put his arms around her.

"Just leave," she ordered, pushing him away.

"But, Terry, it was for your own good," he tried to explain.

"I want you to go," she said repeatedly, growing angry.

Tom reluctantly stood up. "Are you sure?"

Unable to answer, except for a nod of her head to confirm, Terry continued to sob.

Tom reached the door and opening it, turned, hoping that he could somehow help her, but he realized she didn't want him around. He left quietly, closing the door softly behind him. He stood in the hallway and leaned against her room. Thinking this would be the last time he would see her, he whispered softly, "Goodbye, Terry."

Tom turned and walked away slowly as if his very soul had been taken from him. He felt nothing inside but a deep sadness at the thought that he'd lost the love of his life. He walked to his car, climbed in, and slowly drove away.

# Chapter Twelve

"Slow down," the hunter told himself as he drove up the gravel road towards the den of the monsters.

"You must not be heard or seen coming," he is reminded by the Old One. "If you spook them you'll make them scatter, you don't want a chase. Take them as quiet as the night. The hunt is almost over," he said looking in the rearview mirror. "You have lost again."

"There they sit, just like always. The trap worked," he said.

He walked into the room to see the monsters subdued. "I'll be back for you," he said lifting one of the monsters and carried it out of the room. He tied up the sleeping monster.

"There you go, now you'll be no trouble for the ride."

"Come, you she bitch," he said lifting up the last of his prey and carried her out to the van. "Join other monsters in death."

"See, I can find and trap them all, none of them can escape the hunter," he said looking in the rearview mirror as he drove back down the lane.

"It won't matter how much you howl, you can't wake the monsters," he yelled and turned to look in the back of the van.

"They are under my spell. I'll have their power, you'll torment me no more."

"You can't trust the prey, make sure they're tied tight and lifeless before you travel," the Old Ones words rang in his ear.

"Stop the truck, you idiot," the Old One yelled. He feels the sting of claws on the back of his arm. "They're getting out of the ropes."

The young hunter looked back to see a pair of wild boars awake behind him. They struggled to get loose from the ropes tied around their legs.

"Get back there and knock him out before he gets loose," the Old One said and slapped the young hunter across the face.

"No more am I the small one you tormented. I am the hunter, and I'll take your power." He rubbed his face.

"You're tied tight and still asleep," he told the prey in the back of the van.

"I'll make you watch me kill them," he said looking into the rearview mirror as he drove away into the night.

"Now I have the power," he said once he'd dispatched the monsters. "Now we must prepare you for your eternal prison."

He lifted the head of one of the monsters.

"No more will you torment young ones. No more will I feel your hot breath burn my face. No more will I feel the lash of your claws tear my flesh. I am the hunter."

He placed the head of the beast on the body of the other.

"You will spend forever looking for your body, trapped with no way to find your power," he said as he finished his work.

"It's time to place you back in the den, a warning to all monsters that the hunter has found you."

He carried one of the monsters back to the van. "You won't be the last." He laid the second monster beside the other.

"How many do I have to kill before you stop?" he asked looking into the rearview mirror.

"It matters not how many you face, only that the hunter returns from the hunt with the prey," the Old One said.

"You must always bring them home. If the hunter doesn't return, then the Old Ones will go hungry," the Old One said with a sly grin.

"He didn't beat me," the young hunter thought to himself. The only time the old monster hadn't struck him. "He's getting old and weak," the hunter told himself. "Soon I'll be strong enough to kill the monsters."

"This is how I'll kill all the monsters," he said. He put the monster back in the den. "No more will I wait in fear of you. No more will you make me cry. I am the hunter, and I have your power."

He left the room leaving the monsters trapped in their own den forever.

"See, they can't escape the hunter," he said and looked into the rearview mirror. 'Now, I need rest, soon the hunt will begin again."

He drove away from the den.

# Chapter Thirteen

"Morning," Tom muttered in a despondent lifeless tone. Steve turned to Tom and realized the cheery upbeat young detective, who usually came in so happy, was in a state of funk.

"I guess it didn't go well last week?" Steve asked. He set his glasses on the desk.

"No, most of it was great, was even going to be a Friday night to remember. Right up to the point where we're in her room and the news report came on covering the beheadings and everything went south. She just clammed up, turned cold, and blamed me for not telling her. She got on a plane the next morning and left without so much as a goodbye. I've tried to call her all weekend, but she won't answer."

"Tried to call who?" Jerry asked taking his seat.

"Nobody," Tom snapped.

"Give her some time, that's all you can do. She'll come around," Steve said in a reassuring tone.

"He's hit again," Sheriff Lester announced when he burst into the room... "Mogodore, a town just outside of Akron, a retired couple in their sixties. I spoke to the State Police and the FBI; they're all on their way there. Steve, you and Jerry go pack a bag and get on the road."

The two detectives jumped from their chairs.

"Take my car," Lester told them handing Steve the keys.

"What do you want me to do?" Tom asked his attention back on the case.

"Just keep looking. When we get more information

we're going to need you on that laptop," Sheriff Lester said.

"I'll pick you up at your place," Steve told Jerry when they rushed out the door.

\*\*\*

Steve pulled up in front of Jerry's house. Jerry stood on the front porch and hugged and kissed his family goodbye. It reminded Steve of the family he once had. His children would run out to say goodbye and get one last hug from their father. Jerry said goodbye to his family, opened the car door, and threw his bag in the back seat before he climbed into the passenger side of the car.

"You know you have it all, right?" Steve told him looking back at Jerry's family standing on the front porch waving at their father.

"Yeah, I sure do."

Jerry smiled and they drove out of the driveway and headed down the road.

"This guy really gets around, doesn't he?" Jerry said.

Steve looked over at Jerry with a serious face. "Yeah, I just hope he left us something to track this time."

Jerry didn't make small talk to pass time. Although they'd worked together for twelve years, Steve had always kept to himself. He wasn't one for opening up to people, even after he got to know them. The two men drove most of the way with little conversation. Every time Jerry would ask about Steve's past, he would change the subject to some other topic of non-importance. Jerry finally got the hint, it was an off limits subject. He respected the quiet Steve obviously wanted.

They arrived at the police station and parked in the lot among the other police vehicles. They stepped out of the car and stretched from the long ride.

"I hope they have a bathroom close," Jerry stated.

\*\*\*

The two detectives walked into the station. "May I help you?" the officer behind the front counter asked.

Steve retrieved his badge from its case and showed it to the officer. "I'm detective Steve Belcher and this is detective Stevenson from the Springfield Sheriff's Department."

"We've been waiting for you," a familiar voice said from behind them.

Steve turned around to see Special Agent McIntyre.

"About time you got here. Are you ready to go see the scene? We can discuss it on the way," McIntyre said.

"I have to make a stop first," Jerry said. Turning to the officer he asked, "Where's the men's room?"

"Right this way," the officer gestured leading Jerry to his requested destination.

"Be right back," Jerry said and walked away briskly, following the officer.

"Wouldn't stop on the way up, huh?" Agent McIntyre snickered.

Steve smiled. "I think I'll follow them."

The detectives walked out with Special Agent McIntyre, climbed into the agent's black suburban SUV. Jerry climbed in the back seat.

"I didn't think you FBI guys really drove these in real life," Jerry said with a laugh.

"Some things the movie people do get right," he answered.

As McIntyre drove out of the lot Steve asked, "Special Agent?"

"Call me Herb or Mac," he interrupted Steve.

"Okay, Herb," Steve said. "What's the story?"

"Well, it's our killer alright. Retired couples, names are Frank and Mildred Browning. Their son, Phillip found them in the house at 08:00 this morning. They're in the same condition as the other victims." Herb wheeled around another corner looking both ways as he ran the light. "Last seen Friday afternoon, as far as we know, at the local VFW where they usually spent Friday afternoons playing bingo, according to the son. We have a team at the VFW now, talking to anyone they can find and retrieving the member list. The son, Phillip, owns his own construction business and stops every Monday morning to have breakfast with the folks. We're checking into the background of the Brownings. They've been retired for seven years according to the son."

"Any clues from the scene?" Steve asked.

"Our crime lab should be getting to the scene about now. When it came across the wire this morning, we sent a team from the local office to secure the scene, and I jumped on a jet up here."

"That would have been nice," Jerry said. "Maybe you can give us a ride next time." Jerry said.

"Have the bodies been moved yet?" Steve asked ignoring Jerry's comment.

"Not yet," Herb said. "We wanted to keep the scene intact until the crime lab got there. And the locals aren't pleased about us taking over, either."

"I guess they want their picture taken, too," Steve said.

* * *

They arrived in Mogador, just a stop sign in the middle of the road. At one corner, a gas station and general store, on the opposite side a broken down feed mill that looked ready to fall in on itself.

"Well, you've seen the town," Herb said.

Herb continued to drive the county roads, finally, they left the paved road and turned onto a long gravel road that led through a stand of trees.

"It's a little off the beaten path," Herb commented.

"I guess they liked their privacy," Jerry said.

They continued the drive through the twists and turns

of the tree lined country road. They started up a steep grade and Steve looked out his window. A break in the trees revealed a panoramic view of the lake. It had a calming effect on him.

"What a nice view," Steve said.

They reached the top and turned onto another side road. They came upon the police barricade set up to stop any traffic from entering the area. They drove through the standing group of reporters and cameras trained on the vehicle.

Steve looked over at Herb. "Didn't take them long to get here, did it?"

"No, they were here almost as fast as the first officer on the scene."

Herb cleared the barricade and drove about another one hundred yards to the couple's house. The three men exited the vehicle and Jerry and Steve stood and looked over the view. The house, sitting on top of the hill, overlooked the entire valley and lake. The view went on for miles.

"They picked the right place to retire," Jerry said.

They walked up to the house and met the local county sheriff.

"You the detectives from Springfield?" he asked. "Sheriff Lester called and said you were on your way, the names Fred Macy," he said.

"I guess you boys have seen this before, but I'm gonna tell you, this is creepy," Fred said.

"It sure sounds like our guy," Steve said.

"Your crime scene boys are in there now, so the rest of us just cleared out of their way," Fred told Herb.

"How long have they been in there?" Herb asked.

"About an hour," Fred said. "Really didn't want to stay in there," Fred admitted. "Seen a lot of things in my time, but this is the first makes me wish I hadn't quit drinking."

Steve looked at the house. It was a fairly new A frame,

with a porch extending around the house, which was perfect for this location. It had large glass sliding doors the entire length of the front facing the lake. Steve looked inside the house at the crime scene. The couple had been placed sitting in their chairs, facing out of the house, looking at the lake.

"He's got a sick sense of humor, doesn't he?" Fred said.

They waited outside for the crime lab to finish.

"He didn't kill them here. There's very little blood inside, heads cut off and re-sewn on each other's bodies. The son told us he hadn't talked to them since Friday," Fred said.

"Fits our guy," Steve said. He looked at the others. "We need to know everywhere this couple worked, went to church, and even which grocery store they used. Somehow the murders are connected, but how is anyone's guess," Steve said. "How much does the press know?"

"Just that there's been a double murder. We put a blackout on all information after the first call this morning," Herb said. "I saw that reporter's piece last week," Herb scowled. "Makes you want to burn that first amendment, doesn't it?"

"Or at least control what they report, like every other country on this planet. There's just some things that don't need to be reported," Steve said.

\*\*\*

"All clear," the group heard from an officer exiting the house said.

"Let's take a look," Steve said.

Steve led the team into the house and along the hallway.

"Look here," Steve said pointing to a picture on the wall.

*Browning Company Picnic 2000* a sign in the picture

said.

"What did Mr. Browning do for a living?" Steve asked.

The son, who sat in the kitchen of the house, clearly distraught over finding his parents, spoke up. "Dad ran a cleaning company for thirty years. He sold it, when he retired, to his partner. It still goes by the name Browning Cleaners."

"What type of cleaning did they do?" Steve asked.

"They did contract cleaning of office buildings and other businesses. Why would someone do this to them?" he asked losing control of his emotions.

Steve didn't want to admit he didn't have a clue. He briefly put his hand on the son's shoulder before he continued his walk through the house. The group entered the room where the two bodies had already been removed and placed on gurneys. The attendants wheeled them past the men who stood and stared at the black body bags.

They turned to the room where the picture window overlooked the valley. They were approached by the crime lab tech.

"Find anything?" Herb asked.

"Not much, except for some trace on the chairs we'll have to sort out at the lab to see who it came from. It's as if he sanitized the room before and after," the tech said.

They looked around the room and found the same scene. The victims had been undressed and placed in chairs, but this time they'd been left facing the view of the lake instead of the television. It seemed to be the only difference.

*Was it a clue?* Steve thought. *No, it's just a matter of convenience to have them looking out at the lake. The killer's sick way of setting the scene to say, Take your last look. But why?* He looked around the room. *What was the connection between these two retired people and the other two families? Could it be random?* He didn't think so. He turned to Jerry.

"Just look at the view," Steve said.

"Sad, but maybe that's the last thing they saw," Jerry said.

"They looked for months to find this place," the son said joining them from the kitchen. "I helped them build the house. They always wanted to retire on this hill. They were so happy sitting here looking out this window. Even in the winter, they wouldn't come off the mountain. When you find out who did this, tell him I'll be waiting to meet him." A cold look of hate shone in his eyes.

"Well," Herb turned to Steve and Jerry, "you want to go and check out the cleaning company first?"

They agreed and walked back down the hallway. Steve's gaze caught the picture of the picnic again. He reached up and took the picture from the wall. He turned to the son who'd followed them.

"Can I take this picture?" Steve asked.

"Sure," he replied. "Whatever you need to catch who did this."

"Thank you," Steve said.

The three men climbed back into Herb's SUV to leave and Steve turned to Herb and Jerry. "Too bad we can't give that boy his wish," he said, but he thought, *an eye for an eye, sounds good to me too.*

# Chapter Fourteen

Steve, Jerry and Herb drove back to Akron. They decided to have a late lunch and stopped by a small diner outside the city limits. Inside the diner Jerry noticed a sign listing the daily specials.

"Meatloaf and mashed, $5.85." He laughed, telling Steve, "You think it's as bad as Gretta's?"

"I don't think I'll find out." Steve snickered and walked to an open table.

The three men sat down and the waitress approached with menus. While they looked over the menu, Herb turned to Steve.

"How is he doing it?" The two men looked up from their menus with blank stares. "We've all seen the reports, the ME's are as baffled as we are. I've been involved with every serial killer case in this area in the last twenty five years. This beats them all. No DNA, no fibers, no tracks, no prints. Unless this guy wants us to, I don't see a way to find him," Herb said.

Steve set down his menu and with a lifeless tone said, "I'll find him." He turned his attention back to his menu.

"And how are you going to do that, if I may ask?" Herb scoffed.

"Because good always wins over evil in the end," Steve said with a weary smile, having absolutely no clue how they would catch the killer, but knew they had to. "He's not going to stop until we catch him. But how many more will he kill until we do, is what consumes me."

\*\*\*

Having finished their lunch, they drove up to the front of

the Browning Cleaning Company and watched crews loading up to start the afternoon shift. Inside the front doors a sign still read: *Browning Cleaning Company, Frank Browning, Owner.*

"May I help you?" an older man who sat behind the front desk asked.

"Yes," Herb said pulling his badge from his coat. "I'm Special Agent McIntyre from the FBI and these are detectives Belcher and Stevenson from the Springfield Sheriff's Department. We need to speak to the owners, are they around?"

"Gary Benton, I'm the owner. How can I help you?"

"Have you watched the news today, Mr. Benton?" Herb asked.

"No, what's this about?"

"Do you know Frank Browning?" he asked. Several workers filed out of the hallway.

"Yes, he was my partner for twenty years until he wanted to retire and sold his half to me."

"Is there someplace a little more private we could talk?" Herb asked.

"We can go into my office," he replied. He led them down the extra wide, white tiled hallway.

Passing the workers leaving for their assigned duties, Steve looked them up and down and wondered if any of them could be the killer. They reached the office and Gary walked behind the desk. The last one in the room, Jerry, closed the door.

"Now what's this all about?" Gary asked.

"Frank and his wife, Mildred, were found murdered in their home this morning," Herb told him.

"Oh my god," Gary said and sat down in his chair causing it to jerk backwards. "What happened?"

"We're looking into that. When's the last time you spoke to the Brownings?" Herb asked.

"Just last week. We play golf once a week. How did it

happen?"

"Is there anyone you know of who had an issue with them, who wanted to harm them?" Herb asked.

"My god, no!" Gary said.

"We're going to need to look over your employee files and company records. Where do you do business?" Herb asked.

"All over, from Akron to Youngstown. We have clients in a wide range of locations and types of businesses," Gary said. "The employee records, well, we only have twenty five employees, but most of our workers are through temp agencies."

He leaned forward and took a drink of his coffee before he continued. "You can look at anything you like. Most of our records are on computer now. If you guys will follow me, my secretary can help you with anything you need."

The four men left the office and walked down a hall to another office where Gary's secretary worked. Walking in, Gary said, "Tina, these officers need to look at our employee files, would you please help them find everything they need?" Steve walked over to where the secretary stood.

"How can I help?" she asked.

Steve introduced himself and Jerry and Herb, "Let's start with a list of all the employees and temp agencies. Also, a list of all the clients the company has done work for in the past twenty five years," he said to the dismay of the woman.

"That's going to take a while," she said.

"I know," Steve said.

Gary walked back into the room. "Special Agent, I think we can set you up down in this other room we use as a training room, it's a bigger space and you can have more room to work, if you like."

"That would be great," Herb replied.

"I'll have the files brought to you and Tina can assist with any computer information you need. If you gentlemen will come this way." He gestured for them to follow him.

They entered a room filled with tables and chairs arranged in rows facing the front of the room that resembled a high school class room complete with cork boards covered with posters and a television hung on the wall.

"Will this be okay?" Gary asked.

"It'll work just fine," Steve said.

"I'll do anything I can to help you find the bastard who did this, whatever you need, just let me know," Gary said and shook the agent's hand and then retreated back down the hallway.

Tina entered the room. "Gary asked me to help you with any of the computer files you might need."

"I'll help you with that," Herb said. He jumped to his feet.

"I've brought a laptop and we can plug in over here," she said.

"What would you like to see first?" she asked Herb.

"Can you bring up a list of all the temp employees over the years?"

"How far back would you like to go?" she asked.

"How far back do your records go?" Herb asked.

"This year we started converting all the files, they should be all up to date from 1990 up to current. Before that we have to go to the paper files." she explained.

"Let's start with the last twenty years and see what we find," Herb said.

She typed with such speed it made the three men look at each other in wonder as the list compiled and popped up.

"All of the temps are separated from the agency they worked for and the third column is what jobs they're assigned." She pointed to the columns on the screen, sliding her finger across the monitor. "It goes on to list how long they worked here and when their work ended."

"Can you print this for us?" Herb asked.

"Yes, of course," she said and hit the print button. "It'll print in the other room. I'll be back in just a moment."

Steve turned to Jerry. "Remind you of anyone we know?"

"Yeah, I think we found Tom's sister," Jerry said.

She returned to the room and handed the print out to Herb. "Here you are agent."

"Can you also run a list of the companies you've done work for, and a list of all regular employee's?" Herb asked. "Absolutely," she said and sat back down in front of the laptop and pulled up the requested files.

Herb handed the copy of what she had handed him to Jerry, but when he reached the second page, he stopped, his eyes focused on one name.

"Wallace Holt," Jerry said. "He worked with a temp company from 1996 through 1998 working as a laborer on a crew cleaning a hog slaughter plant outside of Youngstown Ohio.

"Steve," Jerry said, "come over here and look at this. Remember the guy that got into the fight with Carl Peterson at the Plastics plant? Here he is, he worked for the Brownings."

Steve stared at the list over Jerry's shoulder.

"But I thought you said he was killed in 2002," Steve said surprised.

"Well, according to the reports, he did," Jerry said.

"Let's get Tom on the phone and have him confirm that," Steve ordered.

Tina pulled up the other reports and gave them to Herb.

"Let's go over all this at the hotel tonight and get out of the way here," Steve said.

They walked up the hallway and when Gary noticed them pass the office he called out to them, "Find what you needed?"

"We have a lot to go over," Herb replied.

Steve asked, "Do you remember someone by the name of Wallace Holt?"

"No, not that I can remember. Is he a suspect?" Gary asked.

"Not yet, just thinking out loud," Steve said.

Once back in the SUV they drove off the lot and Steve called Tom.

"Sheriff's office," a voice answered.

"This is Detective Belcher, can I speak to Detective Jensen, please?" He waited for Tom to come to the phone. Herb looked over at Steve.

"Tom? Hey, this is Steve, I need you to look into something. Wallace Holt, we looked him up on the first murder. Check into him some more and see what you can find out. His name came up on a list up here from a temp agency working for our dead couple." Steve nodded. "Okay, I'll check in later."

Steve turned to Herb. "You think they've finished with the autopsies yet?"

"Let's go see," he said and drove towards downtown.

***

Tom hung up the phone and started a search for the original file on the case. He'd read over the file several times and knew Wallace Holt had supposedly died in a car accident that resulted in a fire that burned down twenty square miles of forest in Lancaster county. He pulled the file from the bottom of the desk and located the page of information he wanted. One of the uniformed officers walked into the room carrying a file folder.

"Tom, this came in from Wilson Meats for you," the officer said and handed him the file.

"Thanks," Tom replied, laying it in front of him.

He searched through the file for all the information on

Wallace Holt that they had. Tired of searching through the paperwork, he yawned and rubbed his eyes. Sheriff Lester stood in the doorway.

"Time to call it a day," he said. "You've been at this too long today, go home, get some rest, and see some sunshine. It's a nice day out there."

"I still have a lot of files to go through, and Steve just called and asked me to check out something for him. Just need to check out a few more things before I go," Tom said.

"It'll be here in the morning," Lester said, ordering Tom to go home.

***

While Tom drove home, he wondered how Terry was doing. He remembered how he felt with her, feeling her soft hands in his while they walked and the taste of her lips. Unfortunately, it was all overshadowed by the hurt he'd witnessed in her eyes. That memory kept popping up in his mind every time he thought of her. He couldn't forget the look in her eyes when she thought he'd betrayed her. But in his mind, he hadn't. He'd done everything he could to help her.

She hadn't answered any of his calls and that made him feel even worse. He remembered her pushing him away with such sorrow on her face. The expression she wore wouldn't leave his thoughts. Not being able to comfort her weighed heavy on his mind.

He reached home completely depressed. He walked into his apartment, kicked off his shoes at the door, and placed his keys on a hook on the wall. He hung up his coat and put his shoes in their proper place before he went to the kitchen to find some kind of frozen meal for dinner. He'd been preoccupied thinking about Terry and had forgotten to stop to get something. Nothing in the freezer seemed good. He closed the door. The menus he kept perfectly stacked on the counter caught his attention. He thumbed through them and picked one out.

"Chinese," he said to himself, "haven't had Chinese for a while." In the living room he sat down in his favorite chair and reached for the phone. After he placed his order, he settled into his chair and turned on his game system.

"Some needed distraction," he said to himself while playing his favorite game.

The doorbell rang and he ran to the door. After he served up his plastic plate of General Tso's Chicken, he returned to his chair and began to eat. Just as he was stuffing his mouth with a very hot piece of chicken, the phone rang.

"Helrow," he tried to answer with his mouth still on fire from the sauce.

"Tom?"Jerry's voice came through the phone.

"Yes, I just burned my mouth on some hot spicy food. What can I do for you, Jerry?" Tom said recovering.

"Did you get a chance to look into Wallace Holt any more today?" Jerry asked.

"No, the sheriff ran me out. Tell Steve I'll look into it first thing in the morning. How's it going up there, find anything new?" he asked.

"Just going over the autopsy reports. We'll catch up tomorrow back in the office. We should be there around noon."

"Okay, Jerry, see ya in the morning," Tom said. He hung up the phone and settled back into his chair with his plate of food. "Why is it every time I eat Chinese someone calls me?"

The first time Terry had called him, he'd been sitting in this chair eating Chinese food. He looked back to the phone. *Should I try again?* He shook his head and decided not to, at least until he finished the food.

\*\*\*

"Is there anything you can tell us?" Steve asked when he,

Jerry and Herb met with the ME. They looked at the bodies with the heads still separated in the autopsy room.

"Nothing, other than what you already know. We found no bruising, no other signs of trauma. We don't have the lab reports back, but it looks the same as all the others. Whoever this is, he is very good at hiding himself," the ME reported.

"Damn," Steve said. "Thanks Doc."

"Can you send a copy of the report to our ME in Springfield when you get the reports back from the lab?" he asked. "Sure thing," the ME responded.

The three men left the room with their frustration rising. Jerry turned to Steve.

"Let's go find a hotel that has a bar. I think we could both use a drink right about now."

Steve nodded in agreement. "We booked you rooms where we're staying, if that's okay?" Herb told the two detectives. "And it has a bar."

They checked into the local HOJO with a nice restaurant and bar attached, even though the building itself was still the traditional orange and blue. Their rooms had new thick blue carpet and surprisingly the television was a new large flat screen. Apparently the owner thought inside improvements were more important than outdoor ones. Steve agreed.

Steve knocked on the door, and hollered, "Last one down buys the first round."

Jerry quickly ran out of the room and caught Steve just before the elevator door closed. Steve laughed at him. "You're never one to buy."

Jerry smiled. "Not if I can help it, spent too many years with soldiers to get stuck now."

They walked into the small, quiet bar that would only hold twenty people or so. Only one female bartender stood behind the bar waiting for any customers to arrive. Herb already sat at a table.

Steve turned to Jerry. "Looks like you're still on the hook."

The two men joined Herb at the small three top where he already had a scotch on the rocks.

"What can I get you gentlemen?" the bartender asked.

"Crown and 7-Up on the rocks for me," Steve said.

"And the beer on tap for me," Jerry said.

While they put back a few, they talked about everything but the case. They tried to have a few hours of life without what they'd seen running through their minds.

Jerry turned to Steve. "Maybe we should fix Tom up with that pretty little Tina," he said with a smile. "They would be perfect together."

"Yeah, but he's still stuck on Terry. I think she broke his heart last Friday," Steve said to Jerry's surprise look.

"What, last Friday?" Jerry asked.

"Well, he didn't want you to know, but he took the whole week off to spend time with her and help her deal with all the stuff with her parents. On the last night, they were at the hotel and about to make his dream come true and she found out about the whole head thing and that kind of ruined the mood. Now she won't take his calls at all," Steve said.

"He didn't say a word about it," Jerry said shocked. He sat there with his mouth open.

"And you're not going to say a word about this either," Steve ordered Jerry. "He's afraid you'd follow him around dressed in your camouflage." Steve laughed.

With the drinks making them all relax, Jerry said, "Yeah, I probably would have, just to mess with the kid. But this sounds bad. I wondered why he was so down in the dumps this morning. Even on the phone he didn't sound like his usual self."

"Now I feel bad for the kid," Jerry said trying to hold a straight face as the three men burst out in laughter.

# Chapter Fifteen

The next morning, Steve and Jerry went downstairs and met Herb in the hotel restaurant. "Sit down, boys," Herb said when they joined him.

They took their seats and Herb turned to Jerry. "Not looking so good this morning."

Jerry had partaken in one too many drinks the night before and looked somewhat sheepish.

"I thought army boys could hold their own?" Herb scoffed as the two men settled into their seats.

Steve smiled and Jerry looked over at him.

"It's been a while," he said. The drained look on his face told the story of the pounding in his head.

"That's what being married will do for you, takes all the fight out of you," Steve said with a snicker.

"You boys headed back today?" Herb asked.

"Yes, we need to get back, and match up everything we have, and see if there are any leads to follow. After the autopsy reports come in, we'll need to have a conference call with all the medical examiners so we can try to put this all together," Steve said.

"Tell you what, why don't we all meet back down at Sheriff Lester's office. I'll bring all the people involved from my end. The report should be ready by Thursday, so let's meet at 13:00 on Friday. That okay with you?" Herb asked.

"That'll work fine, it'll give us time to run a few more things down," Steve said.

\*\*\*

Tom grabbed a fresh cup of coffee and gazed out the

window.

"Morning, Tom." Sheriff Lester greeted Tom with a smile when he came in.

"Morning sheriff," Tom said.

"How's the search going?" Lester asked looking at the stack of files on the table.

Tom sat back down and returned to the file he was looking at. "More of the same," he said and turned another page. "Well, here's something," he said picking up one of the pages from the file. He reached over for the other file on the table looking for the list he'd printed out

Tom compared the two lists. "Wallace Holt," he explained. "This is a list of the temp staff employees from the Wilson Meat's company. Wallace Holt worked as a temporary laborer through a staffing company from 1992 to 1994. He also worked at the plastics plant where Carl Peterson worked. He's in one of the files the company gave us after the first murder," Tom said excitedly.

"Well, sounds like you may have found our guy," Lester said.

"Not exactly," Tom said. "Wallace Holt died in a car crash in 2002 in Lancaster, according to the police record."

"That makes it kind of hard for him to be our killer, doesn't it?"

"Steve and Jerry wanted me to look into him again because his name was on a list of employees from the Browning companies," Tom explained.

"Just as soon as the boys get back, I want the three of you on the road down to Lancaster. I'll call the local sheriff and get the process started. Steve said they should be back around noon, until then, you get on this and track down everything you can about this guy. No one knows about this yet, so let's keep it under your hat. Understood?" Lester said.

Tom pounded away on his laptop thinking he'd found the killer, even though he was supposedly dead. With every stroke of the keys, his excitement grew. Searching through web pages, the only information he found at the Department of Social Security were his work records. He found no record of him, at any school, no criminal record, not even a driving record. He searched in disbelief of what he *couldn't* find, his frustration growing.

"Did you miss me?" Jerry asked announcing his and Steve's arrival.

Tom looked up from his computer. "I can't find anything on this guy, Wallace Holt. No records of any kind, except for his work record through Social Security. Don't you think that's a little strange? No schools, no driving record, no police record of any kind. The only reason I found his date of birth was through the SSN provided in the file from Plastics Plus," Tom said, his voice filled with his frustration.

"It's nice to see you too." Jerry said and sat down across from Tom.

Steve listened to every word Tom said. "So, the only lead we have has no background to look into, and is supposedly dead, sounds about right for this case," he said. "What other places did this guy work?"

"About sixty places, according to this list," Tom replied and slid the list across the table to Steve. "And according to the call I made to the Lancaster Police, they're sure it was him in the crash, but the sheriff wants us to get down there and check things out."

"Welcome back, boys," Sheriff Lester said as he walked into the room. "I just got off the phone with the sheriff in Lancaster. He'll meet you guys in the morning. It's only an hour's drive. By the way, I viewed the reports from yesterday. Anything different you guys saw about this one?"

"They had a much better view to look at," Steve said and told the sheriff and Tom about the scene they'd found at the house. "The FBI will be here on Friday for a meeting to discuss the case, by then we should have the report from the ME up there to see if anything else was found," Steve said.

"Okay, I'll let you boys get back to work," Lester said.

Jerry looked at Tom. "Back to the salt mines."

"I'm going to get a fresh cup of coffee," Steve said. "You guys want anything?"

Both Jerry and Tom shook their heads in response without taking their attention from the files they were reading.

After Steve left the room, Jerry turned to Tom.

"Sorry to hear about Terry," he said. "I know you really liked her."

"Thanks, but I don't think it's going anywhere. She hasn't returned my calls and she won't answer the phone. I guess it's just water under the bridge."

"It's just, well, I've never heard of anyone being shot down that close to the target." Jerry turned his sympathy to sarcasm.

"I'm glad you're enjoying this so much," Tom said and sent Jerry their usual sign of friendship by flipping him the bird.

Jerry smiled. "Look kid, if she doesn't come around, I found you a new girlfriend yesterday. She's really pretty and knows computers as well as you. She's just your type."

"No thanks," Tom said.

"About time to call it a day." Steve said. He laid his glasses on the desk and stood up from his chair.

Tom picked up his phone to order some food to pick up on the way home and noticed he had a message he had missed. He pushed the button to retrieve the message.

"Why don't you guys come over to the house for dinner tonight and have some real home cooking for a change?" Jerry asked.

Tom heard Terry's voice on the phone and his mood changed instantly. He almost jumped for joy. Steve and

Jerry watched him and must have seen the transformation.

They turned to one another and at the same time said, "It must be Terry!"

He hung up the phone and looked at the two men who stood and stared at him in wonder.

"What? Oh yeah, dinner sounds good. Just let me go clean up and I'll be right over," he said trying to cover his elation over the message.

"No, no," Jerry said and the two men blocked his path out the door.

"Let's hear it," Steve said. "You've been moping around here for the last two days like you lost your dog and now you almost dance out. Give it up."

"It's just something I have to check out," Tom said trying to talk his way past the men.

"Not getting out until you spill your guts," Jerry repeated and pushed Tom back from the door.

"What is this, high school?" Tom scoffed glaring at the two men blocking his path. They reminded him of being bullied in school.

"If it was, you would've already had your head in a toilet," Steve said and they all laughed.

"Okay, it's from Terry. She wants to talk, satisfied?" Tom said giving in to the pressure, but he really wanted to get out of there so he could call her back.

"That's great," Steve said and stepped aside to let him go.

"Dinners at 18:00 and don't be late," Jerry yelled.

Tom hurried down the hallway. He glanced back to see Steve and Jerry high five each other, and heard Jerry tell Steve, "That was fun."

"Hey, Jerry," Tom called and threw up another bird as he ran out the door.

Tom rushed to his car, jumped in and dialed Terry's number. He tried to calm himself and not seem too excited. He took a deep breath when the phone rang. While he waited, his anticipation grew with every ring. Finally she answered.

"Hi, this is Terry. I'm not able to come to the phone right now, but please leave a message."

"Terry, this is Tom. I got your message, you can call me back, or I will try you later. Bye," he said. Still excited at the possibility of a relationship, he drove home feeling a rush of adrenaline pumping in his blood. He reached his apartment and hurried to change and get to Jerry's for dinner.

"She wants to talk," he told himself. *This is great, she's thought it over and she wants to get together, or she just wants to tell me to quit calling. But she could have said that in a message, no, she wants to talk to me. I could tell by the tone in her voice.* All these thoughts ran through his mind while he changed his clothes. *It was only 13:00 in LA. She's still at work and couldn't answer the phone, but she called, that's all that matters.* He walked out and closed the door headed for Jerry's.

***

Tom pulled up in front of Jerry's craftsman style house at the same time Steve did. They left their cars parked under a towering oak at the curb and walked up the stone path to the glass double door.

"Thanks a lot, Steve, I thought we were friends," Tom said.

Steve laughed and said, "We are. You know we care about you. Did you get to talk to her?"

"No, not yet," Tom said.

"Can't wait to see what Jerry has planned for me next," Tom said.

"Well?" Jerry asked, "don't keep me in suspense."

"Nothing to tell, I haven't talked to her yet, but I'll give you a full report when I do," Tom said.

Jerry laughed and they walked into the house for

dinner. "By the way guys, let's leave all the work details outside, okay? I try not to bring any of that home."

The three agreed. Jerry shut the door and they followed him into the kitchen.

"Great dinner," Tom said trying to talk over the noise of Jerry's three young boys.

"Thanks," Jerry's wife said as they all heard the music from the other room.

"Bad boys, bad boys, what you gonna do."

Tom jumped up to get his phone and almost spilled everything on the table.

Jerry's wife said, "That must be a girl." She smiled at Jerry.

"Oh, we hope so," Jerry said.

Tom reached his phone and answered it just in time.

"Tom, this is Terry. Did I call at a bad time?"

"No, no," he stammered, "this is a good time, just, ah, hold on for a second."

Tom turned to the others sitting at the table. They were all looking at him with grins on their faces.

"Guys, thanks for dinner, thank you Mrs. Stevenson, but I really have to be going. See you guys in the morning," Tom said.

Jerry turned to his wife. "Yeah, it's a girl." He and Steve laughed.

Tom left the house holding his phone to his ear.

"Hi, I've been hoping you got my message. I was afraid you didn't want to talk to me," he said not letting her get a word in. He stopped to take a breath.

"Tom, I just wanted to say, I'm sorry."

Tom's heart dropped in his chest thinking the worst.

"I blamed you for not telling me about my parents, but I know you couldn't," she said.

Inside his car, he stuck his Bluetooth in his ear and switched the phone to hands free before he started the car.

"I really miss talking to you."

\*\*\*

The next morning Tom arrived at the station first. He'd brought a box of donuts for the ride down to Lancaster. He wanted to have a chance to do some more research on Wallace Holt's background before they left. He brought up the file on his computer and found the birth certificate and Mr. Holt's parents' names, Earl and Betty Holt. He started a search for them and found that Earl had worked in a lumber yard from 1979 to 2001 in Lancaster, but there was no work history on the mother, Betty. There were no police reports on either name, but he did find a last place of residence for them in about 2002.

"Well, that's something," he said.

"Sorry about leaving so abruptly last night," he told Jerry when he came in.

"Don't worry, kid, I would've done the same thing. Everything okay?" Jerry asked.

Tom, with a big grin on his face, replied, "Yeah, we talked most of the night, it was fun."

"Well, maybe today we can get some work done," Steve said from the doorway.

"Already on it, I've located the last place of residence of his parents, who also disappeared from the planet in 2002. Sounds a little strange, don't you think?" Tom asked after reminding them that 2002 was the year Wallace had died in the crash.

"Let's go," Steve said and the three men headed out to the parking lot. Tom grabbed his laptop and the box of donuts for the ride. They piled into Steve's car and Jerry looked at Tom.

"You can tell us all about the phone call on the way down."

"No way in hell," Tom said.

\*\*\*

Steve, never one to obey the speed limit, found his way to the sheriff's office in Lancaster in a very short time. They got out of the car and spotted a man in a sheriff's uniform coming out of the front door of the station. A chubby short fellow around five foot five inches or so. He waddled from side to side as he walked toward the men.

"Morning, I'm Sheriff Charlie Boon," he said with a big grin that revealed gold dental work. "You're the detectives from Springfield, I presume?"

"Yes, we are, I'm detective Steve Belcher and these are Detective's Jerry Stevenson and Tom Jensen," Steve said.

"I spoke to Sheriff Lester yesterday, but he didn't give me a lot of information about what I can help you with, come on in the office and you can fill me in." He led them into the station to his small office in the back. It was just big enough for all of them to stand around his desk. Boon sat in his arm chair behind the desk.

"You're aware of the killings that began five weeks ago?" Steve asked. Boon nodded. "None of them have given us so much as a hair of evidence to go on. The only thing we've found is related to a man named Wallace Holt. Who, according to the county records, died in a car crash down here back in 2002. By some strange coincidence, a Mr. Earl Holt and his wife, Betty, disappear from here at the same time. Wallace Holt has shown up on every case so far, working for or around the deceased. We haven't tied it together in any way yet, but it's the only lead we have," Steve said.

"Kinda thin, huh?" Boon asked.

"Yes, but this killer has us chasing our tails. This may lead to nothing, but we have to look anyway," Steve said.

"Where would you like to start?" Boon asked.

"First, we'd like to see the crash and autopsy reports, if we can," Tom said.

"Let me get someone to pull that for you, anything else?" Boon asked.

"Yes, I've located the last place they lived here in town, at 1429 Wicker road. Could you give us directions to find it?" Tom asked.

"I'll do better than that, how about I drive y'all out there," Boon said. "You've piqued my interest, kinda like to see where this all leads."

"Sheriff Boon, is there anything you can tell us about the Holt's?"

"Not really. From what I gather, no one knew them very well. We couldn't find any family after the crash, and no one ever came to collect the remains, but there wasn't much left after the fire from what I can remember. It had burned for so long all they found were a few pieces of bone."

"Did anyone from where Mr. Earl Holt worked give you any ideas?" Steve asked.

"No, the lumber yard closed down in 2002 about the same time. We figured that they took off to look for work somewhere else," Boon said.

"Tom, you stay here and go over the files," Steve said. "We'll go with Sheriff Boon and see what we can find." The three headed out of the station as Tom sat down with the files.

***

Outside the sheriff told the detectives, "Let's take my truck." He walked the men to his four wheel drive patrol vehicle.

"Now, this is a police car!" Jerry exclaimed. He and Steve climbed into the big black truck with Boon.

"That address is a trailer park on the south end of town. It's still owned by the same people that owned it in 2002, so we should stop in and talk to them first."

They pulled up to the park. Most of the trailers were

old and run down, sagging on their concrete blocks and broken skirting. *Not much more than a slum*, Steve thought to himself. They walked up to the office and Boon knocked on the dented aluminum door. A young, stout woman dressed in grime covered clothes, and carrying a wrench, opened the door. Her hair escaping the ponytail it was tied loosely in.

"Can I help you?" she asked.

"I'm Sheriff Boon and these are detectives Steve Belcher and Jerry Stevenson from the Springfield Sheriff's Department, can we ask you some questions?" Boon said.

"Come on in," she said. "What do you need, Sheriff?"

"Are you the owner of this park?" he asked.

"Yes, my husband and I have owned it for about fifteen years, since his daddy passed away."

"Can you tell us anything about a family named Holt that used to live here back a few years?" Steve asked.

"Yeah, I can tell you a lot, they lived here most of my life. I played with their boy, Wallace."

"When did they move in?" Steve asked.

"Not sure when they moved in, but the boy only stayed here until he was around six years old. I went over to play with him one day and his momma said he went to live with their folks for a while. But the couple stayed until 2002 just before Wallace died in that crash. That is, until they just up and left without any of their belongings and without paying any of the back rent they owed. We never heard from them again. We even tried to find where to send all their stuff, but after a while we just sold it off to recover the rent money, but we didn't get much," she said.

"Was there anything strange about the boy?" Steve asked.

"He was only a kid when I knew him, but he always acted kind of odd. Wallace always seemed jumpy, you know, always looking over his shoulder, kinda weird for a little kid now that I think about it," she said.

"Well, if you think of anything else, you can reach me at this number." Steve said. He handed her his card.

The three men left the office and climbed back into Boon's truck. "Is there anyone still around that could have worked with the Holt's back then?" Steve asked Boon.

"There might be. I'll take you to where all the old timers meet for breakfast," Boon told Steve as he drove to a restaurant in town.

It was a small old building in the center of town. Walking in you could smell the bacon cooking on the grill and the aroma of strong coffee over everything else. Most of the tables full of old men in coveralls wearing farm logo'ed baseball caps with the three day old gray growth on their worn faces.

"Morning boys," Boon said. "These two are detectives from the Springfield Sheriff's Department. The whole restaurant got quiet, as everyone in the restaurant gave their attention to the sheriff and the two strangers who stood in the middle of the room.

"Is there anyone here who remembers Earl Holt, who used to work at the Lumberyard?" Boon asked.

Everyone looked around at each other and one man from the back of the room raised his hand.

"I remember Earl, worked with him for a lot of years, until the yard closed down," the man said.

The three men walked back to the table where the man sat.

"You mind if we ask you some questions?" Steve asked.

"Have a seat. The names Harley Mason."

"I'm detective Steve Belcher and this is Detective Jerry Stevenson. We're here looking for any information we can find on the Holt family," Steve said. "Mr. Mason, what can you tell us about Mr. Holt?"

"Call me Harley. What would you like to know? He was a nice enough guy at work, quiet, did his job."

"Did he talk about his family?"

"Not much, mostly talked about how mean his wife was," he said.

"What do you think he meant by that?" Steve asked.

"He told me one time that if he wasn't so afraid of her, he'd just pack up and leave," Harley said with a laugh. "Now that's a mean woman."

"Did he ever talk about their son, Wallace?"

"I didn't know he had a son, not until I read in the paper about how he died in that crash."

"Did Earl ever talk about his parents?"

"Only that they lived somewhere around here a few years before the lumber yard closed, and a couple months after that, Earl just disappeared."

"Thank you for your time and if you think of anything else, here's my card," Steve said. Steve got up from the table and the three men left the restaurant and climbed back into the truck.

"Does that sound strange to anyone else?" Steve said. "Man works there twenty-four years, it closes down, they disappear, the son dies in a crash, and no trace of them is ever found?"

"Yeah, sounds a little hinky to me," Boon said. "Where do you want to go next?"

"Back to the station and check in on Tom to see what he's found," Steve said.

*** 

Tom sat going over the reports. The crash report said the vehicle driven by Wallace went through a guardrail, crashed into a stand of trees and caught fire. Pictures of the scene showed the vehicle completely burned out and just ashes and a few bone fragments remained. The vehicle was described as a 1980 model Dodge two door, two wheel drive truck belonging to Earl Holt. Wallace was seen driving it from where he filled up at the gas station just before the crash. A real autopsy couldn't be performed and all the ME could tell was that they were burned to bad for DNA. The sheriff's office tried to notify the Holt's, but they couldn't be located. After time passed, the remains were turned over to the county for disposition.

"Can you tell me where to find these remains?" Tom asked an officer in the room.

"I can call the county morgue and see," the officer told Tom.

Tom pulled out his laptop and searched for Earl and Betty Holt. He tried to find any other relatives living in the area. While he continued the search the officer returned with the information from the county morgue.

"The remains were never picked up. They're still in a small plastic evidence bag in a box at the morgue," the officer explained.

"We're going to need to retrieve those remains. See if we can pick them up," he told the officer.

Tom made copies of the files. His search on his laptop revealed the birth certificate of Earl Wallace Holt, born 1934, to Walter and Marion Holt at a Columbus Hospital.

"Did you find anything?" Tom asked Steve and Jerry when they returned to the station with Boon.

"Not a lot, just more tail chasing," Steve said. "How about you?"

Tom told them his impression of the reports and what he was searching for. The three men sat down while Tom shared the information.

"So, we have a guy they think was driving, gets burned up beyond recognition. His parents disappear, there's no family left and the only body parts are in a bag in the morgue, have I got it right, Tom?" Steve asked.

"Yeah, that's about right."

"What about bank transactions, they had to use a bank somewhere?" Steve asked.

"I'll have my boys check into that," the sheriff said.

"Looks like we should have done some more checking back then."

"Don't kick your boys too hard, Sheriff, with that little to go on, we might have done the same thing," Steve said.

"You can stop on the way out of town and pick up the remains of whoever was in the car. I'll call the ME and tell them to release them to you," Boon said.

***

"What a bunch of worthless information. The whole family seems to have no past, no one knows anything. What the hell did these guys investigate?" Steve said as he drove to the morgue to retrieve the remains. "Tom, you keep searching. We get back, I want to know everything you can find about that family, go back to the Mayflower if you have to, but find them."

"You think this could be our guy? It wouldn't be the first time someone faked their death and showed up later," Tom said.

"We don't have enough to know for sure, yet," Steve said.

"But you're thinking that way aren't you?" Jerry said and looked over to Steve who drove faster than before.

"Just find the family," Steve said.

Tom looked at Jerry but stayed silent for the ride home.

# Chapter Sixteen

"Welcome everyone. You all know each other, so let's get right down to business. Steve, will you bring everyone up to speed?" Sheriff Lester said.

Steve walked to the front of the room where he had laid out the timeline of the murders on the board.

"The killings started five weeks ago. The six victims, two at each location, were all found in the same fashion. They were drained of blood with very little or no evidence of the killer. His signature is to switch the heads of the victims on the bodies and place them in their homes. There isn't any evidence that they were killed in their homes, so we can assume he is transporting them back and forth to wherever he is doing the killing."

Steve pointed to the board with the map showing all of the locations of the victims. "We can also assume he watched his victims prior to abducting them. Most of the locations were private. The first one, the Peterson's, had a secluded drive and a fence covered in ivy to hide entrances and exits from the property." He pointed to a picture of the Peterson's home.

"Both of the other two locations were in rural areas and secluded by location. So unless someone drove by at the right time, the killer had all the private time he needed to complete his work. The profile given to us by Doctor Harris suggests the killer has a delusion he is carrying out based on some sort of revenge. He won't stop until he is caught or he is finished with whom or whatever is driving his delusion. He must be strong in stature to carry the victims, due to the lack of any drag evidence at any of the crime scenes. We still have no good suspects to consider. However, we are looking into one name that has come up in the investigation. Have I left anything out?" he asked.

Doctor Harris stood up. "Is there any reason to think it could be a pair, or even a group of killers? Looking at all the case files, and the distance traveled, one person would have to search out the victims, watch their routine to figure out when to take them, figure out how to transport them to the location where they're killed, complete his work and return them before they were missed. That's a lot of work for one killer." She sat back down and moved the file in front of her.

"The killings have occurred every two weeks, so far. We can surmise that he takes two weeks to locate, plan, and carry out his delusional fantasy and move on to the next one on his list. They have to be related in some way. But as of yet, we only have speculation on what we're dealing with. Is there anything else you can add to the profile, Doctor Harris?" Steve asked.

"Looking at the pathology, the only findings are still the GHB, Coumadin and a trace of Quaternary ammonia on the bodies, is this still correct?" She pushed her glasses up from the end of her nose.

"Yes," Steve answered.

"We know he has to get into the food or drink of the victims, and collect them without being seen. He has to get into their lives for a short time to do that," she said.

"Or he could just break into their house and put it in something. Wait for the circumstances to be right and abduct them without any problem," Steve said.

"That's possible, but there's no sign of forced entry at any of the scenes," she said.

"Doesn't mean he couldn't get in and leave no trace," Jerry said. "Especially if he's stalking the victims for that long while he waits to strike. A good hunter will watch his prey, learn their habits and strike on his terms."

"The report from Doctor Singer details his thoughts. He believes they were hung up to drain their blood, like a hunter would after a kill in the field. We've all seen deer hung in the yard or a shed, hell, even in slaughterhouses the carcasses of animals are hung for the blood to drain while they are moving down the line." He walked over to the end of the room. "Our killer either has a fetish for blood or just wants to be sanitary in his work. He's done his homework, he knows where, when, and how to do what he's doing. We're playing his game. He's not concerned with the media. There haven't been any notes left behind or any riddles to solve, because he doesn't care about a cat and mouse game with the police. From your assessment, Doctor Harris, this guy is on a mission, be it from god or just in his own mind. We have to find him before he runs out of the people he is after or we won't catch him, will we?" Steve asked.

"That's correct, in my opinion," she said.

"Where are we with suspects, anything new there?" Sheriff Lester asked.

"We're taking a strong look at Mr. Wallace Holt. Born in 1961 to Earl and Betty Holt. From what we can find, he was sent to live with his grandparents in the Hocking Hills in southern Ohio at the age of six. We presume because the parents didn't want him. There are no signs of him ever going to school. He just showed up working at the Plastics Plant in 1984 where Carl Peterson and he got in some kind of conflict and Carl fired him. Then he seemed to drift around from temp agency to temp agency. He showed up at one company that did work for Wilson Meats and Browning Cleaning services, the owners, are the victims of the last two killings. No one remembered him or where he lived. All the information he gave at the time is outdated or false," Tom said.

The group sat up in their chairs and hung on every word.

"That's until he's listed DOA at the scene of a crash in 2002 in his father's truck. He was the only one seen in the truck when it left the gas station just prior to the crash. At which time, both of his parents go missing. Now, it could be because they're all together on this, or because they're killed in pairs, we could find them in the same shape. Bank records show the couple's account was closed the day before the wreck and Wallace Holt never opened an account, anywhere. Most of the checks we could track down were cashed at check cashing operations or wherever he worked. All Wallace had was an ID card, and the last time it was updated, was in 2000, so we're stuck at this point. I'm still looking into the parents' pasts to see what turns up there," Tom said.

"Any thoughts?" Sheriff Lester asked the group.

"It fits," Doctor Harris said. "Wallace Holt, for whatever reason, secluded from everyone, sent away from his parents, hidden away with no outside influence, could manifest any number of delusions. When he was old enough and went to work, had to take menial labor jobs because that's all he could do," she said. Again pushing her glasses up from her nose. "Think about it, no schooling, and no interaction with other children to help him conform to society, thrust into adulthood where he has to find a way to live. We're looking for the catalyst. Look back into the jobs he performed. Most of them he probably left because he was let go or he had a conflict with someone he didn't know how to handle. But somewhere in that line of events, he snapped and took the only action he knew."

"That all means nothing if he's deceased," Sheriff Lester said. "Carol and Doctor Singer are still working on the remains, until they find something, we keep looking into Wallace Holt and his missing parents. Remember, outside of this room no one speaks a word. We find something definite, we will discuss what to tell the press, until then…"

"No comment," the entire group said together.

"Remember, we have one week before he kills again," Sheriff Lester warned and the room grew quiet.

***

The group broke up and left the room. Steve, Jerry, Tom and Herb stayed behind. Herb turned to Steve. "I think I'll wait a while and let them run the gauntlet of vultures outside. Maybe seeing them leave, I can get out without being seen."

Steve laughed. "Don't bet on it. Now let's get to it, from here, we focus on the Holts. By Monday, we need a list of all the jobs Wallace worked in the past. We need to contact everyone we can find. From what was said here, he's already out there picking out his next target. We need to find him before he takes them."

"I already have the list," Tom said. "So all we need to do is start calling Monday morning and locating them."

"No, I think we need to contact all of them in person. I know it's going to take a lot of manpower, but if we contact them in person, and if the killer's watching, it might throw him off his game. He might screw up or maybe get scared off," Steve said. "Herb, let's go grab the sheriff and Sergeant Winslow before he gets out of here. Jerry, you and Tom work on separating Tom's list by location, so we can split into groups."

Steve left the room to catch up with the others and found both Sheriff Baker and Sheriff Lester around the corner talking with Sergeant Winslow.

"Sheriff Lester, could I interrupt? We need to see all of you back in here for a minute," he told the three men.

They followed Steve back to the room where Tom had already done the search on the computer file and separated the listings by area.

"We have a game plan for Monday, but we're going to need some additional officers to carry out the canvassing on this," Steve told Lester.

"How many?" Lester asked.

"Sixteen," Tom answered before retrieving the pages from the printer.

"That was fast," Steve said with a grin when Tom handed him the pages.

"Sixteen according to wonderboy here. We're going to contact all of the employers Wallace Holt ever worked for. Hopefully, we can either get in the killer's way or find out some more information about him," Steve said.

"A lot of man hours looking for someone you're not even sure is still alive," Lester said.

"Yes, but what if we don't do anything and he's out there and he kills again and we've sat here and done nothing? If it's not him, we're chasing our tails anyway," Steve said.

"Sheriff Lester," Carol called to him when she came into the room. Doctor Singer came in behind her.

"Nice of you to join the meeting, finally," Lester said.

"Sorry sheriff, I believe that's my fault," Doctor Singer said. "But with good reason. You might want to sit down for this, gentleman." They all gather at the table. "Carol, will you inform the sheriff of our findings?"

"Well, Sheriff, the remains the detectives brought back from the crash in Lancaster were of little use, really, they were burnt to the point of not being able to retrieve any DNA," Carol said.

"So how does that help us?" Lester said.

"Well, looking at a cross section of bone under the microscope Doctor Singer noticed something strange. Doctor Singer?" She gestured for him to continue.

"The bones are not compatible with the cell structure of human bone tissue, in other words, what they found in the car and thought were the remains of Mr. Holt, while they are close in structure, if you look, you find they are actually a few pieces of a domesticated pig," he said.

"What? Pig bones?" Steve said and slapped his hands on the table.

"Yes, it was confirmed just a moment ago by a colleague of mine that works in animal pathology," Doctor Singer confirmed. "Seems they found someone's last meal instead of their remains."

"Hot Damn," Steve yelled and jumped out of his chair.

"Great work, Doc, both of you," Lester said. "Now we have somewhere to start. You'll have your men Monday."

"Tom, give me all the information you can on this guy. We'll let the press have the story. They can help hunt him down or maybe scare him off long enough for us to get close. Steve, you want to handle the press this time?" Lester asked.

"No way in Hell," Steve said. "I'll leave that to you guys who need your picture in the paper." He gave a nod to Jerry and Tom. "I'll work with Jerry and Tom to lay out the search grid for Monday."

"Shall we go?" Lester gestured to Sheriff Baker and Sergeant Winslow and they walked out of the room. Steve was happy that they got to go and announce they finally had a person of interest in the case.

Steve turned to Jerry and Tom. "You boys have earned a night out on me. What do you say?"

"Sounds good to me," Jerry said.

"What about you, Tom?" Steve asked.

"I sorta have plans," he said.

"Okay kid, spill your guts," Jerry commanded and the two of them stood on both sides of Tom blocking his path.

"Okay, okay, I'm taking the red eye to LA tonight. I'm going to see Terry for the weekend. I'll be back late Sunday night," he confessed.

"Good boy," Jerry said. He rubbed his hands on Tom's head messing up his hair.

"Have a good flight, but before you go, set up the grids for Monday," Steve said.

"Already done." Tom handed him the area assignments he had already completed.

"Show off," Jerry said. "I told you we should have gotten him and Tina together."

Tom looked at Steve. "Who's Tina?" he asked puzzled.

"Nobody kid, just get out of here and have a good time," he said. Tom bolted out the door apparently in a hurry to start his weekend.

Steve sat down. For the first time in weeks he looked at the board of pictures without feeling lost. "I got you, you son of a bitch. It's just a matter of time now."

\*\*\*

Steve set up the first round of drinks and stood up from their table at the local bar called "The Spot", a place all the locals went to at the end of the work week to blow off steam. The sound of pool balls being struck and the local sports teams on the television filled the room.

"A toast, may the skies be free from bad weather from here to LA, smooth flight Tom." They all lifted their glasses.

Jerry and his wife sat with Carol. Carol leaned over and whispered in Jerry's ear. "You ready to fill me in on this?"

"Our little boy is all grown up." He laughed and he and Steve bumped their glasses together.

Carol punched Jerry in the leg. "Tell me, you ass!" Carol said to the group's laughter.

"Okay."

Jerry told the story from the very beginning, of course in Jerry's version, which to him was much funnier. He completed the story, which took a few more rounds of drinks to complete.

Carol, amazed, sat back in disbelief.

"You're kidding," she said. She moved her hair back

out of her eyes.

"I don't know why you're so shocked, my dear," Doctor Singer said in a funny alcohol induced tone of voice.

"We hooked up on the same case," he announced to a roar of laughter from the group.

Shocked by his admission, Carol's face turned an embarrassed tone of red. Carol hid her head like a teenager who had just gotten caught kissing in public for the first time.

"Way to go, Doc!" Steve and Jerry yelled. They stood up to high five each other and almost spilled their drinks.

Doctor Singer sat back with a look of conquest on his face. Carol reemerged from hiding her face and reached for her drink. Her face still the same shade of red as her blouse.

Jerry's wife looked at Carol. "Don't let these clowns get to you. They're just blowing off steam," she whispered to her. After the laughter subsided, Carol did her best to change the subject.

Steve's attention went to the television over the bar where the nightly report was playing. In the corner of the screen a picture of Wallace Holt flashed on. Although several years younger than now, it was the only picture anyone had found of the suspect. Steve's gaze trained on the eyes of the man in the picture. The other four turned their attention to the broadcast, and the entire bar quieted down to hear the report.

"Is that the guy?" Jerry's wife whispered.

"We think so," Jerry whispered back. "And we're going to find him, thanks to the docs here." He stood and toasted the two doctors before he ordered another round. Slapping Steve on the shoulder, he broke the hold the picture had on him.

"Set us up again!" Jerry yelled to the waitress who headed in the group's direction.

\*\*\*

Tom had made his way home and rushed to pack for his trip. Excited, he wondered what it was truly like in LA. He looked through the closet at his neatly hung clothes. The irremovable smile on his face told the whole story of what he was thinking. Over packing his suitcase full of clothing he stood back for a moment.

"Dude, you're only going for a day and a half," he told himself. He unpacked the case. He reached into the closet and pulled out a small carryon bag and continued to pack, this time being more selective in his choices. The packing complete, he replaced what he wasn't taking with him in their properly assigned areas in the closet. Tom grabbed his bag and headed for the airport.

He waited for the plane to take off, phone in hand while he pondered if he should call her or not. He'd decided to fly out to see her on a whim. *What if she'd changed her mind? What if she was trying to make him feel better and she really didn't mean for him to come?"* All the disastrous possibilities constantly ran through his thoughts. They called for the boarding of his flight and he stood and got into the line to board. His phone rang.

"It's her," he said looking down at the phone screen. He slid his finger over the screen and apprehensively answered.

"Hello."

"Hi Tom," Terry said.

"Hey Terry."

"You're coming, aren't you?" she asked.

"Absolutely, I'm coming," he said in an excited tone.

"Are you on your way yet?" she asked.

"Yes, I'm in line to board the plane. Is something wrong?"

"No, be safe, and hurry up. I can't wait to see you," she said.

"Okay, I'll see you then, bye," he said and hung up the phone. He handed the gate steward his boarding pass with the biggest grin he'd worn all day.

"Excited to be flying to LA?" the steward asked.

"You have no idea," Tom responded and walked down the jet way almost skipping as he hurried to get on the plane.

*\*\*\**

Tom's plane landed at LAX and he jumped up out of his seat, impatiently waiting in the line to get off. He walked up the jet way, with every step his pace quickened. He reached the security checkpoint and pulled out his phone to call Terry. Before he could dial the number, he spotted her standing outside the entryway.

She looked amazing. Her smile seemed to light up the entire airport. She wore the same black dress she had worn the first time they'd met, her long, soft red hair fell around her face. He was completely entranced. He shoved his phone in his pocket and walked toward her. When he reached her, he dropped his bag and reached up to touch her face. Not a word was spoken, but the conversation between them was obvious to everyone around them. They both leaned forward and their lips touched with the softest kiss.

"Hello," he said after their kiss ended.

"Hi, really glad you came," she said with a radiant smile.

He reached down for his bag, she took his hand, and they walked through the airport.

"How was the flight?" she asked.

"Way too long," he said with a smile, "but way worth it." He put his arm around her as they walked.

When they reached her car and she asked, "This is your first time in LA, right? The night has just begun out here. Where do you want to go first?"

"I guess I should find a hotel," he told her. "I never got the chance to book one before I left." He closed the door to her side of the car. He walked around to the passenger's side of the vehicle, climbed in and commented, "Nice ride." The deep grey exterior and dark grey leather interior caught his attention. He rubbed his hands over the leather dash as he nestled back into the soft bucket seats.

She turned the key on her BMW and drove away.

"I know the perfect hotel for you to stay at," she said.

He looked out at the lights of LA, with the wondering amazement of a little boy.

"Wait until you see it from your room," she told him.

She drove up to an apartment building and parked the car at the curb. "Coming?" she said and stepped out of the car. "Grab your bag."

She opened the door to her apartment and walked through the door. He stood outside, nervous, like he was sixteen again and didn't know what to expect. They made their way into a dimly lit hallway. She turned to him and took off her jacket.

"I thought you could stay here," she said with a sweet smile.

She reached behind him and closed the door. Taking his hand, she led him into the dark front room where the open blinds revealed the LA lights glowing in the distance. The apartment perched on the side of a hill and hung over the edge, with a perfect view of L.A. from the windows that made up the back wall of the main room. She turned to him.

"Now, where were we?" she asked and reached behind her to slowly un-zip her dress. Their gazes locked. They moved closer together and softly embraced. Their bodies pressed against each other in the soft shimmering light of the LA skyline. Tom forgot about the case.

# Chapter Seventeen

Monday morning brought a flurry of people to the police station: FBI, State police and officers from the sheriff's department. Steve had worked out the assignments and gathered all the officers together in the squad room.

"Good morning," Steve said once everyone was seated. "We're going to split up into groups, along with the officers from the Akron, Cincinnati, Lancaster and Columbus police departments. We're going to contact every person on this list to find out two things. Number one, we need to know anything they can remember about Wallace Holt. What he was like, did he have friends, even as far as what he liked to eat. Anything that could lead us to him. Second, have they seen him recently?"

He held up the black and white glossy of Wallace.

"Along with your list of assigned contacts, there is a picture of Wallace Holt. If you receive any information as to his location, call in immediately. Right now, he's just a person of interest, presumed to be involved in the killings. If by chance, you run into Mr. Holt, don't try to take him down by yourself. Watch him and call for backup."

He tapped a picture on the board behind him of the Holt's burned out truck.

"Wallace Holt was presumed dead. We think the accident was planned so he could drop off the face of the planet. Maybe he was already planning the killings or maybe he just wanted to disappear. The reason at this point doesn't matter, we need to find him and his parents, Earl and Betty Holt." He paused and scanned the room. Everyone was focused on his words.

"Any questions?" When no one asked anything, he went on. "Okay, Special Agent McIntyre will hand out the assignments on your way out the door. Go find Wallace Holt." Steve concluded the briefing and the officers lined up to receive their lists.

"Where do you want us to go?" Jerry asked Steve with Tom in tow.

"Jerry, you and I are going to check out a few contacts ourselves. Tom, I need you to stay on the trail of the family. Find any addresses you can for them. Go back to great grandparents if you have to, this guy is hiding somewhere, find him," Steve ordered.

Tom turned and left to continue his search.

Steve and Jerry headed out to their first location, Metric Shipping, a small shipping company, on the west side of Columbus, handling LTL shipments around Ohio. Steve drove in his normal fashion, dodging traffic while Jerry held on to the door handle trying not to spill the coffee he brought with him. He sped to the location like they were going to find the clue they needed on their first stop.

\*\*\*

"Any luck?" Steve asked Herb when they returned to the station after an exhausting and unfruitful day of searching.

"No. You?" Herb asked.

"Nothing," Steve replied. "This guy is a ghost. No one remembers him, or anything about him. Showing his picture just draws a blank stare from anyone I showed it to. If we hadn't had the records to show these people, they would have sworn he was never there. Not even the temp agencies we spoke to had anything to say. It's been eight years since he's worked anywhere. Most of the people he worked with are working somewhere else or retired," Steve said.

"Same story here, from the ones we contacted, it's as if

the guy never existed," Herb said.

"I had no luck looking into the parents and grandparents either," Tom told Steve. "I'm going to have to go down there," Tom said. "I have to go through about fifty years of county records they won't give me over the phone. That's the only way we're going to find any trace of them."

"Can we call Boon and see what he can find out?" Steve asked.

"Not if we want the information. This is going to be a long search, and I don't want someone just looking through files because they're told to. We need someone who is good at research." The officers around him smiled.

"I know, that's why I'm going tomorrow morning," Tom said sarcastically.

"I knew there was a reason we keep you around," Steve said and they walked back toward the squad room.

A list of all the locations and names that needed to be contacted was up on the wall. The day drew to a close and the final calls from the teams came into the station.

"That's all of them from today," Steve said and he marked off the last of the names. "thirty-two of the sixty, contacted, and from all reports no one has anything of interest."

"Maybe we'll get lucky tomorrow," Jerry said.

"We better, because someone on that list only has a few days left," Steve said staring at the pictures.

"By the looks of it, you didn't have much luck today," Sheriff Lester stated.

"That's an understatement," Steve replied.

"I want to have another talk with Doctor Harris. Herb, can you see if you can get her over here on Wednesday?" Steve asked.

"Sure, what's on your mind?"

"Something about this just bugs me and I need some questions answered. I don't really believe in all this mumbo jumbo about delusions, there has to be a pattern, but I can't figure out what it is," Steve explained.

"I'll call her now, 09:00 good?" Herb asked Steve and Lester.

"That's perfect," Steve replied. "Let's call it a day.

# Chapter Eighteen

"The hunt begins again," the hunter told himself. The cold dark expression on his lifeless face never changed. He went unnoticed sitting in the shadow of the trees that secluded his van from view. He sat for hours, watching. The prey was unaware of his presence. His calculated stare was enough to chill the air around him. His mind filled with sketchy, blurred memories of a little boy hiding from the monsters that ruled the tormented hallways of his mind.

He ran around every corner, only to fall prey to the never ending onslaught of pain inflicted by the monsters. This drove him to lash out against the heartless beast that could only be there to kill him.

He must strike first, and he had, but it hadn't stopped the beast. He must go on stalking the monsters until all of them were gone. He must save himself and any other small ones on which the monsters fed.

In the distance he spied the prey, out in the open at last. He must follow it to its den. Catch it in the night while it sleeps. It was the only way not to be eaten alive, when he could take both of them together. He followed his prey cautiously to avoid detection, but the beast was trying to get in his head.

"You must go on," the voice of the Old One tells him. Finally, the den of the beast is in sight. He drove down the lane and surveyed the target like the hunter he had become.

*"It's not time yet. I must continue to watch carefully, can't be seen, must find the back way into the den. This is too far from my home,"* he thought. *"But so was the last hunt."*

It didn't matter how far the hunt lead, only that the hunter came home. He watched the house and waited for any signs of movement. He studied everything that moved in the surrounding area. Looking for how the prey could elude his trap, but also how he could escape if the prey turned to attack.

The den was located near many others, but was still hidden from view of the rest. The hunter could get in and out quickly and quietly while the prey was away. But first, he must survey the den, to see how many monsters were inside, this would take more time. He pulled over and parked hidden from view. Silently, he learned by being watchful. Night time fell and the hunter, concealed in darkness, was free to move closer to the monster's den. He crept through trees and yards, making no sound. He left no footprints as his steps were soft on the ground, soft enough not to break the leaves that had fallen from the trees. He was skilled in the hunt. Since he was little, he'd roamed the woods, learning and hunting to survive.

He had tracked all manner of wild animals. He knew their tracks, where and what they ate. He had learned to pick up their trails.

*But the monsters aren't smart,* he thought. *They have no instinct for their surroundings. Their trails are easy to follow. They aren't scared, so they don't run, and there is no chase.* But he liked the chase, for now he was the hunter and not the small boy they tormented with all of their yelling and hitting to drive him to go where they wanted. The prey could slip away. He must be quiet giving the prey no chance to avoid the hunter.

He peered into the light of the windows to where the monsters dwelled. "Silent," he reminded himself. He knew if he was discovered they would surely eat him alive. He remembered the howling beast as the memories tormented him.

"Don't let them in." He grabbed his head to keep the

monsters from entering. "They rest," he said skulking around the house from window to window.

"There!"

His keen eyesight had found the way into the den. An open window on the side of the house. "Must ensure it stays open."

He took a twig from the ground and forced it into the side of the window. "Now it won't close on me. Now we wait," he told himself. The monsters must be prepared for the kill. He slipped back along the path the same way he'd come. "Now we wait for them to leave the den," he said and he climbed into his waiting van. "Now I can rest, get some sleep. The hunt continues tomorrow."

# Chapter Nineteen

On the road to Lancaster, Tom decided to call Terry and wake her up. They had talked most of the evening, but talking to her would pass the time.

She answered the phone with a sleepy, "Hello."

Tom remembered the time difference. "Oh, sorry Terry, I forgot the time. Go back to sleep," he said feeling stupid.

"No," she said, "I'd rather talk to you. How's your day going?" she asked. "I saw on the news last night that you guys might have a lead?"

"We're not sure, but it looks good. I'm on my way to look into his background and see what I can dig up," he replied.

"I know you don't want to talk about this with me," Terry said. "But I'm okay now. I want to know whatever you can tell me. And when you find him..."

The phone went silent for several moments.

"Terry, you still there?" he asked.

"Yeah, just find him and put him away," she said.

"How about we talk about you and me?" he said changing the subject.

"What about us?" she asked.

"Well, like when you might be coming back out here, or when I could come back out there?" Tom asked in his little boy voice.

While the conversation continued his mind drifted to part of the file on Wallace Holt's past, about having to stay with his grandparents in Hocking Hills.

"Terry, just thought of something I have to check out,

got to go, but I'll call you later, okay?" he said.

"Okay," she said.

Tom made another call to Sheriff Boon's office and asked him to meet him at the county records office. He was only ten minutes away and excited to get there.

He pulled up to the front of the building to see the sheriff leaning against his car.

"Morning, Detective Jensen," Sheriff Boon said before he leaned over to spit tobacco juice out of his mouth."What can I do for you this morning?"

"In the file it says Holt was taken to his grandparents place somewhere in Hocking Hills, but he doesn't show back up until 1984 in Columbus where his work record starts. We need everything we can find on the property records for his grandparents, Walter and Marion Holt, here and in Hocking Hills," Tom said.

They entered the building and followed the clerk to the record's room.

Boon asked, "How do you plan to go through all these records?"

"Well, hopefully they'll be in some sort of order," Tom said.

"What records are you looking for?" the clerk asked.

"We're looking for anything we can find on property owners named Holt," Tom replied.

"Let's see what we have in the land records for them. That should give us any properties they've owned around the county," the clerk said.

She led them to the section, through rows of files.

Tom turned to Boon. "You know the sheriff down in Hocking Hills?"

"Yes, I do. His name's Clifford Warner. He's been the sheriff down there for a long time. Would you like me to call him?" Boon asked.

"Yes, sir, and please ask him if he can meet me later today, that will be my next stop."

They followed the clerk farther back into the store room. She reached the location and fingered through the files. "Holt you said, right?"

"Yes, that's correct," Tom said.

"Well, there's nothing here under that name."

"Nothing?" he asked.

"It just means they didn't own any property in this county," she said.

"Thanks anyway," he said and turned to leave.

Tom and Boon walked back out to their cars.

"Let's go over to the office and give Sheriff Warner a call from there, maybe we can save you a drive down there."

"Good idea," Tom said.

# Chapter Twenty

The hunter had watched the sun come up and watched the prey leave the den.

"Now is the time to enter, both monsters have left," he said. Quietly, he stalked through the trees leaving no trace. He reached the window from the night before and gained entry swiftly. He stalked like a cat through the den, peering around every corner like he expected to attack a mouse for his dinner. His mind drew a map of every room as he made his way around the house. Only then could he be sure there were no monsters still home. After mapping all the possible hiding places, he relaxed enough to walk around the house studying it. He must know everything he can about them to defeat them. In the kitchen, he pulled a bag from his shirt pocket.

"We must make ready," he said. The morning breakfast dishes were stacked in the sink. He picked up a half full glass of orange juice.

"Perfect," he said and went to the refrigerator to find the container of orange juice. Taking a vial from his bag, he dumped the contents into the orange juice. "This will make things easier," he said. He remembered the old one and how he took this medication after his heart attack, "I have to take this stuff to thin my blood," he remembered the old one saying. He'd found it would make the process easier to complete.

"The monsters are vicious, but they're unaware," he thought. After replacing the container back in the refrigerator, he picked up the bag and pulled out the other vial. Holding the vial in his hands, he relished his magic weapon against the monsters. "Not yet, first we must wait." He replaced the vial in the bag. The flood of memories returned to torment him. He grabbed his head.

"Don't let them in," he said. The pain twisted his face showing the conflict raging in his mind. He fell to the floor as if struck from behind. With the faces of the monsters all around him, the first ones, and every other one he had killed, all of the monsters attacked him at the same time trying to control him. All of them screaming and attempting to beat him. Not him, but the little boy he used to be.

He watched the female monster, standing back, yelling for the bigger male to do her bidding. All of them surrounding him, all screaming and clawing his flesh.

"No more," he yelled out.

Opening his eyes, his face returned to the same cold mask from before.

"They are getting closer," he told himself. "I must not fail." The hunter left the house as stealthy as he'd entered. He moved in the shadows to reach his van, where for now, he felt safe.

"It won't be long now," he told himself. "I must follow the beast." He drove back to where he first picked up the trail.

Again, outside the Pearling Bakery, he hid in the trees. A good hunter, he blended in with the trees. Waiting all day, never moving, hardly breathing. He had learned to sleep and watch at the same time. All things he had to learn to survive after the monsters first sent him away. But he returned a better hunter, and it was the monsters who would perish, not him.

*** 

The hunter stalked the prey back home from work following the same routine. "Easy to track this one, so unaware of his surroundings," he thought. They reached the house. The prey went inside. He drove past and parked away from the area.

"I can't be seen, the prey can't be aware of the hunter. I must watch the den. The time is close for the trap to be set." His mind focused on the task before him. He slinked again unnoticed through the trees, becoming part of the landscape. The camouflage he wore hid him from view when he climbed the tree he'd already scouted to view the den. He sat in complete silence watching the monsters, there were only two.

"Good, I can take them both at once, like before, they make it easy staying together in the den." He carried out the planned details of the hunt in his mind. "I must study them, must make sure there is no way of escape. If they escape, they're sure to warn the others still out there. I must capture them all, it's the only way I can be safe."

The cold expression left his face as the monsters in his mind attacked him once again. He ran down the hallways of his dreams, frantically trying to escape them. The small boy never knew the loving safe harbor of protection from anyone. He'd had to fight them on his own. With each attack, his mind struggled in vain only to be ravished once again by the beast.

"No more," he said to regain control of his tormented mind. "I am the hunter." His cold demeanor returned. "I will hunt them all." His vigilant watch continued through the growing darkness.

# Chapter Twenty-One

Sheriff Boon and Tom were back in the sheriff's office. Tom held the phone to his ear and leaned back in the black, fake leather chair.

"Sheriff Warner, have you ever heard of a Walter and Marion Holt down in Hocking Hills?" Tom asked.

"Well, let me think. You know I do remember Walter. He and Marion lived way back in the woods on the outskirts of the Wayne National Forest down here. But I haven't seen them for years. They would be in their nineties if they're still alive," Sheriff Warner said.

"I need to find any records there might be for them and their grandson Wallace, could I meet you in an hour and see if we can find out where they could have gone?" Tom asked.

"Sure, I'll have an officer run over to the county seat and pull the records on them. I'll see you in an hour," Sheriff Warner said.

Tom hung up the phone. "Thanks for your help Sheriff Boon, my search continues," Tom said. He shook the sheriff's hand.

"You know it's only an hour down the road. How about I ride along and see where all this plays out. I got nothing going on here and the boys can handle whatever comes up," he said.

"Great, I could use the company."

The ride down was full of stories from Boon on local lore, most of it just talk to fill the time. Boon was one who loved his own stories and folklore. He didn't stop talking the entire way. Tom, not one to interrupt his elders, much less a superior officer, was trapped by circumstance and had to listen to every story for sixty miles. Tom nodded and smiled and occasionally laughed at a joke Tom didn't even get. But he didn't mind, he filled his thoughts with Terry and that made the ride bearable. They reached the Sheriff's Station in Hocking Hills and Tom parked the car and he and Sheriff Boon entered the building.

They introduced themselves to the officer inside, Sheriff Warner walked around the corner. A tall man, around six foot five inches tall walking with long strides, he could cover long distances with very little effort. He approached Tom and Sheriff Boon.

"Detective Jensen? Sheriff Boon?" he said in a deep voice that would command attention in any room.

"Yes, Sir," Tom answered almost snapping to attention. He reached out to shake Sheriff Warner's hand. Tom's hand was engulfed in the bear paw sized grasp of Sheriff Warner's hand.

"Hello, Sheriff Boon," Warner said. He reached out to greet Sheriff Boon. "You boys follow me." He led them down the wood paneled hall to his office.

"This is Officer Lambert, I sent him to pull the files you gentlemen required. Now how can we help you, Detective Jensen?" he said. He sat down in his chair behind the desk.

Feeling somewhat like he was back in school and sent to the principal's office, he said, "Well, Sheriff Warner, this serial killer case we're working on has led us to look into the Holt Family. The son, Wallace, was believed dead when his father's truck was found burned out after it ran off the road." Tom reached up and loosened his tie, still feelling nervous from the overshadowing stature of Sheriff Warner. "He was the last one seen driving it away from a local gas station. Finding very little evidence, and the parents disappeared soon after, there was really no reason to question it. But now, we've determined the bones found in the wreck are not Wallace's. We've reason to believe he could be involved in the case."

Sheriff Warner leaned back in his chair with his hands folded behind his head, pondering the information Tom was giving him.

"We need to locate anywhere they could have lived down here. He has to have a secluded location to carry out what he's doing to the victims," Tom said.

"Well, there sure are some areas down here that fit that bill," Sheriff Warner said.

"We can't find any school records for Wallace, anywhere. He must have never gone and lived out of touch for most of his life," Tom said.

"Why don't we take a ride up to the Holt's old place? The records tell us all the taxes have been paid, so the land is still in their name. It's a good bet he, or all of them, could still be up there," Sheriff Warner said. "We also did a search for vehicles the Holt's owned. They own a 1980 brown panel truck, and a 1978 four door Chevy Cavalier."

"Let me call the lead detective on this and let him know what we've found," Tom said and picked up the phone.

After reaching Steve, Tom placed the phone on speaker so they could rely the new information.

"Hold off until we get there in the morning. I want to have a SWAT team and the FBI with us before we go into the woods. I'll have the whole crew down there," Steve said on the other end of the phone.

"Will do," Sheriff Warner said. He hung up the phone.

"I know this is your jurisdiction, but…" Tom said.

"Don't worry about that. If I'd been hunting this guy, I'd want to be there, too. Lambert, you and Jones go out there and keep an eye on the area until the rest of the bunch gets here. If you see any movement, call it in," Sheriff Warner ordered.

"Okay, Sheriff," Officer Lambert responded and

151 • Hunting Monsters

headed out the door.

"Tom, I guess you'll need a place to stay, and you'll need a ride back up north, Sheriff Boon. Let me get someone to take you back," Sheriff Warner said.

"No way. I think I'll stay right down here and see the show," Boon said. "I just need to let my people know." He picked up the phone to call his office.

\*\*\*

"Let's go pull the team together and you and I get on the road tonight. I want to be ready at first light tomorrow," Steve told Jerry. They walked into the squad room.

Sheriff Lester heard the news and called the two men into his office and shut the door. He sat down in his chair, dialed up Sheriff Warner, and put him on the speaker.

"Sheriff Warner, this is Sheriff Lester. I hear you have some good news for us."

The plans made for the next morning, Steve felt a lift in his spirit. For six weeks they had been chasing what seemed to be an untraceable killer. Steve informed the group around him about what Tom had found. Sheriff Lester looked at the two detectives from across the desk,

"Make no mistake, make sure he's the right guy, and don't let him get away," he told them.

"You got it, Sheriff," Steve said.

"We need to call Herb and get him up to speed and see how many of his boys can get down there. The more officers the better," Lester said.

"I'll call Sheriff Warner back and make sure we get a warrant for the property. I don't want anything to go wrong with this, no mistakes," Lester said.

Leaving the office, Steve and Jerry met Herb coming into the building. They quickly caught him up on the latest information and he agreed to have officers there right of way.

"How about we all go together? I'll pick up my case

from the hotel, that should give you guys time to pack a bag. We can be there in two hours," Herb said.

"Just have to grab something from the weapons locker," Jerry said and headed down the hallway.

"Pick me up at home in a half hour," he told Steve.

"What's he getting?" Herb asked Steve.

"His sniper rifle," Steve responded with a cold stare.

\*\*\*

Steve, Jerry and Herb arrived at the motel in Logan, Ohio where Tom had booked rooms.

"Hey, guys," Tom said as they exited the SUV. "I already have your rooms." He handed them the keys.

"How about we unload and go find some dinner," Steve said.

"Sounds good to me," Tom said in agreement. "There's a little diner down the road, we probably won't get too sick eating there." The group grinned at Tom's joke.

"It's not too bad a place." Tom said. "It's kinda like Gretta's, just a dive by the side of the road." Tom said. He led the group into the diner.

"We meet the sheriff at his office at 06:00," Tom told the group at the restaurant.

"All of the other officers will be here at 05:00.," Herb said. He took a long drink coffee from the chipped white cup.

"There are two officers watching the location tonight, but as of an hour ago there hasn't been a sighting of anyone." The food arrived and so did Sheriff Warner, who followed the waitress to their table.

"Sheriff," Tom said surprised.

Warner pulled up a chair and sat down with the group. "I thought you boys would be here, not much else around here and the food really won't kill you, at least not right away," Warner said with a grin.

The waitress brought another coffee cup and filled it

while she chewed a wad of gum like a hungry cow.

"Okay," Warner said, "I know this is my town, but how do you boys want to run this? There can only be one leader giving directions, now I don't care if it's the FBI," he looked at Herb, "Or you guys from the Springfield Sheriff's Department, but let's decide now before all this starts in the morning."

Jerry, Tom and Herb looked over at Steve.

"Well, Sheriff Warner, you know the lay of the land. We haven't worried about jurisdiction between any of us so far. We just want the bastard caught. Jerry is the leader of the SWAT Team and I would prefer he leads the assault. But the rest, I think we can let you handle that. I think we're all on the same page with this," Steve said and looked around the table at the rest of the group, who nodded their heads in agreement.

"Okay then," Warner said. He dumped more sugar in his coffee and gave it a hard stir. "We'll have a briefing at the office at 06:00 and all the ground rules will be laid out, fair enough?" Sheriff Warner asked.

"Sounds like a good plan to me," Steve said.

"I'll see you guys in the morning then, have a good night," Warner said. He gulped down his coffee and left the group.

"Now that's a big old boy," Jerry said.

"Yeah, kinda makes you feel real small standing next to him," Tom said.

"I'd feel that way, too, if I was still in third grade," Jerry said and slapped Tom on the back.

"I might be less than six foot, but it's not the size that counts," Tom said with a smile to the group's laughter.

"That's reminds me, you never told us how the trip went, Romeo," Jerry said on another fishing trip for information.

Tom sat silently looking around the table at the grinning faces for a moment. He started to speak, but stopped himself. Knowing if he opened his mouth, it would be all over the station and most likely the town before they got back. He took another bite of his grilled chicken sandwich and smiled at Jerry who was still trying every way to get the goods on the weekend.

The men finished the meal and returned to the motel and separated to their rooms, agreeing to meet at 05:00 to drive to the sheriff's station. In his room, Tom pulled out his phone to call Terry. When she answered he sat on the side of the bed, pulled off his shoes and leaned back against the headboard.

"Just thought I'd call before I went to sleep. I wanted the last voice I heard to be yours," he said.

"And what are you up to?" she asked. Their conversation continued on but he mentioned nothing about where he was not wanting to change the mood he could feel in her voice. They talked until he had to say goodbye.

"I have to get up in a few hours so I'm going to sleep but I'll be dreaming about you," he said.

"You better, talk to you later," she said and hung up the phone.

Tom lay back in the bed and pictured her standing in front of the glass doors in her apartment. "Good night," he said and drifted off to sleep.

# Chapter Twenty-Two

"I see the FBI made it," Jerry said to Steve when they pulled into the parking lot. Exiting the SUV they joined the groups that filed into the sheriff's office where Sheriff Warner had set up a map on the wall.

"Morning boys," Sheriff Warner said in greeting. Sheriff Boon, who had also stayed for the event, already stood in the front of the room. The room full of men quieted and Sheriff Warner moved to the front of the room. When he spoke, his booming voice filled the room, commanding the attention of the group.

"Good morning, we're all here for one reason, to catch a killer." He indicated the map behind him. "We're going to surround the property of Walter and Marion Holt. We're looking for this man," He tapped the picture of Wallace on the board. "Wallace Holt, who is believed to be involved in the serial killings that have taken the lives of six people already."

"Detective Jerry Stevenson will lead the assault team from the west side. Detective Belcher and I will lead the team entering from the south. Sheriff Boon has the north, Tom and Special Agent McIntyre will lead the team covering the east section." Again he indicated the map and pointed to a satellite image of a wooded area where the roof of a house could faintly be seen. "The house is surrounded by woods and thick overgrowth, so we should be able to arrive at the location without being seen." He pushed his cap up on his head and leaned on the table with his long arms still propping him up above the group. "We want this guy alive, but either way, he doesn't get out of there. We have twenty men, no one gets trigger happy. If we have to take a shot, Detective Stevenson is a trained SWAT commander and he will make that call. But only as a last resort," Sheriff Warner told them. His words were a command.

Stillness fell over the room and Sheriff Warner continued with the assault plan.

He turned to Steve, who nodded in agreement with Warner's description of the events about to unfold.

"Any questions?" Warner asked. "Okay, let's load up and go get this guy."

They all filed out of the station, all wearing their bulletproof vests showing FBI, SHERIFF, and POLICE in bold letters identifiable to anyone around.

***

Stopping about one hundred yards from the entrance to the driveway of the residence, the convoy pulled to the side of the road. The teams unloaded and gathered around Sheriff Warner who laid out the map on the hood of his car.

"Okay, we are on foot from here. In fifteen minutes Detective Stevenson and his team will make their way up the driveway to the front of the house. Stay in the woods until all the teams are in place. Detective Belcher, there is a small barn your team will need to clear before we go in, after you secure it, radio us to begin the assault. Everyone knows where they're going?" he asked and the group responded with a confident, "Yes, Sir."

"Okay, let's move."

Jerry removed his weapon from its case and loaded it. He turned to Steve and said, "Just give me a chance, one clear shot and this will all be over."

Steve nodded and the teams headed off into the dense woods. Twenty men prowled through the woods, all carrying loaded weapons, a few of the officers with shotguns, but most with their service weapons. Jerry, the only one with a sniper rifle, stopped and peered through the scope looking for the target.

Steve's team approached the barn, split up, and entered it from both sides. They moved in, guns pointed sharply in front of them, making swift moves around the perimeter. Steve waved to one of the officers to climb the ladder to the loft of the barn. While the others trained their weapons on the open loft. Silently, the officer climbed the ladder to confirm it was empty. Without a sound, hand signals relayed the message to the team that all was clear.

With their positions secure, Steve broke radio silence. "Team one in place," he said.

***

"Team two in place, all clear, all clear in front," Jerry's voice over the radio.

"Team Three in place," Tom's voice came over the radio.

"Team four will be on location in two," Boon's voice came over the radio.

The other teams waited and watched and the anticipation built.

"Team four in place," Boon voice again comes through the radio.

"Okay team two, advance, everyone else spread out and hold the perimeter," Steve ordered.

Jerry led his team like a commando unit headed into a war zone. "Team two on the porch," came over the radio.

"Hold your position, we're going to breach, no signs of anyone in the house." The groups had assumed positions that completely surrounded the old farm house. Jerry stood up in front of the door with the other officers on each side slung his rifle over his shoulder and pulled his sidearm.

"Okay to breach," Steve said.

Jerry kicked open the door with one swift move and was inside before it hit the door stop on the other side of the wall. His 9mm pointed where his sight lead him. The other officers filled in behind him.

From room to room they searched. Steve, Tom and the rest of the officers waited anxiously to hear the outcome.

"All clear," Jerry said over the radio and walked back out onto the porch followed by the other officers.

Steve and Sheriff Warner joined Jerry at the front of the house,

"There's no one in there, no one alive that is. Better call the crime lab Herb," Jerry said.

***

Inside the house, it appeared like no one had been there for years. Dust a quarter of an inch thick covered everything. Old pictures and furniture in the house looked to be from the sixties. They walked into the kitchen and discovered a horrific scene. Two bodies sat at the table wrapped in plastic, almost mummified. Their dried up bodies posed as if they were having dinner. Their skin was shriveled and covered in dust and cobwebs, it looked like a scene out of a mummy movie.

"My god," Steve said to Warner and Herb when they joined him.

"How long have they been here?" Herb asked.

"Long enough for them to shrivel up like that," Steve said.

Even from the decayed remains, they could tell the bodies' heads had been switched and sewn on in the same fashion as the other victims.

"This is one sick son of a bitch," Warner said.

"Okay, everyone out of the house," Steve ordered.

"Herb, call the team in and call Doctor Harris, too. I want her down here. Sheriff Warner, can your boys seal off this place?" Steve asked.

"Sure can," Warner answered and left the house ordering all of his men to follow.

"Sheriff Warner, use all the FBI men you need," Herb said.

Steve, Herb and Tom walked through the rest of the house. They found a small bedroom down the hall. The room wasn't as dusty as the rest of the house.

"He's been here," Tom told the others who were looking around the room.

"Don't touch anything until the lab gets here," Steve reminded Tom.

A box sat on the table by the bed. Steve walked over to the table and a cold chill ran up the back of his neck when he peered into the box.

"Look at this," he said.

Tom and Herb walked over and looked in the box. Four dolls lay inside.

Two male and two female dolls posed sitting at a table with all four of their heads switched to the opposites bodies. There were no cloths on the dolls in the old paper shoe box. Only a table and four chairs for the dolls.

The pictures hanging on the walls of the room were of a small child being chased by monsters drawn in crayon.

"What the hell went on in this house?" Steve said. He took off his cap and wiped the sweat from his forehead.

"Okay," Steve said, "Let's get out of here." Steve led the group out of the house.

*** 

"How long until the crime lab gets here?" Steve asked Herb.

"I had a feeling they'd be needed, so they're only thirty minutes out."

Steve smiled and nodded.

"Who do you think those two in the house are?" Jerry asked.

"It's either Walter and Marion Holt or the parents, Earl and Betty Holt, would be my guess," Steve said. "Sheriff

Warner, are there any more buildings on the property?"

"Not that we're aware of, but we're bringing in some dogs. We'll go on a hunt after they get here," Warner replied.

\*\*\*

Jerry, Steve, Herb, Tom and Sheriff Warner stood talking about what they had just seen inside. Jerry stood as if he was on guard, looking out at the surrounding woods like he expected an enemy attack.

"Here come the lab boys," Steve said when he saw a black van coming through the trees.

Steve's phone rang. "Detective Belcher," he answered.

Silence fell over the group and Steve turned quiet listening to the voice on the other end.

"You've got to be shitting me," he exclaimed. "Thanks sheriff." Steve ended the call. "You're not going to believe this," he said turning to the group of men. "Lacy James just broke the story of this raid, along with video of the entry with close ups of all of us five minutes ago. How the hell did she find us?"

The puzzled group stood there shaking their heads.

"Sheriff Warner, will you put a couple of men down on the road to close off the area? I figure we have about an hour before this place is surrounded by reporters, so much for setting a trap," Steve said. He walked off the creaking porch still cursing.

"Who is Lacy James?" Sheriff Warner asked.

"A burr in his saddle," Jerry replied and walked away from the front of the house to allow for the crime team to enter.

"Do you know when Doctor Harris will arrive?" Steve asked Herb.

"Not for a while, she was on her way to our office when we called her," he replied.

"Nothing here to do now but wait for the crime scene

folks to finish. How about we head into town and grab some breakfast?" Sheriff Warner asked. "The boys have the place surrounded, no one's going to come in here even if he was hiding in the woods."

The men agreed and the six of them headed off to town.

*\*\**

Walking into the diner, Steve spotted Lacy and Tim sitting back in a corner booth having coffee. He started to walk back to confront her, but Jerry grabbed him by the arm and stopped him from going.

"Nothing good can come from this. Just stop right there, act like you don't even know," Jerry told him. "It's going to come out anyway. For all she knows we found nothing, so there's no reason to let her know we did, okay?"

The group picked out a couple of tables and pulled them together. The six men sat down and talked about what food looked good. Small talk, just to set the mood that nothing bothered them.

Lacy walked up to the table.

"Good morning, Detective Belcher," Lacy said in a smug tone.

"Well, good morning to you. What brings you down this way?" he asked.

"Oh, I followed you boys from the sheriff's office last night and this morning. Thanks for the breaking story," she said with a smug smile.

"Well, not sure what you mean by breaking story. We've known about that place for a week, but no one was ever around. All we found there was dust and spiders, so whatever you want to report is okay by me. That okay with you Sheriff Warner?" he asked looking over at the sheriff.

"That would be just fine," Warner said. He laid his hat on the table in front of him.

"Would you like to join us for some breakfast, little lady?" Sheriff Warner asked in a patronizing tone.

"No, but thanks anyway. We have to be going," she said and left the diner with her camera man scurrying after her. Steve walked over to the window and watched them go across the street where they climbed into her van. He watched as she tore out of the parking lot headed north out of town. Smiling, he walked back to the table and told the group.

"Boy is she going to be mad after we give a press conference this afternoon and she's the only one not here." The group erupted into laughter.

"Now, let's get down to some southern cooking," Steve said.

"So where do you think this guy is now?" Jerry asked.

"Out there somewhere, and by now he's picked out his next victims," Steve said with a chilling stare.

***

After the group of officers finished their breakfast they returned to the crime scene where the lab techs had gone over every inch of the house. The lead tech approached the group before they were all the way out of the SUV.

"We're done," he told Steve. "We'll have the bodies sent to the Columbus lab where Doctor Singer is waiting for them. The rest of the evidence is being loaded to be sent back to the FBI lab for testing."

"Thanks," Steve said.

"No way to tell how long it's been since someone's been in there, but it's been awhile."

Steve watched Doctor Harris come out of the front door with some of the drawings in plastic evidence bags. She held up the bag.

"Detectives, you might want to see this," she said. "In the bedroom we assume was for a small child, we found all these drawings on the wall."

"Yes, we saw them, too," Steve said.

"We also found a bunch more under the mattress on the bed," she said.

Looking around at the group and showing them two of the drawings, she continued.

"I think you'll find a hide out somewhere in the woods. In the drawings, it looks like he has a place where he feels safe under a large tree. If we can find that place we might be able to find some more clues," she said. She placed the evidence bags in the car.

"Sheriff Warner, how long before the dogs get here?" Steve asked.

"Another couple of hours, they're coming from Columbus," the sheriff responded.

"We're not going to wait that long. Jerry, grab your gear." He turned to look at Herb. "Herb, get a few of your men and let's go for a walk in the woods," Steve said.

"Tom, you stay with Doctor Harris and go over everything before it leaves here, find us a clue to where this guy is. Sheriff Warner, if we're not back in an hour, come and find us," Steve said with a smile. The group headed into the woods at the back side of the house.

"Jerry, you're the tracker, find this hide out," Steve said.

Jerry led the group into the woods and returned to the sniper he once was. Steve watched as he moved cautiously and quietly as if he hunted someone who hunted him. Using the scope on his rifle, he peered into the woods ahead of him looking for any sign. He knew no one had been at the house, but someone who could pull off the murders he had seen, could hide underneath a leaf and not be discovered. Turning around several times to tell the group behind him to be quiet he finally stopped.

"Look, Steve, I'll find it. You guys stay here until I call you. If this guy is out here somewhere he'll hear you coming from one hundred yards away. Stay put and stay quiet," Jerry whispered to the men before he moved off silently through the trees ahead of him.

In seconds, without a sound, he disappeared. Steve and the other officers sat and waited for fifteen minutes. Herb turned to Steve and said in a whisper, "Who is this guy, Rambo?" he said with a smirk.

"I'm just glad he's on our side," Steve said. They both smiled.

"I thought I told you to be quiet," Jerry said startling the two when he appeared out of the trees beside them.

"Where the hell did you come from?" Herb said in surprise.

Jerry just smiled. "The tree is about two hundred yards straight north from here. There's no one around within five hundred yards, follow me," Jerry said and led them back into the woods.

Steve and Herb looked at each other, shook their heads and followed Jerry into the deeper woods. They reached the tree and found a hollow section between two very large roots of the old oak tree. The tree had been hollowed out with time, and there was enough room for someone to hide inside. Inside the base of the tree they found some more pictures, crayons and a few articles of clothing.

Most of the pictures had degraded with time and weather from being in the woods, but one of the pictures they pulled from the tree brought a look of fear to all their faces. On the paper, drawn in crayon, the picture depicted a little boy holding the severed head of a monster. The flaming sword in the boy's hand dripped with blood. Written on the bottom of the page, in a child's rough handwriting, were the words, "Now I have your power."

"We need to get this to the Doc," Steve said.

\*\*\*

With all the evidence at the house collected and the tree location, Steve, Tom and Jerry made their way back to the motel. Loading up to head back to Springfield, Steve turned to see Doctor Harris pulling up behind them.

"Detective," she called to Steve, "I'll meet you down at your office tomorrow, but first I need to go and research some cases. I'll have a new profile for you tomorrow."

"Okay," Steve said and then watched her drive away.

"What more can she add? We have a nut case killing people, it don't matter why, just that we have to stop him," Steve told Jerry and Tom.

The men loaded up Tom's car and headed for home. Steve rode in the passenger seat and remained quiet, his mind drifted through the last six weeks of events.

"How can no one remember seeing this guy?" he said with frustration. "There have been officers to every place that guy worked, and not one person remembers him. I just don't get it," Steve said and became silent once again.

# Chapter Twenty-Three

He sat once again outside the fence at the Bakery. The hunter stared, waiting and watching. His unwavering stare remained constant and clear. In his thoughts, he's in the woods watching the game he's tracking to bring food to the table. But the monsters appeared, yelling and hitting, and he turned back into the little boy running for his life.

"You're worthless, you little piece of shit," he heard over and over again until his head hurt with the pain he couldn't stop.

He ran farther out into the woods. Far enough to lose the monster chasing him. He'd hidden for hours in the woods. The words still repeating in his thoughts.

He shook from the terror striking every nerve of his body. Tears streamed down his face until they dried in lines from the wind passing over his cheeks. He ran franticly, deeper and deeper into the woods, the only place he felt safe.

Alone, he sat underneath the trees, holding his hands over his ears thinking this would stop the words from coming and stop the yelling. Night fell and he was still rocking back and forth, holding his hands over his ears. Calm finally came and he believed he could slip back into his room unnoticed. The monsters should be asleep. Scared to wake them, he crept in through the kitchen for whatever he could find to eat. Hiding in his room, he laid awake in his bed most of the night and waited for the monsters to come and get him. He drew the shapes of the monsters in his tormented mind. "Someday I'll be big enough to fight the monsters," he believed. He would be just like the men in the story book he kept under his bed. But for now, all he could do was hide from them.

He woke early. "Must be gone before they wake up," he thought, but it was too late, he heard the monster coming. The screams set him into a panic to find a place to hide. He crawled under the bed and hoped they couldn't find him. But the powerful grasp of the monster pulled him out, crying and screaming, from under the bed to be beaten again.

"If I knew you would turn out like this, I'd have jacked off in the John," the monster yelled. He was thrown down the hallway, his cries for help went unanswered, just more screams from the monsters.

Awakened by the sound of semi-truck's brakes, the hunter returned to his present hunt. His eyes were wet with the tears of fear from his dreams.

"I fear no monster, I am grown and will kill them all," he told himself. "Now is the time. I will wait no longer for this hunt." He returned to his hidden van and drove away. "I know enough about them, now is the time to set the trap. Then we'll see who cries for help."

Again, he stealthily moved in and out of the trees to find the window he'd entered before. With the monsters gone, he could move in and set his trap. Entering the house, he made his way to the kitchen. Having watched the routine of the prey for ten days, he knew their daily habits. He reached into the refrigerator and pulled out a half full gallon of milk. "This is where we set the trap," he said out loud. "They always have a bowl of cereal every night before they sleep. They make it so easy." He pulled a vial from his pocket and emptied it into the plastic jug of milk and replaced it in the refrigerator and closed the door.

"I have you now," he said. "All I have to do is wait."

He left the house the same way he'd entered. Back out through the window and into the woods. "Must wait until dark to return, that will give plenty of time for the trap to work." He disappeared into the woods.

\*\*\*

The night continued to grow darker and the hunter waited in the tree line watching the monsters go through their nightly routine.

"Always the same, such creatures of habit, that's why they're so easy to kill," he said.

He watched them pour their nightly bowl of cereal. "Yes, take the bait," he said and watched them pour the milk in the bowl. His excitement built. "That's good, devour your last meal, monster." Now it's time to wait, it won't be long before he'd move in and claim his trophy. He settled back in the trees to wait, his mind wandered again. Trapping the monsters was much easier here than in the woods where he learned to hunt from the Old Monster.

The one who taught him to listen to the woods, the monster he was sent to live with was just as big and scary, but he was old and weak. He didn't beat him as much, and when he did, it didn't hurt as long. But the Old Monster showed him the woods, how to hunt, how not to be seen. To learn how to know the prey.

"We don't hunt with guns," the Old Monster said. "We hunt with our minds, we think like the prey, we change ourselves to look like the prey. Pay attention to me," the monster would tell the little boy. "If you want to live, you will learn the woods better than the animals you're hunting. You must learn to hunt with only your bare hands and your head. When you do, you can take the power from the prey and add it to your own just like our ancestors did thousands of years ago," he told the young boy.

Being with the Old Monster was still scary, but better than the others. Still scared to sleep at night, he hid in his room and watched for the monsters to break down his door. But the hunter grew bigger, and with each day he learned more of the woods. He could hunt unseen by even the trees themselves. He brought back game he had tracked and killed with his bare hands, but nothing stopped the monsters from chasing him in his dreams.

"You're worthless, I should have killed you at birth," the monsters screamed they beat him.

The young hunter woke in his bed screaming in terror, with tears dried on his face, his pillow wet from the sweat of fear from his tormentors. No matter how big he got, or how strong and silent of hunter, he couldn't drive the monsters from his dreams. In the light of day or the darkest of night, in the woods he feared no animal. He had become the perfect hunter, taking the power from every kill, he grew stronger. The small boy grew into a young man, and he was no longer held by the monsters that kept him captive all these years. One night, he left for the hunt and didn't return. He left the woods in hopes of leaving the monsters behind. He needed to make it in the big world he'd heard about from the Old Monster.

He tried to fit in, not to be noticed, but it wasn't like the woods. There was nowhere to hide. Finding work was hard. He lived doing the one thing he knew. He never went hungry. "You can find food anywhere if you're a good hunter," he told himself. He roamed from place to place, working where he could, but always the monsters were there.

"Get out of here, you worthless piece of shit," the monsters told him.

He was too big and strong to beat, but the words they spoke were all the same.

"Pay attention, are you too stupid to understand?" the monsters told him.

So he learned from everywhere he went. He learned what the monsters taught him as he had done from the Old One. For years he tried to run from them, but there was nowhere to hide. He must go back and kill the monsters in his dreams or they would haunt him forever. He returned in the night while the monsters slept.

The hunter woke from his dream to a howl in the distance. Not a wolf but a dog out barking in some back yard. His prey was ready to be taken. He slunk through the trees back to his van. Quietly, not to wake the monsters in the surrounding dens, he pulled the van to the back of the house. He entered through the same window, creeping through the house silent as the dust settling in the moonlight, floating softly down to the floor. The prey were right where he thought they would be, sitting in their chairs in front of the television. Passed out from the bait he had used to render them helpless.

"Not so powerful now," he thought, He picked up the small female over his shoulder, and carried her to the van. After opening the door, he laid her on the floor of the van. Returning to the house, he started to pick up the male when the news on the television caught his attention.

"And next the story that broke today in Hocking Hills Ohio, where FBI and Police raided the home of Walter and Marion Holt. They are still looking for Wallace Holt and his parents, Earl and Betty Holt, for information of their involvement as persons of interest, with the death toll grown to eight murders. Wallace Holt is considered a prime suspect at this time."

He watched the old picture of him on the screen. "Now the monsters are hunting me," he said watching the report. "They have found the house, but they're looking in the wrong place." He carried the male monster to his van. He tied them up so they shouldn't get away in case they woke up. "We have a long way to go," he told them, climbed into the driver's seat, and silently drove away into the darkness without leaving a trace of himself behind.

# Chapter Twenty-Four

Doctor Harris, the FBI's criminal psychologist, arrived at the Springfield sheriff's office along with Herb for their meeting with Steve Belcher and Sheriff Lester.

Steve was already in the conference room with Tom and Jerry. He had posted the information from all the teams' interviews and the new pictures of the bodies found in the farm house. Sitting back in his chair, he looked at the board.

"He's got more victims out there," Steve said.

"Yes, he does," Doctor Harris confirmed and put her black leather briefcase on the table. She opened it and pulled out a thick file.

"Good morning, Doctor Harris," Steve said.

"Sorry for being curt, I'm just concerned about what you've found." Her blue eyes were filled with resolve.

"And what's that?" Steve asked.

"You have a focused killer with a specific goal in mind with his delusion. From the pictures and the information we have on Wallace Holt, he's a loner. He never went to school, so he didn't learn any social skills. He spent his childhood running from the people that should have been teaching and protecting him. They beat and abused him to the point where he saw them as monsters. He was isolated from the time he was born, until he showed up trying to live a normal life, trying to work like everyone else." She tapped one of the pictures with a blood red fingernail." Someone at each of these places put him back into the situation, in his mind, that he went through as a child. Look at his work record, no longer than a year at any one place.

He can't feel comfortable or safe out in the real world. In his mind he's still a small boy running from the monsters. Look at some of these pictures we found in the farm house and the woods." She took one of the crayon drawings down, her razor thin brows drawn together.

"'You're worthless. Get out. You'll never be worth anything.' Just a few of those at that age would send any of us right over the edge," Doctor Harris said. She stuck the child's drawing back on the board.

"But why now? Why start killing people? He's in his late forties," Steve said.

"For almost forty years he fought off the monsters in his mind, but the constant bombardment of abuse as a child was released by a trigger, one moment in his life too strong to ignore. Something took him back in a way that the past became his reality." She touched another of the crayon drawings. "Look at this picture, he's a hunter chasing the monsters through the woods, next we have him watching them from outside the house, and the third," she drew her finger across another drawing, "is him cutting off the monster's head and taking its power. He believes the monsters are still after him and until he kills all of them and takes their power, he will never be safe," she said.

The men in the room had sat silently while they listened to Doctor Harris. No one had spoken or even blinked while the reality of what she said sunk in. Steve tried to imagine what it was like for this child to grow up in this fashion, alone and afraid, always looking over his shoulder, like the trailer park manager in Lancaster had noticed.

"Just think, how would any child act if they were put into the same circumstances? All you've known is violence and fear, you grow up learning to hunt and live alone, the monster is always chasing you. Your mind is never at peace. What are you going to do one day when you finally snap?" she asked. She waved her hand across the drawings displayed on the board. "Some of these drawings are old, but some of them are recent, they can't be over a year old. He has regressed in his mind to the past where the monsters are still chasing the little boy around. He is acting out the delusion that had been locked away."

"But why the gap in the killings? The victims we found in the farm house were several years old, why start again? Why go after the ones he has?" Steve asked.

"He's most likely a very intelligent person. IQ off the charts. All of the jobs he has held from the list your investigation provided, are all places that have provided him the means to learn. Somewhere along the way he had to be shown how to use a computer. Just walking into a library you can sit down at a computer and find whoever you want. And with the detailed mind this killer certainly has, his memory would be phenomenal. He has a list, not on paper, but in his mind of everyone he considers to be a *monster,* and he is hunting all of them. Look at the way he kills, the meticulous way he prepares the body. He is using GHB to subdue the victims, to control them because he has to take them back to what he knows. He has worked on his plan for years, the cleaning of the bodies, draining them of blood, which he considers to be their power. The dolls you found in the box," she said and she pulled the picture from the file and passed it around the table. "All of the male and female heads are switched. He believes either the male or the female is the dominate of the two. If he switches the heads, there is no way for the monster to come back to life if he or she can't find their head because it's on the other body. He doesn't see people anymore. All he sees are monsters. None of the drawings has any other people in them," she said. She spread out the pile of childlike drawings on the table. "He's trying to rid the world of monsters."

"You feel sorry for him," Steve said. "He may have had a rough childhood, but so did a lot of others. They don't turn out to be serial killers, doc."

"No, they don't, but the continuous damage to him, both emotional and physical did," she said. She handed him the stack of pictures showing the child being beaten and yelled at by the monsters. "I'm not here to condone his actions, but give you the reason behind them, Detective," she said. A look of contempt marred her face. "And yes, I do feel sorry for him, because this won't end until he's caught or killed. Either way, it won't be an easy capture. He can disappear into the woods and live unnoticed, he's already done it. That's where he feels the safest. He won't come in, because anyone who approaches him will be a monster in his eyes. So, detective Belcher, if you get close enough to him, you had better put a bullet in him, or he'll just slip away into the woods until he feels safe again. This isn't his fault, he's the product of these two." She pointed to the latest group of pictures from the farm house. "And his parents you will find in the same shape, if my guess is correct. He returned to where it all started to find the worst monster of them all," she said and pointed to the pictures of the mummy wrapped corpses on the board.

"Didn't mean to piss you off, Doc, just asking a question," Steve said. He smiled and leaned back in his chair.

"Any idea where you think we should look, Doctor Harris?" Sheriff Lester asked.

"In the woods, that's where he feels safe," she replied.

The meeting broke up and Lester escorted Doctor Harris out of the room leaving the three detectives.

"I think it was love at first sight between you two," Jerry said.

"Yeah, maybe if she pulled the mumbo jumbo stick out of her ass," he said to the laughter of the men. "Don't get me wrong, I know people's minds can get messed up by things in their childhood. But that doesn't mean they turn into killers. We all have the same choice, it's no excuse. All it does is make his insanity defense a lot easier so we get to pay for him to stay the rest of his life in some hospital, while the families of the people he killed get no help. That I can't accept," Steve said. He buried his face in another report and Jerry returned to his desk.

# Chapter Twenty-Five

"They found the house, must make sure they're not around," the hunter told himself, looking back at his captives who were still passed out but alive. He left the van in the woods and scouted the location. He returned in a few moments and climbed into the driver's seat and drove through the open door of one of the buildings. He parked the van and closed the door behind him. He opened the back door of the van. The monsters were still under the spell of the drug. He pulled out the male of the two. "It's time to prepare you," he said and lifted him over his shoulder and carried him into another room. He returned and picked up the female and took her into the same room.

Inside the large, dimly lit room, the male was laid out on a clean shiny table. He placed the female down in a chair against the wall. He reached up and grabbed her by the chin and turned her head from side to side looking for any sign she might be waking up. His hands covered in thick plastic gloves, he used one hand to lift her eyelids to confirm she was still out. *"Sometimes they can fool you,"* he thought.

Returning to the male and grabbing a large knife from a holder on the side of the table, he cut through the clothes, removing them from the man. Having removed all of the clothes, he pulled the body of the man to the edge of the table until his shoulders met the edge and his head and neck hung off the end of the table. He walked over to the corner of the room and returned with a roll of plastic. He wrapped it around the man and the table. So tight there was no way for the man to escape. Many times he wrapped the beast, all but the head and neck. Finished with the male, he returned to the female in the chair. He lifted her over his shoulder and carried and he placed her on another table. He reached again for the large knife and cut through her clothes and began to remove them. It doesn't matter if they are male or female, they are both monsters. He finished with wrapping the female and placed the roll of wrap back in the corner. The knife replaced in the holder on the table, he arranged the tables in a line.

The room was clean, not even a dust bunny in the corner. He stood at the head of the two tables.

"Now I wait for them to wake," he said and turned and opened the door to another room.

He walked into the room and turned on the lights that only lit up part of the room. He sat down at a table inside the lit area. He sat down and looked at the other side of the table.

"I have brought two more of the monsters you set loose. You will watch them die, too," he said to the dead and dried up bodies of his parents, Earl and Betty Holt. "You'll hear their screams and see me take their power. Never again will you hurt anyone. I'll hunt them all and you'll see them all die before your eyes."

The bodies were chained to the wall, sitting in chairs behind the table, but his mind still saw his parents alive and squirming to get out of the chains. Their mouths were sewn shut so he wouldn't have to hear them scream at him. "You can no longer hurt me!" he told the corpses. "I am in control now. I will make you and the ones like you suffer." His attention was interrupted by the sounds of the two on the table starting to wake from the drugs.

He walked back into the room where the two were on the table. The male was the first to open his eyes.

"Where am I?" he asked holding his head up from the end of the table. "What the hell is going on?" he screamed.

Coming into the light, the hunter imagined the man

saw a tall man in his forties, wearing a plastic apron over his set of old army camouflage clothes. He wore a ball cap on his head mostly covering his sandy colored hair, the bill of the cap shadowed his face.

"Who the hell are you?" the man screamed and looked around the room calling for help.

The hunter watched as he discovered his wife on the table next to him and his panic increased. He jerked hard to try to free himself. "What do you want? Who the hell are you?" the man kept repeating.

The noise woke the wife. The hunter waited as she also realized she was trapped and couldn't move. She called her husband's name,

"George! George!" she screamed.

He could see terror fill both of them as they watched him stand at the foot of the tables. Quiet, and still not speaking, he just stared at them while they struggled to get free.

"What do you want? Where are my clothes?" they shouted in turn when they realized they were naked and strapped to the table. Silence filled the room and George looked over to his wife who still struggled to get free.

"Mary," he called to her, "calm down." He turned back to the figure standing at the end of the table. "What do you want? We have money we can give you, please don't kill us," he pleaded.

Breaking the silence the hunter placed his hands on the table. "You don't remember me," he said and removed the cap from his head.

"No, I don't, please let us go," George said and looked at his wife who sobbed while still trying to get free.

"I worked for you until I realized you were one of the monsters," the hunter said.

His mind returned to George telling him, "Are you stupid? How could you screw this up, it's not that hard." The younger hunter from fifteen years ago stood beside a mess made from a box falling and breaking the bottles inside. He cowered to the screams of his tormentor and his mind told him he had found another monster. The man's appearance turned to one of the beasts that roamed his dreams. "You can't hide any longer from what you are. I am no longer afraid and I can see through your disguise. You've haunted me for years in my dreams whenever I close my, eyes you're there to chase me. I will run no more, I am the hunter," he screamed. "I will have your power." He rolled the table through the doors.

Mary screamed George's name as he was wheeled out of the room and she was left alone.

George was wheeled into the room where the corpses were chained to the wall.

"Soon you will join all the monsters in death after I take your power," the hunter said.

He rolled George into the room and the hunter locked the table into place.

"I don't know you," George said.

The hunter heard the cries of Mary in the other room. He walked over and pulled a cord. The sound of a motor starting up and the smell of gas fumes filled the room. He slid a large metal stand over George and he grabbed his hair. He could see the pain in his eyes as he pulled his head out straight and the large metal frame slid over his head down to his shoulders.

"That will hold you still," the hunter said.

"Please don't do this," George cried.

"You are one of the monsters, you must die. You will never hunt and feed on the small ones again!" He picked up a large, razor-sharp sword. With one swift stroke, he sliced through the neck of George and separated his head from his body. The blood of the monster sprayed through the air and landed on the hunter. He rubbed one finger through the blood that landed on his apron. He looked at the blood on his glove. He licked the blood from his finger. "Now I feel your power," he said. The smell of blood and death filled the room.

A dark crimson flood covered the floor and ran down a drain in the middle of the room. He returned to the room to watch Mary, who struggled to get free. "Where's George?" she asked.

The hunter looked into her eyes. "You will see him again in death, she-beast. Now I am the one with the power, not you," he told her and moved her into the other room to the sounds of her screams of terror.

A day had passed since he'd taken the power from both monsters when the hunter began his ritual of cleaning the bodies. They'd been on the tables with one end raised up almost vertical, to allow for all the blood to drain. The sound of the power sprayer engine starting filled the room. He picked up and turned on a power sprayer to sanitize the room. The hunter went about it like it was just another day on the job, cleaning the room from top to bottom. The chemical foam from the spray washed away the dark crimson blood from the floor, turning it to a soft pink flow running to the drain in the floor. He washed all of the horrific happenings away like the room had never been used. He turned to the tall stand holding the equipment he used to remove their heads and cleaned it like he was washing down a car on a Saturday morning. He showed no sign of emotion as he continued his work. He walked over and flipped a lever on the power washer to shut off the concentrated flow of chemicals, and clear water rushed through the nozzle of the wand. Fanning out a spray, clearing away all of the trace of foam and remaining pink tint, he removed the last of the life force of the two monsters.

He changed the spray nozzle to a soft stream and covered the bodies with water to clean them off. The water ran from the tables to the floor below, the last traces of their life ran down the floor drain and away. Turning off the sprayer and setting down the spray handle, he turned to the bodies and, one at a time, lowered them from the inclined position. The heads of the beasts hang from a chain in the ceiling. A clip in their hair held them over the drain. He washed and placed then on the table. He placed the female's head on the table of the male. He grabbed a small tool box and brought it to the table where he worked. He opened the box and removed a spool of thick, light blue fishing line. He pulled out a large curved fishing hook. Threading the line into the eye of the hook, he pressed the pointed end of the hook into the skin. He lined up the head, and began to stitch the head on the body.

He completed the task once he made a full circle around the head and secured the end with a very tight knot, "That will hold you in hell forever, she beast," he uttered and cut the line. He moved to the body of the female and performed the task on the male in the same cold manner. Once finished, he removed the heavy plastic gloves from his hands. He turned to the two dried up bodies of his parents chained to the wall.

"Here are two more of your monsters, they've joined you in hell." He grabbed the end of the table and wheeled it back through the doors to the waiting van. With the van door open and the floor covered in plastic, he slid the body into the van. Returning with the other body, he repeated the process and covered them with the plastic. Closing the door, he said, "Now I must put you back so all the other monsters will see I am coming for them, too." He shut the door on the van. He removed the apron.

Now in his camouflage and boots, he put the cap back on his head and climbed into the driver's seat for the trip back. This time he wasn't concerned about them waking up. He pulled out of the building and stopped to close the doors behind him. Returning to the van, he drove away with a smile on his face.

"One more set of monsters who won't hurt anyone

else," he said.

# Chapter Twenty-Six

"Hey Docs, how's it going?" Steve said when Carol and Conrad entered the squad room.

"What did you find?" Steve asked.

"Not a lot," Doctor Singer said. "Both in the same shape as the others, only wrapped in plastic wrap, not sure why. All of it's been sent to the lab, but I don't think they'll find much more than we did. Most of the soft tissue has been eaten away, of course, by insects and time. We think they'd been there for between six and ten years. I know," Doctor Singer said looking at the detective's discouraged faces, "that doesn't help much, but it is the same killer. From the rest of the evidence we found, it appears from the level of dust in the house, and even in the bedroom, it's been vacant for at least two to three years. There wasn't much to go on, either," Doctor Singer said.

"So we're back to square one?" Steve said.

"I'm afraid so," he said.

"We know who he is, we know where he's worked for the last twenty five years." Steve said looking at the board on the wall that listed every one they had talked to in the last six weeks. "No one remembers this guy, or anything about him. He disappeared years ago, and now we have eight bodies and at least two more we think are out there, but don't know where. This guy could turn up anywhere and vanish again because we have no idea where he is. Have I got it right?"

Silence filled the room. No one seemed to have anything to add to his rampage.

"How the hell are we going to catch this guy? Will

somebody please tell me?" His voice carried down the hall to where Sheriff Lester stood.

"There has to be something on one of these bodies to tell us where he is," he said.

"It's not their fault," Lester said talking over Steve who paced back and forth in the room.

"Excuse us for a moment," Lester told the rest of the group.

They all filed out of the room like a pack of dogs with their heads down and their tails between their legs. Steve turned to the sheriff.

"Just listen." Lester stopped him from speaking. "Now I know this is a bastard of a case, and I know you are taking this hard. But the people around you aren't him. They're as frustrated as you are. You need to take the rest of the day and the weekend off. Go call your kids, get your mind off this for a while. I know that's not going to happen," he said in reaction to the look of disbelief on Steve's face.

"I can't help it," Steve said, "I'm eaten up with this guy. He's baffled me from the start."

"Not just you," Lester said. "There are a whole bunch of FBI, State police, and sheriff's offices around the state that are just as in the dark as you are. I don't want to pull you off this case, but I will if you don't get a grip on yourself."

Steve sat down in a chair and put his head in his hands almost in defeat.

"Now get out of here and I don't want to see you again until Monday morning," the sheriff told Steve.

Steve rose from the chair, grabbed his coat and headed out of the room. Jerry and Tom scrambled down the hallway from where they had been listening outside the door. Jerry and Tom sat in the squad room and tried to look like they'd been there the whole time.

"You okay, Steve?" Jerry asked.

"Sorry guys, I guess I need a break."

"No need to be sorry," Jerry said. "Just go get some rest."

Steve walked by Tom and placed his hand on his shoulder before he left the squad room.

\*\*\*

"Jerry," Tom called. "Come take a look at this."

"What you got, kid?"

"You know according to the doc this abuse had been going on since birth. The statement from the trailer park manager in Lancaster says she played with him. If he had a place to hide in the woods at the farm house, what about at the trailer park? What was it like in Lancaster?" Tom asked.

"As I remember," Jerry said, "it was surrounded by woods, too." He picked up the phone and dialed. "Yeah, this is Detective Stevenson from the Springfield Sheriff's Department. Can I speak to Sheriff Boon?" Jerry asked and put the phone on speaker.

"Nice thinking, kid." Jerry said to Tom. He gave him thumbs up.

"This is Sheriff Boon." Boon's voice filled the room.

"Sheriff, this is Jerry, how's your day going?" he asked.

"Good, real good, but I get the feeling you're about to ruin it," Boon said.

"Well, not really," Jerry replied. "Can you send a team back out to the trailer park and comb the woods around it for the same thing we found in Hocking Hills? We think there could be something in the woods like we found at his grandparent's place that might lead us closer to this guy," Jerry said.

"I'll lead the team myself. I'll call you back if we find something," Boon said before he hung up.

"Boon is on the trail," Jerry said. They both laughed.

The two detectives worked going over the information,

and laid out everything on the table. Jerry looked at Tom.

"You know this is going to end with us or someone else killing this guy?" Jerry said knowing Tom had never had to fire his weapon in the line of duty. "Are you going to be able to handle that?"

"If I need to kill him, I won't hesitate," Tom said.

"Where's Steve?" Herb asked as he walked in the room.

"Out for the day," Jerry said. "What's up?"

"Call him and get him in here, we might have a lead," Herb said.

"We better go see the sheriff before we do that," Jerry said before he and Herb walked down the hall to see the sheriff.

***

"Sheriff Lester," Jerry said when he, Herb and Tom walked into his office. "Herb has some good news for us."

"Thursday morning, a couple, George and Mary Grayson of Lima, Ohio, didn't show up for work. As of last night there has been no contact. The local police were called to the scene by the family." He handed the report to Lester. "They had plans to see them on Thursday night. They got to the house and found it open, no signs of a struggle, keys and cars all there, no sign of them around, so they called the police. This is a switch in his pattern, if this is our guy. Right now, I have ten agents combing the area, looking for clues. Contacting everyone they know, running credit cards and checking every store, park and motel to see if they can be found. If we get lucky, this guy will try to bring the bodies back and we'll be waiting for him," Herb said with excitement.

"How can we be sure it's our guy and that these two didn't just sneak off for the weekend early?" Sheriff Lester asked.

"The bakery George works at hasn't heard from him

either. The wife works at a preschool and has never missed a day of work, until now. I think this is our guy. We're checking employment records to see if Holt shows up," Herb said.

"What do you need from us?" Sheriff Lester asked.

"More man power on the scene. Honestly at this point, I think they are already dead. But there is always a chance he hasn't killed them yet. We think he does all his work at night to avoid being seen, so starting tonight, if we haven't located them yet, we'll set up look outs. The house is in a wooded section of the neighborhood, so there is plenty of cover to hide in," Herb said.

"You can bet he knows every tree in those woods, too," Jerry said. "He's already mapped it, walked it, and knows where every leaf is. If you go in there with a normal police force, he'll walk right past you and you'll never even see him," Jerry said.

"What do you think we should do?" Herb asked Jerry.

"Put cameras in the house, if he has the couple, I agree they are already dead. For some reason he took them early, so if he stays to his M.O., he'll bring them back tonight. But you need to be gone by sundown. You can station your team in the houses around the neighborhood, but if he sees a police car he's going to bolt. If the neighborhood is changed in any way, he'll notice. A strange car, a person on the corner that doesn't belong, he'll notice. He's hunted for forty years, he'll tell from five hundred yards away if something is wrong, and he'll disappear into the woods," Jerry said.

"How are you going to keep the press out of this?" Lester asked.

"The call came into the local police station where the police chief called us first. So far there hasn't been a leak. All of the neighbors have been contacted, and as far as we know, no one has spoken to anyone," Herb said.

"Jerry, why don't you get packed and go with Herb,

I'll call Steve and you can pick him up on your way out of town. Make sure you're not followed this time," Sheriff Lester said. He pointed his finger straight at Jerry.

\*\*\*

Tom sat back at his desk going over the employment files, trying to see if Holt showed up anywhere else. He was interrupted by the returned call from Sheriff Boon.

"Tom, you might want to ride down here and see what we've found," Sheriff Boon said. "I'm standing in the woods one hundred yards from the trailer park. We found another hideout. Covered by thick woods, a makeshift fort, filled with drawings and pages of writings in crayon. Hidden under tree limbs and covered in leaves." The police scoured the surrounding trees for clues while Boon relayed what he found to Tom.

"Make sure your boys don't touch anything until the crime lab gets there. I'll call them from the FBI lab in Columbus. They should be there in an hour. Thanks, Sheriff Boon," Tom said and hung up the phone. Dialing another number, Tom sent the FBI crime team down to collect all the evidence. He was forming a mosaic on the wall of all the pictures that had been found.

Tom informed Sheriff Lester of what they'd found in the woods as they stood and looked at what had already been discovered.

"This kid was really messed up," Sheriff Lester said. He raised the brim of his hat to see better, then rested his hand on his gun belt.

"Yeah, I don't think he had a chance," Tom said. They stood looking at the wall covered in the drawings of a small child being chased, beaten, and locked up by monsters. It showed the progression of the boy's growth as he followed and tracked the monsters. The boy hid behind trees and peeked out, hunting them. The most disturbing of them all, the last in the line, was where the little boy stood over the slain body of the monster with the sword in one hand and the head of the monster dripping blood in the other. The two men stood and stared at the picture. They tried to hide their own monsters. Monsters that all people have lurking in their dreams, but somehow were able to control.

"There were just too many for him to handle," Sheriff Lester said in a compassionate tone. "Now, he's gone from being hunted by monsters to being the monster, and being hunted by us," he said.

"Does that make us monsters, too?" Tom asked.

"Where was the help for this once little boy, the once innocent child who by the age of six had already endured more pain and terror than most people see in a lifetime? His future all laid out by the physical and psychological torment from the ones that should have protected him. And we have to hunt him down, because he's become the tormentor."

"No," Sheriff Lester said, "we have to stop him, that's not being a monster. Our help has come forty years too late for him, but there has to be a way to help him and stop the killing. The people he's killing most likely didn't even know what they said to him. People today just don't care about anyone any more. There's no respect for anyone. It all plays into the fact the world has become a place of self absorbed, 'it's all about me,' people concerned only with themselves, most of them just trying to get through life and survive. We're not the monster, but we have no choice but to stop the ones we can," Sheriff Lester said. He pulled his hat back down over his forehead, turned and walked out of the room.

# Chapter Twenty-Seven

"See, this was perfect for him, secluded from view on all sides, even being in a neighborhood full of houses," Steve said as they arrived at the house where the couple had gone missing. The team of agents had already set up the cameras around the house and neighborhood. Steve parked and walked up the driveway to the house.

"They're all separated by large stands of trees," Jerry said.

A short, blonde, female agent approached the group and said "Agent Winslow, George Grayson worked at the bakery for the last twenty one years, but before that he worked at a *Market Meats* slaughterhouse in Columbus, Ohio until it closed in 1988, and then he got a job up here."

"That was on the list of places where Holt worked," Jerry said. "This is our guy."

"Jerry, where do you want to set up?" Herb asked.

"It's about two hours until dark, let me go look around and we'll set up an hour before dark," Jerry told Herb and Steve.

Jerry walked away and into the woods. Steve watched as his demeanor switched back to the hunter/killer training embedded in him from years of Army life.

After an hour, Jerry reappeared, walking out of the shadowy woods into the light. He walked up to Steve and Herb, who were completing the checks on all the surveillance equipment.

"The officers sure made their presence known in the woods. Any junior tracker could tell there'd been a search in there. They made tracks out two hundred yards from the house he's sure to spot." He pointed to a large ash tree on the corner of the lot. "He watched the house from the tree over there. He made fewer tracks watching them for a week and a half than these men did in a few hours." He nodded his head towards the edge of the woods. "I'll be out about three hundred yards from the point where I believe he entered. All these cars need to be gone. Steve, you and Herb hide upstairs in the house. The rest of these guys need to be out of the area. They need to be close enough to set up a roadblock if he shows, but not close enough for him to see them," Jerry said.

With night quickly approaching, Herb sent all the officers away from the scene. He and Steve took their places inside the upstairs of the house.

Jerry disappeared into the shadows of the tree line and in a moment Jerry's voice come through the radio, "Eyes in the woods. It's going to be a long night."

Steve and Herb, who had settled in, looked at each other in the gathering darkness. "Yep, it sure is," Steve said.

# Chapter Twenty-Eight

"You still awake out there?" Steve called to Jerry over the radio. Daylight was showing over the treetops.

"I don't think he's going to show in the daytime, boys. I think we can call it a day," Jerry said.

"I think he's right, let's call it in," Herb told Steve.

"Okay, come on in, we'll meet you in the back of the house," Steve told Jerry.

"I think we should have a couple of officers stay and watch the house. We can go get a room, grab some sleep and stand watch again tonight," Steve told the men.

Herb assigned a team of agents to watch the house. "Stay out of sight just in case, we'll be back this afternoon to take over," he told them. The three loaded up and left the scene to go into town.

"What if he comes back in the daytime?" Jerry asked.

"He needs the cover of night to get in and out, I don't think he'll be here on such a beautiful day," Steve said looking at the sun shining in a clear blue sky. "If he does, we have officers there to grab him. You did tell them to shoot to kill, right?" he asked and looked at Herb in the driver's seat.

"Don't worry about them boys, good marksmen both of them," Herb replied with a smile.

\*\*\*

"Carol, good morning," Tom said when he called Carol from the office. "Sorry to bother you on Saturday morning, but can you come in? I need you to look at something."

"Right now?" she asked.

"Yes, I need you to look at some of the drawings they found yesterday," Tom said.

"Okay, I'll be there," she said and Tom hung up the phone.

Tom was still working on the mosaic of drawings, and had covered the wall from one end to the other.

"Oh my God!" Carol exclaimed when she walked into the room with Doctor Singer. Looking up at the wall, she examined each picture in a row. "It's the story of his life he's telling," she said.

"Look at the beginning," Tom said. "Tell me if I'm crazy, Doc, but he starts out as a little boy, hiding under his bed from the monsters. As he grows, they chase and beat him, lock him in rooms, and even withhold food, if I read this right?" he said pointing to the scribbled words in crayon, *I'm so hungry*, at the bottom of the picture. "The child grows and walks with the monsters in the woods. He learns to hunt, catch and kills animals, and feeds the monsters. Then one day, grown, he goes out in the world and tries to work," he said pointing to a drawing of a man pushing a broom in what you would think was a warehouse or some kind.

"Sorry guys, I've been staring at these all morning. Is this making any sense to anyone besides me?" he asked the two doctors.

"I think you are right on track." Doctor Singer said. "The story of Holt's torture is documented in these pictures. Please go on with your impression of them."

"Well, from here," he touched one of the pictures in its protective evidence bag, "you see him fighting the monsters, and you see him kill the monster in this one," he lifted the corner of another drawing, "where he's holding the head in his hand with the blood dripping. '*Now I have the power*'," Tom read the scrawled words at the bottom of the page.

"Good work, young man," Dr. Singer said. "If I didn't

know better, I'd think we were looking at old cave drawings from some lost tribe. I must take pictures of these for my records," Conrad said.

"Don't sound so excited," Carol said. "These are the drawings of a killer who has taken the lives of eight people we know of," she said sternly.

"I'm sorry, but this is psychology 101," he said. "Look at his progression. He has it all recorded in his own handwriting, from a very early age to adulthood. I know it sounds coarse, but however unfortunate, this is a fascinating study in human behavior," he said.

"Doctor Singer, I hate to interrupt your *King Tut* moment, but you need to see the rest of the story," Tom said.

"There's more?," and it's Conrad, Dr. Singer insisted.

"Yeah, a lot," Tom said and slid the stack of pictures he had over to them.

The two doctors sat down and looked through the pictures, the excitement drained from Conrad's face. He stopped, his gaze locked on one of the pictures, and turned to Carol sitting beside him.

"This is going to get really bad," he said and handed her the picture.

"Most of the stack is the same picture of him killing a monster and holding up its head, there must be twenty of them. Then I found this one," Tom said.

They silently gazed at the picture.

"Well doc, am I right?" Tom asked again.

"I think so, it's going to get a lot worse," Conrad said looking down at the picture of the boy standing on top of a pile of monsters, all beheaded with the heads of the boys on one side and the girls on the other.

"The bodies are going to pile up on this, I'm afraid," Conrad told them.

Tom had spent the morning in the office going over the drawings and feeling drained. He stepped over to get a cup of coffee. "You guys need a cup while I'm up?" he asked.

"No, thanks," Carol said. She and Conrad continued poring over the drawings.

"While you're at it, Doc, see if you can read anything in that to tell us where he is," Tom said and sat back down. He rubbed the back of his neck and then loosened his tie.

The silence in the room was interrupted with the ring of Tom's phone.

"Good Morning," he answered after looking at the readout to see Terry's name.

"How's your morning going?" she asked.

"Just sitting at work going over reports," he said. Hearing her voice changed his mood for the better.

"What about yours?"

"I'm just getting out of bed and thought I would give you a call to see what you're up to," she said.

"We should take these down to my lab," Carol said with a smile. Conrad waved to Tom and left him talking on the phone.

***

The hunter drove back to the lair. His mind continued to battle the rage of the monsters plaguing him. No matter how many he destroyed, they still tore at him. His feelings of satisfaction from the kill were gone from him and they again chased him. He looked back at the two dead bodies in the van to confirm that they were actually dead.

"You won't win," he said and looked in the mirror to confront the monster from his dreams. "I will chase you all down until I have rid the world of your kind. Just like the knights in the story he'd read as a child who hunted down the dragons to free the kingdom of their terror. I will destroy all of you." The rage in him grew with each pair of monsters he killed and the battle in his mind grew stronger. The stronger he got, the more monsters attacked his mind.

"I must wait until dark," he told himself as he drove

into town with the sun still showing high above the trees. He took the route he had taken before. He drove through the town, and close to the entrance of the neighborhood, he spotted two police cars. One of them was exiting the street leading to the house, and another entering. They were stopped driver's window to driver's window, so the two officers could talk to each other. His senses peaked and he drove slowly past the two officers looking at them. He'd watched this area for two weeks, and there'd never been any officers around here. He drove to an old gas station down the road and parked behind the closed building. He left his van, alert and watchful. "I must find out what the monsters know," he said.

He moved across the street and entered the woods. He moved through the trees with speed, but with silence. Making his way to the section of woods behind the house, the hunter came across a trail of foot prints. He followed them to the very tree where someone had spent the night.

"Another hunter," he thought. The tracks were hard to follow, they'd have been missed by most people in the world. He followed the tracks through the woods back to the front of the house.

He remembers the teaching of the Old Monster. "This one is a good hunter," he told himself. "The tracks don't lead straight and they're constantly changing direction with the smallest of moves to elude being followed."

"You must hide your path in the woods, no one should be able to follow you," the Old Monster would tell him as he practiced eluding him in the woods.

Fifty feet from the place where he had sat in a tree and watched the monsters for two weeks, he watched one of the agents leave and take up a post to watch the house. "He's not even hiding," he thought, when the agent leaned against a tree. The agent's sniper rifle rested against the tree like the agent wasn't expecting anything to happen in the day time. The hunter sat and watched the agent watch the house for an hour.

"Should I kill him? He's one of the ones chasing me, trying to stop me." He debated with himself. "There must be more around." He peered through the woods looking for hiding monsters, ready to pounce at any minute.

The silence was broken when the radio the agent carried squawked. "Pete, you ready for a break?" a voice came from his radio.

Picking up the radio from the ground he said, "Yeah, I'm ready for some food. I'll be right in, they know this guy isn't going to show up in the daylight but they keep us grunts out here anyway."

"Just consider it a day out in the woods," the voice answered.

He picked up his rifle and walked towards the edge of the woods, stopped and unzipped his pants to relieve himself.

"Stupid," the hunter whispered to himself.

The agent finished and continued out of the woods. The hunter returned the same way he'd come. He didn't make a sound while he traveled through the trees and brush. He reached the tree where he knew a hunter had spent the night, smiled and reached in the pocket of his shirt and pulled out the red crayon. He left the woods and returned to the gas station for his van. He laughed at the sight of the agent peeing in the woods.

*"He's not the hunter he was tracking,"* he thought. *"The monsters are getting close. I can't let them find me. I must leave the monsters. I can't get to the house, but I can get close."*

He climbed in the van and drove across the road and into the woods. He opened the doors and pulled the body of the male, lifting it over his shoulder carrying it into the woods. He set the body down and returned for the female. Returning to the tree and setting her down by the male under the message he had left for whoever was hunting him. He returned to the van and was quickly gone. Driving down the road, the struggle raged inside him, he looked in the mirror to see the monster. "See, I am the true hunter, your beast can not stop me," he said and drove away.

***

"This is where it comes to an end," Steve told himself looking in the mirror at the hotel. "He has to come back and place the bodies in the house, and I'll be waiting for him."

He climbed in the shower to wake up and clear the fog from his mind. Standing under the running water and letting it clear away his lack of sleep, his mind ran over the pictures of the dead bodies on the board in the squad room. All of them were imprinted on his mind and the flashes in his memory replayed each photograph. He saw the killer in his mind, carrying around the separated heads of the victims. Knowing this was the closest they'd come to the killer, he hoped this would be the end. He turned off the water, stepped out of the shower, and looked into the steamy mirror. "You have to get him tonight," he told himself.

Steve picked up the phone and called Jerry,

"Hello," Jerry said when he picked up the phone.

"Are you about ready to go get some dinner before we head over?" Steve asked.

"I'll be ready in ten," Jerry said.

"It's show time," Steve said. He reached for his 9mm pistol on the table, ejected the clip and checked the load, then slid it back in the handle of the weapon. He snapped the weapon in the holster sling on his left side, grabbed his jacket, and headed out the door.

***

Meeting Jerry and Steve downstairs in the lobby of the hotel, Herb had already heard from the teams at the scene that nothing had happened during the day. They left the hotel and decided to hit a drive through and grab some burgers on their way to the scene. Riding along and eating, Jerry loaded up some extra burgers in his bag.

"It's going to be a long night and I might need a snack," he told Herb and Steve while they laughed at him.

Jerry tapped Herb on the shoulder. "Go straight up here a little more," Jerry told him. "I'm going in the back way. At the end of the tree line there's a field where I can slip in while you guys go in the front to the house."

Herb drove to the end of the trees and let Jerry out. By the time he turned around Jerry had vanished into the trees and out of sight.

"That guy is a ghost. I think I'm going to get him a job on my team when this is over," Herb told Steve.

"Over my dead body," Steve said. They laughed as the two men traveled down the street headed for the house. They pulled up front and watched the agents from inside walk around the back with the agent from the woods.

"Steve, it's over, walk about five hundred yards straight out from the back door. Herb, call the crime lab out here," Jerry's voice came across the radio.

"What?" Steve said in surprise. "You got him?"

"Not exactly," Jerry said and the men ran back to where Jerry stood in front of the tree where he had spent the night before.

Walking up to the tree, where the two bodies were laid back against the trunk, they saw above their heads in red crayon were the words;

*I WILL KILL THEM ALL, THE MONSTERS MUST DIE.*

"He drove up about thirty yards from here and carried the bodies by the looks of the tracks," Jerry said.

"Where in hell were you guys?" Herb yelled at the agents.

Jerry looked around the ground. "It wouldn't have

mattered," he said. "Look at this," he showed them the trail the killer took, "first he walked in to look at the scene. One of you was in the woods, so you would have had no reason to think he would come from behind." He led the team through the woods following every turn the killer made. "He watched from here, he saw you standing over there." He pointed to the spot where the agent had stood.

"How the hell do you know where I was at?" the agent asked.

"You can see where you paced and disturbed the ground. You leaned your rifle up against the tree," he pointed to a spot in the dirt and leaves, "see the indention in the dirt?" He walked over to another spot and pointed to the trees. "This where you took a piss. He watched you from here until you left your post. He traveled back the same way he came. You're lucky he didn't feel like killing you," Jerry said and walked towards the house.

"Damn it, he beat us again," Steve said.

"I'll take care of the scene. You take my car and head back if you want, there's nothing we're going to find here now," Herb said.

"Send us a photo of that writing on the tree," he told Herb and took the keys from him.

Steve walked around the front of the house to catch up with Jerry, who sat on the front porch.

"Hey, it's not your fault. We had no way of knowing," Steve told him.

"Yes, we did. We should have had better trained people out here. We thought we knew his pattern, he has no pattern. He adapted to us, like he's tracking us. I won't make that mistake twice," Jerry said with a cold glazed stare in his eyes.

"Come on, let's go. We're taking the truck. Herb is staying to run the scene with the crime lab," Steve said and headed for the truck.

Jerry stood and grabbed his bag and placed it in the

back seat. "How's he going to get his truck?" Jerry said. He stood up, grabbed his bag, and placed it in the back seat.

"I really don't care. Got to hand it to those FBI boys, they really know how to guard a crime scene," Steve said and drove away.

# Chapter Twenty-Nine

"You did all you could up there guys, you're getting close, don't give up," Sheriff Lester said when he saw the looks of defeat on their faces.

"I should have stayed in the woods," Jerry said. "I would have got him."

"You might have, but he might have seen you, too. From what you tell me, this guy is as good in the woods as anyone you've ever seen, and that includes you. I know it's tough to take, but what do we do now?" Sheriff Lester asked. He leaned back against the wall and crossed his arms.

"He's looking for his next set of monsters to kill," Jerry said walking over to the wall of drawings.

"There's no way to tell where he's going to strike next," Steve said. "He could be anywhere."

"So how do we draw him out? He knows we're on his trail. He believes he's killing the monsters from his past, so let's give him one," Jerry said. "Let's use the press to bring him to us. If I go on the news and insult him like these pictures suggest, maybe we can get him to come after me and we can take him."

"Not you, me," Steve said. "I'll need your skills to hunt him while he's hunting me. You're the best on the trail. It'll take that to get him if he takes the bait," Steve said. He watched Doctor Harris, Carol, and Conrad enter the room.

They took seats around the table. "Good morning Detectives," Conrad said. "I've asked for this time to go over what we found examining the drawings. I've also asked Doctor Harris to join us, due to the nature of what we have found." The room was silent except for Doctor Singer's voice. All of them gazed at the mural on the wall of the drawings.

"As you can see, and correct me if I am wrong on this Doctor Harris, we see the boy being tormented by what he sees in his mind as the monsters. This group of pictures was found in the woods near where he and his parents lived in the trailer park, by Sheriff Boon, at the insistence of young Tom there. The next group shows the progression to being hunted by the monsters to walking with them and then the start of the hunt for them, and this is where you come in Doctor Harris," Conrad said.

"We believe when he was sent to live with his grandparents, they are depicted here," she slid the board over to reveal the one behind covered with the next set of drawings, "as the smaller, older monsters. Not as scary, as you can see in the drawings. The next set shows him, we presume, hunting with one of them and tracking it through the woods." She pointed to the lower set of drawings on the board as she caught her falling glasses with her other hand. "These were found in the woods behind the farmhouse where the bodies, of what we know, are his grandparents. This next set, although they were found with the same group of drawings as the first set in Lancaster, show the child's progression through adulthood. These drawings are much newer than all the rest," she slid a third board into view, "even so, they are a few years old. Here's where it gets scary. The last set shows him hunting them, but in this one," she said and pulled it from the folder on the table. "This one shows him standing on a mountain of monsters with his sword held in the air in triumph over the monsters. We think this means he isn't going to stop until all the monsters in his mind are dead. Which brings us to the message he left on the tree this weekend." She placed the new picture of the words written on the tree above where the bodies were placed. "He has, in his mind, a list of the ones he's after." She turned back to the face the group. "There's no way to find out who they are, but the next set Doctor Singer and Carol have been working on might help find him," she said and pulled another set of drawings from the folder. "These were found in the woods in Lancaster along with the others," she said and put the pictures on the wall. "These show a group of buildings and in the first one, it shows the inside of a building, with what we presume are two people chained to the wall. We think it could be his first two victims. As we go on with the rest of the drawings," she pinned more of them to the wall covering up the top row, "they show two tables that the monsters are on. We see some sort of machine and the heads of the monsters in this machine. The next, the same, but the head of the monster is on the ground and we see the killer standing over the head holding his sword in the air." She read the words out loud, *"Now I have your power!"* She turned to the group. "This delusion of his is deep-rooted. We need to find this group of buildings. They're abandoned. It has to have been empty for a long time. He didn't draw anything around them. I know it's not much, but it's the best idea we can get from them," she said and sat back down.

The group remained quiet for a moment, still looking at the killer's drawings.

"That's good information," Sheriff Lester said breaking the eerie silence in the room.

"Tom, you coordinate with both Sheriff's Boon and Warner, start them looking into any abandoned buildings in the area. I'll call Herb and the state police to help with manpower for the searches." He stood up and pulled down a map that unfurled from the mount on the wall. "Steve you and Jerry meet me in my office and let's go over your plan one more time. I don't want any mistakes. Good work, doctors," he said and they all rose to leave the room.

\*\*\*

"Okay, let's hear it," Sheriff Lester said and sat down behind his desk.

"We get the blood sucker involved. By the looks of his drawings, he's going after anyone he believes has done him wrong over the years." Steve sat down across from the sheriff and crossed his legs. "It doesn't have to be anything other than telling him he's worthless, according to the pictures. I attack him on the air, and challenge him." He uncrossed his legs and leaned forward resting his elbows on his knees. "We get the news to run the story on every TV and radio station we can, let him come to me. Jerry will be my shadow the entire time." He looked up at Jerry who stood beside him against the wall. "We know his M.O. is to watch them in their homes, enter, and we know he drugs their food. If we get this on the air today, we might stop him and draw him away from the next set of victims. I keep the same routine for as long as it takes. We can set up watch stations everywhere I go," Steve told the sheriff.

"But, Jerry, as good as he is, can't watch you 24/7. Even super hunter here needs to sleep sometime, what then?" Lester asked.

"I'll make a call," Jerry said. "I know of two others in the field. They're both snipers. We can get a loan from the stations where they work, they can be here tonight. Three shifts, round the clock. He makes a move and we'll drop him before he knows we're there."

"Okay, make the call and see if you can get them. We don't move until that's confirmed. Then you and I will write the statement. But you, Steve, will have to convince, *The Blood Sucker*, aka Lacy James to help," Sheriff Lester said.

"No problem. I'll call her and start kissing ass," he said to the laughter of the group. "You get your guys on the way," Steve told Jerry.

"Report back to me when you find out, Jerry," Lester said.

"Will do," he replied. "Now we're talking," Jerry said to Steve. They walked down the hall with some kick in their step for the first time in eight weeks.

***

Tom watched as Jerry entered the squad room and sat down in his chair and picked up the phone.

"What's up?" he asked.

"Not sitting on our hands anymore," Jerry said before a voice on the other end of the phone answered.

"Hey Raider, this is Scout," Jerry said.

"Scout?" Tom whispered to Steve, who had joined Jerry at his desk.

Holding his hand over the mouthpiece on the phone Jerry said, "It's a long story." He turned his attention back to the phone. "Raider I need you to TDY to us for a few weeks. We have a ghost in the woods we need to flush out. Yeah, I need you tonight. I'll put your captain in touch with mine." Jerry bounced a pencil on its eraser while he talked. "I'm also calling in Smoke. Yeah, this is about the serial killer we got out here. Okay, I'll see you then," Jerry said and he hung up the phone.

"Scout?" Tom asked again.

"It was my callsign in the army, Raider and Smoke were two of my team. These guys are the best," Jerry said.

"I hope so," Steve said.

"Would I let anything happen to you?" Jerry said sarcastically."You just worry about the blood sucker."

"Let me know when you confirm the arrival time of your two friends. I have to go and get my pucker on," Steve said and puckered his lips making kissing sounds. He walked out of the room followed by Jerry's laughter. "Who is he puckering for?" Tom asked.

"Lacy," Jerry said.

\*\*\*

Steve sat in his office, staring at the growing out of control wall of deceased bodies staring back at him. "I will find him," he promised the lifeless faces of the group. Taking out a pad of paper from under the pile on his desk, he began to write the statement he was going to give Lacy. He scribbled on the paper, while his mind flashed to the mural created by the drawings. What Steve scribbled on the paper was not words, but the pile of dead monsters with a child standing on the top.

"It's getting to you," Jerry said interrupting Steve from his trance.

"Yeah, I think it is, that's why we have to get him," Steve said.

"The guys will be here tonight. I just told the sheriff, so I guess it's time to make that call," Jerry said.

"I know I'm going to regret this," Steve told Jerry as he picked up the phone to call Lacy.

"Yes, I would like to speak to Lacy James if I could. Yes, this is Detective Steve Belcher. Yes, I'll hold," he said.

"Get your pucker ready," Jerry said and sat closer so he could hear the conversation better.

"Hello, this is Lacy," Lacy said when she answered the phone.

"Lacy, good morning. I was wondering if I could get you to come to the station. I'd like to discuss the case with you. We need your help and since you're the lead reporter on this case, you're the only one who can help," Steve said and made faces at Jerry. He pantomimed throwing up.

"What do you want, Belcher? You screwed me before, is this another joke?" She said in a voice dripping with sarcasm.

"No, Lacy, this is no joke." His voice had turned cold.

Jerry sat there trying not to laugh and moved the trash

can over to where Steve was sitting.

"Yes, this is for real. How about 15:00 today?" he said in the most serious tone he could find.

"Fine, but this had better be for real, Belcher." Lacy said.

"That's great, I'll see you then, thank you, Lacy," he said and hung up the phone.

"That was very good," Lester said and walked around the door from where he had been listening. "Maybe you're learning some people skills after all," Lester said. Jerry laughed.

"Just be here at 15:00. I really don't want to shoot the blood sucker. I forgot my wooden bullets at home," Steve said, thinking if wooden stakes worked, then wooden bullets should as well.

"Sheriff's Boon and Warner are putting together assault teams and will start the search tomorrow," Tom said as he entered the room. "I was thinking, he has no current driver's license, no vehicle registered in his name, no address, what makes us believe he's in one of those counties? I know, all of the evidence we have so far leads us to one of those two places," Tom said.

"What are you thinking, Tom?" Lester asked.

"I wonder if we shouldn't check around here, too. I mean, the first kill we found was here, not in the other locations. We know he's traveling around and transporting the bodies, but we don't know where. I think we should look everywhere in the state, not just down where he was. I think he's smarter than that," Tom said.

"The kids got a point," Steve said.

"Okay, let's you and me go call the state police and get them on board. After that, run a search for all vacant buildings in the county and start your search. This is your ball, run with it," Lester said and he and Tom left the office.

"You know that kid is going to be a really good

detective someday," Jerry said to Steve.

"If he makes it through puberty," Steve said. "Get out of here so I can write this damn speech." Jerry puckered his lips at Steve.

*\*\*\**

"Lacy," Steve called as he walked around the corner. "Thanks for coming down." He gave her the biggest smile he could muster.

"Okay, what's this all about?" she asked.

"Come with me and we can talk about it, the sheriff's waiting for us," he said.

They walked into the sheriff's office and closed the door behind them. The sheriff stood and reached to shake Lacy's hand in greeting.

"Please sit, thanks for coming in," he said.

"Okay, I'm here, what's up?" Lacy asked.

"Okay, this is what we need" Steve said and laid out his plan to draw out the killer.

"Are you crazy?" she asked. She sat straight up in her chair. "This guy could get close enough to kill you."

"We have all of that in mind and we'll give you the story of your life, but we need you to help us. This has to look like Steve just went off the reservation and blurted it out in a moment of rage," Lester said. "We'll give you the first look at some new information if you'll help us."

"Let's see it," she said.

"Oh no, not until you help us, then I'll give you the story," Lester said.

"Okay, but I get full access before it hits any wire service, deal?" Lacy said in a commanding voice.

"Deal," Steve said.

"I guess you're not as bad as I thought," Steve told her, still playing to her vanity.

"I'll see you later," she said and left the building.

# Chapter Thirty

The hunter woke from sleep after another day on the hunt, stirred from the dark room. Surrounded by drawings on the walls and ceiling of his room, they kept him safe while he slept. Looking at the pictures he had placed on the walls, he took one down and carried it out to another room and placed it on another wall lined with other drawings.

"Now you join the rest," he said and backed away from the wall of crayon drawings depicting the monsters he'd killed. The room was barely lit from the setting sun. He moved through the place from room to room, turning on small lights casting an eerie glow on the walls covered in the drawings from his tormented mind. He returned to the room with a half eaten carcass of a rabbit he had caught and cooked the day before. He sat and fed his hunger and turned on a small television. He crunched through the charred and burnt flesh, his mind again overtaken by the beasts.

He was running for his life from the howling beast sent to torment his dreams. Out in the woods he ran to his safe place, only to hear the screams in the distance of the monsters trying to find him. The cold he felt overtook his thoughts and he shivered from the night air. Alone, cold and hiding, he sat and rocked back and forth telling himself, "They can't find me here, they can't find me here." He repeats the words over and over, his delusional mind slipping farther and farther into the horror of his past.

"And here's the latest on the horrific serial killings that are continuing to baffle the police and FBI," Lacy's voice is heard from the television set.

Snapping out of his tormented dream, he reached over and turned up the volume on the small set.

"This is Lacy James reporting, the video you are about to see was taken this afternoon by this reporter when the lead detective, Steve Belcher, was questioned about the failed attempt to catch the serial killer this weekend in Lima, Ohio. Two more bodies were discovered right under the noses of the FBI, watch this." The video changed from Lacy behind the desk to Lacy chasing after Steve. "Detective Belcher," Lacy called to the detective as he tried to avoid the camera.

"Can you tell us why you failed to catch the killer and what you plan to do?"

The detective on the screen stopped in his tracks and turned back to Lacy.

"You want to know what I think?" he said in an agitated tone showing his frustration.

The hunter focused on the little screen as he sat on the floor in front of it. "What this sick worthless piece of crap is doing is a joke. This guy is just some little man who thinks he's going to save the world, but all he's doing is taking his sick delusions out on some old people," Steve raged.

The Detective's rant continued and the pleased demeanor of the hunter changed to a cold lifeless stare as the rest of the video plays out.

"I know who you are and it's just a matter of time," Steve said, looking straight into the camera, looking right into the soul of the hunter. "When I catch you, you'll suffer for your crimes and I'll be the one to stop you." He looked away from the camera. "Now, get out of my face!" he screamed at Lacy, who backed away. Steve jumped in his car and drove away.

"As you've just seen, according to Detective Steve Belcher, the lead detective in the case, they know who the killer is—a worthless pathetic loser—who according to the detective, will be caught by him and punished."

The report ended and the hunter stood up and left the set on. He walked out of the room to where the two bodies were chained to the wall.

"You have sent another monster after me. But I know who he is and where he is," he said. The cold night air added to the chill of his words. "It's time for the hunt to begin." Grabbing his ball cap and coat, he left the room. "It won't be long and you'll see the next monsters die before your eyes."

# Chapter Thirty-One

"That was quite a performance. If I didn't know better, I'd think you actually had her peeing in her pants at the end," Jerry said with delight after watching the newscast with Steve and Lester.

"Scout," Jerry heard from the doorway.

"Hey guys, come on in," Jerry said. "Steve, this is Sergeant Antwan Wells, AKA, Raider and Sergeant Paul Archer, AKA, Smoke. They're the boys I was telling you about." Raider, a tall dark-skinned man in his late thirties, wearing camo and dark sunglasses with his head clean-shaven, reached out to shake Steve's hand.

"One of you will be in my apartment at all times. This guy enters the homes, and watches their every move for two weeks before he kills them. If he comes in the house, you can nail him," Steve said.

"That will be you, Raider," Jerry told Antwan.

"There isn't much room to hide, but you can move about inside with the shades closed and shouldn't be seen. Jerry has to carry out his regular routine or the perp might notice. He'll take the day watch. Smoke, you're the one in the wind." Smoke, who was average height and build, dressed in a tight tee-shirt and jeans with red hair and a beard to match, nodded to Steve. "We have a car you can make your base while you follow me around. We'll all be wired, so if anything happens, or if anyone shows up, everyone can be aware at the same time. We don't know if this is going to work, but it's worth a shot," Steve said.

"Don't worry, if this guy is out there on your trail, we'll find him," Smoke said.

"I have to ask about these colorful names you have, Smoke and Raider, and we learn that you're Scout?" Steve asked.

"Well, Raider got his in college from all the sororities he visited in the night," Jerry said.

"Guilty as charged," Raider said raising his hand.

"And Smoke is the last thing anyone will see if he has you in his sights," Jerry said. Jerry slapped Sergeant Archer on the shoulder.

"And what about you, Scout?" Steve asked.

"He's the best tracker the rangers ever had. He could track a flea through a pack of dogs," Raider said. The three laughed like they'd been out on a mission and returned safely home.

"That I believe," Steve said. He'd witnessed it first hand over the last few days.

"Okay, let's put this in motion. Jerry, you take Smoke and get him set up. Raider, you come with me and we'll get you set up at the apartment. I can drop you off and you can go through the back in case he's watching the front. I'm not surrounded by woods, so it'll be a lot harder for him to hide," Steve said.

"What's the order, Scout?" Smoke asked.

"This guy doesn't escape at all costs," Steve replied before Jerry could answer. His cold stare made his intentions clear to the men.

\*\*\*

"If we can't draw this guy out, then what do we do?" Raider asked Steve. They sat in the front room of the house discussing the case. Raider cleaning his weapon.

"I don't know, but I know he's not going to stop. We found all these pictures he made," Steve said and he recounted the story of the drawings to him.

Raider continued to clean his gun through the story. Steve wondered if he'd even been listening.

"How many times have you had to use that?" he asked.

"Too many," Raider replied coldly. "But I'll use it any time it's necessary. I don't want to kill, but if this guy is what you say he is, the best possible solution is for one of us to get him in our sights and end this quickly," Raider said.

"You should get some sleep so you can watch the house tomorrow, I'll take first watch. I can sleep at the station if I need to in the morning," Steve said.

Picking up the radio he called the other two men. "Scout, Smoke are you in place?"

"Smoke is in play, about one hundred yards from the front door on the north side. Clear view, all clear for now, Scout is down and will relieve in two," Smoke respond.

"That means he's sleeping and will take over in two hours," Raider said.

"You guys have done this before," Steve said.

"Yeah, a couple of times," Raider said closed his eyes to sleep.

Steve watched for hours from behind the side of the curtains looking for any movement and listening for any sound. He peered into the night and his focus began to blur.

"Shit," he yelped when Raider touched him on the shoulder. "You scared the hell out of me. Don't sneak up on me like that! You guys love to scare the shit out of people don't you?"

"Well, if he's out there, he heard you," Raider said with a laugh. "Go get some sleep, I'll take watch."

Steve moved to his bedroom and lay down on the mattress. He drifted off to sleep with his mind still seeing the pictures on the wall.

***

Morning came and Steve left the apartment the same way he did every morning, stopping at the same place for his morning coffee. Followed by Smoke and Jerry, he arrived at the Station at 08:00. Smoke drove past to circle around to take Jerry to his house now that Steve was in the station.

"From here on out, you're on your own," Jerry told Smoke once they arrived at his house. "I'll keep the radio on at all times. If you need a break at night, call and I'll sneak over. Try to get some sleep," Jerry said.

"I know the drill, Captain," Smoke replied to his old squad leader with a grin. "If your man comes knocking, I'll bag him for you." Smoke drove away.

Jerry took a quick shower and returned to the Station at 08:45. He drove into the station parking lot and noticed a car on the side of the street facing the station, but there was no sign of Smoke. He entered the station, pulled his ear piece from his collar and called him,

"Smoke, you with us?"

"In the tree, south side of the station, got a good view," Smoke said.

"Don't fall out taking a nap," Jerry said and continued into the station.

Jerry found Steve and Tom going over the plans for the team looking into all the vacant buildings in the county.

"There are one hundred and thirty we know of for sure, but there could be more," Tom told the group. "I've got a program running that will cross check surrounding counties."

"Remember the picture," Jerry said. "The one drawing showed a group of buildings, I'd start there first."

"Thanks," Tom said.

"Steve, you look like hell, go lay down somewhere and get some sleep. We can take it from here," Sheriff Lester told him.

217 • Hunting Monsters

# Chapter Thirty-Two

The hunter, on the move, entered the town and drove around town, up one street and down another. Finding the sheriff's station and scouting the surrounding areas, he found a quiet place to hide and wait for a sighting. Lurking in the dark, with his mind in turmoil from Steve's rant, he no longer sees Steve's face. He sees the face of a monster repeating the words over and over again, building the rage in his demented thoughts. He waited and watched in the dark for any sign of movement. He must learn the pattern, for this may be the most difficult hunt so far.

He left his van and scouted the area around the station. Looking for the best place to hide and watch. He noticed a shack in the backyard of a nearby house. He entered the yard and watched the people inside the house, an old couple rambling around. He opened the door to the old shack to find it full of old garden equipment and boxes.

*This will be perfect,* he thought. He'd be able to see everything from the shed and not be noticed. *The old people won't be out here. And if they do come, I'm just a bum looking for a place to sleep,* he thought. He returned to his van where it was parked down the street in a vacant lot. He returned to the shed with supplies, food and water for the time he'd watch. The shack would be his home for a while.

He settled in for the night and after watching for a while, his mind still engaged in his delusional battle, he drifted off to sleep, hidden from sight.

\*\*\*

The hunter, awake since dawn, had seen Steve enter the

police station. He knew his target, he noted the time of his arrival, he had to be patient and wait. He saw a car drop Jerry off. He paid no mind to it when it left, and, from where he hid, he didn't see it return. For three days he watched, on the third day, he was out for a better look. He'd moved to another location in the night. One closer. He'd found an empty house behind the station. He hid in the attic of the house. Hiding behind some bushes in the yard, he had a clear view of the area.

He watched Steve arrive at his usual time in the morning. He was ready to move and follow the prey home. He stayed in the attic for the day. While he slept, his dreams were haunted even worse than before. The monsters were real again. He could feel the heat from their breath on his skin. Pain flowed through his body with every strike from the monster's hand. His cries for help went unheard and he sat up from where he lay. Fear woke him and sweat covered his face. He looked around to see that he was alone and in the attic.

It was afternoon and he must clear his thoughts and return to the hunt. He peered out a window in the end of the house and watched Steve walk to his car. Now was the time. He left the house after watching Steve drive out of the lot. He reached his van and climbed inside.

"Must hurry or I will lose him," he told himself.

He pulled out to follow, but he noticed a car turnaround in the middle of the street to follow Steve's car. He held back. His attention on the car ahead of him. He stayed back far enough not to be noticed and followed the car that trailed his prey. Steve arrived at home, parked out front and walked up to his apartment. The car passed Steve and parked about a block and a half down the street. The hunter turned at the street before the apartment building and drove around the back of another building. He sat in the van until darkness came. He wondered what that car could mean. He knew the car had followed the prey. He needed to find a place to watch and see what happened.

He silently moved though the still night and stayed in the shadows. There wasn't much cover to hide him.

"This isn't good for the hunt," he told himself.

He crawled under the porch of a house across the street from the apartment building and he'd stay the night there, watching. He watched the man in the car looking through night vision glasses. He could see the soft glow of the goggles. He stayed under the porch and watched the man in the car.

As dawn came, he watched Steve leave for work. He observed him walk down the sidewalk to his waiting car and drive away. The other car followed.

"They're watching him, they're setting a trap," he told himself. He left the hiding spot under the porch and made his way back to his van. For the first time on a hunt, he wasn't sure what to do.

He drove out of town and back to where he knew was safe. He pulled into the building and closed the door. He walked into the room where he confronted the two monsters still held captive, chained to the wall.

"You warned him. I'll show you who the hunter is. I'll bring him to me," he exclaimed to the two monsters. "But what bait will I use?" he asked himself and took off his hat and scratched his head. He hadn't seen a female, and no small ones. He must think, he must find the right bait. He remembered the Old Monster's words.

"For every animal there is the right bait, you must learn what attracts each one if you want to be a good hunter."

\*\*\*

He's followed every move the prey made. He remembered every stop, every car, every person they passed just as he had done in the woods. *This was no different from hunting wild boar,* he thought. They ran in packs, the small ones protected by the more deadly large ones.

"I can track them and wait for the right time to separate the prey from the pack," he said again remembering the teaching of the Old Monster.

"You must put the prey in the position where they are most likely to lose sight of the pack. If the animal is alone, the prey can be taken without having to take on the whole pack," the Old Monster had said.

A lesson he'd learned the hard way, running into the pack to try to kill one on his own. He felt the old wounds on his arms, "*the scars of stupidity*" the Old One called them. But he'd learned, the next time he took the animal when it was separate from the pack.

"The hunter must watch and be ready to strike at any moment. He must learn when that moment is to be successful in the hunt," the words of the Old One rang in his memory. "The hunter must adapt to follow the prey. He must learn to track them wherever they go. He must look for hiding places to watch from," he said. He needed to use everything he'd learned. "The prey is being watched by other monsters, there are most likely more in the den where the monster sleeps," he told himself. "I must watch for many days. This monster is smarter than any of the others I've hunted so far."

# Chapter Thirty-Three

"Where would I hide?" Steve thought studying the hand colored images from the killer. He found himself in the woods, under the tree where he'd found him sitting in the dark cold of night. The sounds of the woods his only friend. Scared and crying for the monsters to stop. Sifting through the stack of drawings, he was drawn deeper into the woods. He spots the small boy learning to hunt by following the monster. He's in the woods, walking the path, the monster pointed out the signs to read. Hunting the animals he later cooked and ate for food to survive on his own. But the monsters turned on him and again he was being chased. In fear he hid in the tree. He found himself trying to keep his fear under control, because if he cried out, the monsters would hear him. He must stay quiet with the tears streaming down his face. In the tree, with the little boy, he too felt the terror running through him.

"Don't move, don't make a sound, if they find me they'll kill me," the scared child said.

"And they'll kill you, too," he said and the little boy turned to Steve with his face a mask of fear, tears streaming down his face.

"Steve, we're going out for some lunch." Steve jerked awake from the dream to see Jerry standing at his desk.

"What?" he asked.

"Lunch, you want to come?" Jerry asked.

"Yeah, yeah," he replied, the feelings of terror from the dream subsiding. He walked down the hall with Jerry and they met up with Sheriff Lester.

"What about your boy out there?" Steve asked.

"We already took care of him, he's used to meal packs. Besides, we don't want to blow his cover. Don't worry, you'll never be out of his sight," Jerry said.

They walked outside to load up in the sheriff's car to head for lunch. They left the lot. Smoke was already in his car and poised to follow the group.

\*\*\*

"How's it going, Tom?" Steve said when he and the group returned from lunch. Tom and his team's search of the empty buildings and had come up empty. For four days they'd searched from building to building with no luck. Tom sat at his desk mapping everywhere they'd searched. His hope of finding the right one dwindled. With no word of success from the other teams across the state, his plan seemed to be a waste of time.

"The search isn't going so well, I hear,"Lester said.

"No, no luck at all, looks like I've wasted a lot of man hours for nothing," he said.

"We don't think so, you're eliminating the possibilities of where he's been hiding, and you know that's a big part of police work. It may not be glamorous, and it sure isn't any fun. But in order to find him, sometimes you have to look at a lot of places he's not. Now, the way I see it, you have eradicated a whole bunch of places he could be. Keep going, you'll smoke him out," Lester said and patted him on the back.

"Really kid, it's no fun watching Steve's boring life 24/7, but what you're doing is just as important," Jerry added with a smile. They turned to go to their desks leaving Tom feeling better about his task.

"What do you mean boring life?" Steve asked Jerry.

"Well, you don't really live it up any, old man," he replied.

"I'm just trying to make it easy on your boys out there," he said with a smile, then headed down the hall.

"Go take your nap so we can get to work," Jerry said and laughed. He pantomimed Steve falling asleep at his desk.

***

Tom continued his quest to find the killer's hiding place. With every building they searched, his frustration built. The adrenaline built and coursed through his veins with every step through the unknown buildings. Searching from room to room, the team cleared each location. Being startled by birds, and rats, or rabbits in many of the old and unused buildings, his highs and lows of excitement took him on a roller coaster of emotion.

"Stay focused," he told himself and the team. "The next one we walk into might be the one."

Driving up to the next location, a group of buildings out on the outskirts of town, the group unloaded from the car. The eerie calm around him heightened his senses. Pulling their weapons they approached the first building of five on the property. Tom stopped, noticing tire tracks in the dirt leading up to the doors of the building. With hand signals, he motioned to the team to spread out covering all sides of the structure. They moved into position by the doors and surrounding the building. Hearing a noise from inside the building, his heart pumped loud in his ears and he motioned for the team to make entry.

He reached for the handle to open the door. He looked to the officer and nodded. They swung open the doors and rushed into the room.

"Don't move," they screamed and pointed their weapons.

Three teenage boys stood with their hands in the air, shaking in fear, with police weapons aimed at them.

"We're just skipping school," one of the boys told them and the officers lowered their weapons.

"Is there anyone else here?" Tom asked.

"No, just us, we weren't doing anything, honest," the other boy said while they were patted down.

"Call their parents to come and pick them up," Tom ordered one of the officers.

Tom and the rest of the team continued to check the other buildings. They found the same thing they had for the last eight days, nothing.

\*\*\*

More days passed and the group went through the same motions, the daily stop for coffee on the way to the station. Lunch out to expose Steve to whoever may be watching. The nights on "*look out*" at the apartment building lulled them into a routine that had become mundane.

Friday morning came and the normal routine began as always with Steve leaving the apartment and driving to work, followed by Smoke in another car watching every move.

Steve stopped at the normal coffee house, he went in and Smoke called him on the radio.

"Hey, pick me up a cup and leave it on the curb. I'll do a drive and scoop," Smoke said.

Steve stepped in the coffee house to retrieve his morning brew. Smoke, a block back, waited, minutes passed but no Steve.

"Steve, are they growing the coffee beans in there or what?" he asked.

When he didn't get a response, he floored the gas and raced to the coffee house parking lot. Smoke slammed on the breaks in a tire squealing stop. His weapon drawn, he entered through front door to find no one in the building.

"Scout, Raider, target is missing, I repeat, target is missing from Cup-a-Joe's, gone two minutes!" he said running through the back of the little shop. He found no one, nothing out back, no cars, no movement at all. Sirens filled the air and police cars were on the scene within minutes.

"What the hell happened, Smoke?" Jerry yelled from his truck.

"I don't know, Cap. We stopped for his morning coffee and when he didn't come right back out, I called him on the radio. No answer. I entered to find just what you see. I checked out back and nothing. I swear it was less than two maybe three minutes and he ghosted," Smoke said.

Jerry grabbed his radio and called the dispatcher, "Every available officer, we have an officer 10-57, as of five minutes ago. Last seen at Cup-o-Joes, Twenty-third and Maple. Suspect could be fleeing in any direction, stop anything moving," he ordered.

Sheriff Lester arrived on the scene and began a full search of the coffee house. In the cooler they found the regular clerk, drugged, but alive.

"I thought you guys were the best," Lester yelled at Smoke, who stood with his head down.

"Not his fault, Sheriff. I should have known better, this guy has bested us at every turn," Jerry said.

"Damn it, I should have never gone along with this. Now he has one of my officers, not to mention the lead officer on the case. Pack your bags and get out of my town," he said talking right in Smoke's face. "And you better find him before I have your head on a platter!" he screamed at Jerry.

Sheriff Lester stalked away from them.

"I'm sorry, Scout," Smoke said. He looked as though he felt the weight of the whole world crashing down on his shoulders.

"Not your fault, Smoke," Jerry tried to reassure him.

Raider pull up to the scene. He walked up to the two men.

"What happened?" Raider asked.

"I'll explain on the way, load up," Jerry said.

\*\*\*

"How could he have gotten in and out of the area so fast?" Sheriff Lester said. He looked at map of the county.

Tom, who had surveyed most of it over the last few days, walked up to the map. "Well, Sheriff, looking at where he had to start, he had to either go north, or south away from the back of the coffee house. Once he's on the main road, the possibilities are endless. His route could be one of these dirt, back roads. He could have gotten to any of these in less than a minute from where he started," Tom said.

"I know my county, Detective!" Lester said with contempt.

Tom felt the anger in his voice and backed away ready for what he knew was about to be a Mt. St. Helen's size eruption from the sheriff.

The sheriff shook his head and turned to Tom. "Sorry kid, I know you're just trying to help. Where do you think he might go?" Lester asked.

"Sheriff, we have covered most of the northern section of the county, and found nothing. My best guess would be south. There are plenty of wooded sections, areas that are as hidden as you can get. Which one, I have no idea, but if I was running and had to move in a hurry, I'd of gone straight out Twenty Third street, no traffic this time of the morning, and it's a straight shot to Rt. 67 out into no man's land. Within ten minutes he could be gone forever. Sorry, I didn't mean it that way, Sheriff," Tom said.

\*\*\*

"Sam, we need you to broadcast live," Sheriff Lester told the news station manager. The Sheriff explained what was happening and they need everyone in the county looking for Steve.

"Sheriff, we have another problem. Lacy James is missing also. We thought she was out somewhere looking into a story, but she hasn't checked in. The last we heard from her was last night," Sam said.

"I'll send someone to her house, get a reporter over here," Lester commanded.

"Jerry," Lester called down the hallway, "get over to Lacy James apartment and check it out. It seems she's missing, too. This just gets better and better."

Jerry left the sheriff's office and grabbed Raider and Smoke, who sat in the squad room, to go with him.

"Guys, hold up," Lester called, "I thought I told you to get out of my county," he said to Smoke.

"With all due respect, Sheriff, I'm here to find this guy. It was on my watch, and whether you like it or not, I'm not going anywhere until we find that son of a bitch!" he said.

"Then get going and find Lacy, and then you find that bastard," Lester said in a commanding tone.

***

The three men arrived at Lacy's apartment building, a two-story bank of apartments surrounded by trees. A calming water fountain sprayed in the small lake in the front courtyard. "It's number 1420," Jerry said and pointed to the door. They walked up to the numbered apartment and found the front door unlocked and ajar. They pulled their weapons and with a nod from Jerry, assumed positions covering each other. Jerry, aiming high right, Smoke left and Raider following behind, aiming straight ahead. They entered in a flash. After several short seconds clear was heard from all three from different rooms. "Empty," Jerry said. They found no sign of Lacy. Her purse and keys were still on the counter.

Jerry picked up his phone and called the sheriff.

"She's gone. Her purse and keys are here. There's a half drunk cup of coffee on the counter. I'll bet it's drugged just like the others. While we were watching Steve, he took her and then him right in front of us."

"Damn, stay there, I'll get the crime lab on the way. Soon as they get there you get back here," the sheriff's voice came through the phone.

"Okay, I'll wait for the crime lab to get here," Jerry replied and hung up the phone.

"Who is this guy?" Raider asked the other two men.

"He's a ghost, and he has Steve and Lacy. We have less than two days to find where they are. Call in every favor you have, get the team together tonight. Our yearly hunting trip is going to start early this year," Jerry told them with a fierce grin.

\*\*\*

Night fell and the search had to be called for darkness. News reports filled the airways with the story of the abduction of Detective Steve Belcher and news anchor Lacy James. The police were asking for the public's help in finding them.

Lost and not knowing which way to turn, Jerry sat in the squad room going over the maps of where Tom had already searched.

"Okay kid, where do you think I should look? Take your best shot," Jerry said.

"Well, like I told the sheriff, my best guess is to go south down the old Rt. 67." He pointed to a road on the map. "It branches off into several remote areas. Roads that connect with three other counties. He could be anywhere out there," Tom said.

"You continue with your team's search area in the morning. I'll take my team and go in tonight," Jerry told him.

"No, we're getting ready to go now. They are meeting me here in thirty minutes." He stabbed a spot on the map with his finger. "We're starting here at this intersection and working all the buildings to the west from there. Take your

229 • Hunting Monsters

team and work south," Tom told him.

"Okay kid, good hunting," Jerry said.

Outside the station, Smoke and Raider had assembled an entire squad of twenty Army rangers, weapons loaded and in full camo. They stood and waited for Jerry to exit the station. This team of rangers had served together for four years. They had stayed in touch and had gotten together every year for a hunting trip. They were a true band of brothers. They would all come running anytime one of the group needed help.

"Thanks for coming," Jerry said as he approached the group.

"I know Raider and Smoke have filled you in on what's happening. We have less than thirty-six hours left to find this killer before he takes two more lives. He's a ghost in the woods. He can disappear right before your eyes. If you make him, take him, do not hesitate or he will be gone, understood?" Jerry asked.

They responded with a loud military, "*Yes, sir,*" that rang in the night air.

"Mount up," Jerry called and led the caravan down the road.

"The hunt is on," Jerry told Raider and Smoke. He drove south out of town.

# Chapter Thirty-Four

Jerry and his team moved through the buildings they came upon. Silently, they converged on a building.

They moved through the trees like they were back in the desert town, swift and sure, training their weapons on anything that moved. Having searched through the night Jerry called the men together.

"Everybody take thirty minutes. We'll rest and regroup, any one need to take longer, let me know," he said.

"No way, Cap, we're good to go," Raider said.

"Okay, take thirty," Jerry told them and everyone relaxed. Some of the men drank from canteens and others pulled food from their packs.

"You think we'll find him in time?" Smoke asked Jerry. Jerry looked up from the map.

"I hope so, but either way, you can't carry this with you. He got past us two weeks ago after we knew where he was going to be. He still slipped in and out. You didn't have a chance. He's the best I've seen," Jerry said and stared out into the woods.

"I'll keep my money on you, if you don't mind," Smoke said to him and walked away. He settled against a tree and shut his eyes.

Jerry smiled for a second and returned his focus to the map. His mind lost in the faded memories of the past. He'd sat in the same position with a map, hunting a target. This time a lot more was on the line than just him pulling the trigger on an unsuspecting target from one thousand yards away.

"I have to find my friend and partner," he told himself.

Gathering the team, Jerry led them deeper into the woods. They spread out staying close enough that they could still stay in contact. They moved through the dense brush headed for the next location to search.

\*\*\*

With two more hours gone and finding nothing in the woods, Jerry called the team back together.

"Okay guys, let's take five," he said and he sat down and pulled his canteen out for a drink.

"Don't give up, Cap," Raider said and walked over to join him. "We'll find them. We'll stay out here until we do."

Jerry stared out at the trees, his thoughts traveled back over the drawings, searching for anything from them to tell him where to look.

# Chapter Thirty-Five

"You sent them to haunt me, but they will join you in hell," the hunter said. His mind was in a constant struggle with the delusions of the past tearing at him. All the monsters from the past attacked him all at once. He flailed with the knife to keep them back. The screaming and shouting filled the building with echoes that rang in his ears.

"I am in control," he told them, and continued to prepare the bodies. He wrapped them in the plastic, and placed them on the table ready to begin. "Wake up!" he screamed. "Let's get this over with. They have to know it was me who defeated them," he told himself while he sat at the table and fought the raging battle in his head.

He fought the snapping and snarling, lunging monsters all around him. He ran to his bed and closed the door. Surrounded by his drawings, he would be safe until they woke up. He sat rocking back and forth, back and forth, like the small child. *"They can't find me in here, they can't find me in here,"* he repeated over and over and over.

\*\*\*

Steve began to stir in the next room, groggy but with his head clearing, opened his eyes and looked around the dimly lit room. Lacy lay wrapped to the table next to him, and he realized he, too, was constrained, naked and unable to move. He called to Lacy, who was beginning to stir.

"Lacy, Lacy," he whispered.

"No need to whisper," he heard a low voice from the darkness. "There is no one around to hear your screams, monster," Wallace said.

Steve looked around the room but still couldn't see anyone.

"Wallace, Wallace Holt, I know who you are," Steve said.

The only answer was silence. Steve continued, "I know why you're hunting monsters, but we're not monsters. We only want to help you," Steve said and used all of the training from his years on the police force, talking like he was trying to talk a jumper off a ledge. "We had to do what we did, so you would find us, so we could help you escape from them," Steve said.

Still silence, the only sound was the echo of Steve's voice and the moans of Lacy regaining consciousness.

"Where are we?" Lacy asked looking over at Steve wrapped to a table beside her.

"Lacy, just listen and stay calm. We need to talk to him, it's going to be okay," Steve told her. "Wallace, we can help you. We're hunters, too," he said. "We need your help to catch the monsters after us." He looked over at Lacy who looked at Steve as if to say, "*are you nuts?*"

"I know what your parents did to you, and I know what you went through in the woods. We found all of your drawings in the trees. Talk to us, all we want to do is help you stop the monsters," Steve continued to speak even though Holt stayed silent. "Will you talk to us? How can we convince you that we're hunters, too, if you won't talk to us?"

"Tell him why we contacted him the way we did," Steve told Lacy.

"It was the only way to fool the monsters. We had to make them believe we were monsters, too," she told the dark room turning her head all around, looking for any sign someone was there.

"We know the monsters are all around us, we had to make sure you'd be the only one to find us," Steve said.

"Please, help us," Lacy cried softly, "I'm afraid they're coming to get me." She whimpered.

"You don't have to be afraid," Wallace said from the darkness. He heard Lacy's soft whimper and it triggered the memories of the small child in the woods hiding in the cold. He emerged from the darkness and walked around the two on the tables.

"We've been hunted all of our lives," Steve said.

Silently, the hunter walked slowly, reciting the Old One. *"The prey will trick you, lead you one way and turn back on you. You must always be aware so the hunter doesn't become the hunted,"* he said loud enough for Steve and Lacy to hear.

"Please, save us," Lacy said with a whimper again.

"Monsters lie," Wallace said in a cold, calm voice and he disappeared into the shadows again. "I see through your lies. You are monsters and soon you'll join all the others," Wallace said.

"I know you don't believe it, but there are others out there like you and us, hiding from the dark, seeing the monsters in our dreams. We hide, cold and hungry. Always looking over our shoulders for the monsters to come," Steve said and used everything he had learned from the case to try and save their lives. The room was still silent except for the whimpers and pleads from Lacy.

"What do you want?" she cried out.

"I want your power, I want all of your power," the hunter said quickly emerging from the darkness to stand over her and look into her tearful eyes to see her fear.

"We don't have any power, the monsters have it all," Steve shouted at him.

The hunter moved from Lacy and peered into Steve's eyes.

"No, I have the power, I have taken it from them and I will take it from you," he said.

"I have no power, I'm just the weak scared little boy

who hides in the woods. I draw the monsters in my dreams. But they still keep coming. I burn the pages I draw hoping that would kill them, but they still chase me," Steve told the hunter.

"Lies, Lies!" the hunter screamed and ran from the room.

"You told them lies to get to me!" the hunter screamed at the mummified bodies in the other room.

His rant continued and Steve looked over at Lacy, who seemed to be on the verge of breaking down.

"Stay with me, we have to convince him, it is our only chance to get out of this," he said.

Lacy mouthed the words, "I can't," and shook her head no.

"We can do this," he said. "Just stay focused, this is the story of your life."

She shook her head in agreement, relaxed and took a deep breath to calm her out of control fear.

The ranting quieted in the next room and the hunter returned.

"Your tricks won't work, monster, I see through your lies," he told Steve and Lacy.

"We followed all the signs you left for us," Steve said.

"The drawings told us your story, and how we could find you so you could help us," Steve said and tried to go deeper into his mind.

"We need your help, why won't you help us? You're the only hunter to survive the monsters. But you can lead the army to stop them all," Lacy pleaded with every ounce of being.

"Don't you want to stand on top of the pile of the dead monsters after the battle and raise your sword after you kill the last one?" Steve said as he remembered the last of the drawings.

"No, No, you tried to capture me, you had monsters follow you to set a trap, but I was smarter. I used your trap to hunt you. No more of your lies, monster, it will soon be time for you to die like all the others," the hunter ranted at Steve.

237 • Hunting Monsters

# Chapter Thirty-Six

"No news is good news," Jerry told himself after calling in to hear if there was any news. "Okay boys, let's move out," he called to the men.

They continued the search through the woods into the next clearing where the cars waited to take them to the next search point. They loaded into the vehicles and the all but exhausted team still remained focused on the task. The men were happy to be riding even for a few moments while being transported to the next site. While they made their way to the location through the twisting and turning back roads, Jerry spotted the helicopters flying overhead. He communicated with them to locate possible targets and they reported no signs of anyone in the area, but the woods were too thick and too hard to see well from above.

"You're next location is two miles up on the left and one thousand yards into the woods there is a clearing . Only an overgrown dirt road leads up to it," the pilot said through the radio.

"Okay, thanks, keep looking," Jerry said and the helicopter flew away continuing their search.

"Pull over here," he told the driver. They unloaded from the vehicles. "Ready for another walk in the woods?" he called to the men. Again they spread out and moved swiftly through the heavy wooded area. Alert but weary, Jerry led the hunt, tuned in to all of his senses. "I want this guy," he told himself. "You won't get away again."

\*\*\*

"Hello, Sheriff, this is Terry Peterson. I heard about

Steve and Lacy on the news. Has there been any word yet? I've been trying to call Tom all night but I can't reach him and I'm beginning to worry," she said without stopping.

The sheriff, trying to get a word in the conversation, finally interrupted her.

"Terry, Tom's fine. He's out with the search parties trying to find Steve and Lacy. He's probably just out of cell range in the woods. I'll have him call you as soon as I hear from him, okay?" he assured her.

"I'm sorry, Sheriff," she said.

"You don't need to be, I know how close you two have become and I know your interest in this case. But you have to let us get to work," he said.

"Thanks, Sheriff," she said and hung up the phone.

She walked over to the window in her long white pajama pants and matching shirt. She looked out at the city lights. She thought of Tom standing next to her and let out a sigh. "I wish you were here."

***

Terry felt the concern from the sheriff and had decided to fly back. Her plane arrived at the airport and she deboarded and headed for the car rental counter. She climbed into a rental car and headed for the sheriff's station. Her imagination ran out of control and she feared the worst. Her parents were killed by this monster and now Steve and Lacy were missing and Tom was out there somewhere looking for revenge. Afraid he, too, would end up missing and dead, she drove as fast as she could. She entered the building and walked past the front desk to the surprise of the officer.

"Sheriff, is there any news?" she asked.

"It's okay, Jack, she's okay," he called off the officer chasing her. "No word yet, Terry, they're still out there. And, yes, Tom has checked in. He's fine," he told her with a warm smile.

Hearing the news, her fear subsided.

"I know you're upset, but there's nothing you can do here," he told her.

"Can I answer the phone, make coffee or something? I won't be in the way. Please, Sheriff, I just want to be here," Terry pleaded.

The sheriff looked over and saw Jerry's wife standing behind Terry. "Why don't the two of you go get some dinner, feed the kids, and I'll call you when we hear something," he said and introduced Terry to Jerry's wife Cindy. "If anyone is going to find them, it will be Jerry and Tom. Now, go on and let us get back to work," he told them leading them to the front door.

"Terry, would you like to come to my house? I really don't want to be alone and you don't need to be, either," Cindy said with a smile.

"That would be great," Terry replied. She didn't want to sit in a motel room or at some diner fearing the worst.

"Great, just follow me," Cindy said before getting into her car.

They arrived at Jerry and Cindy's house and Terry parked on the street. She walked up the drive to where Cindy waited at the front door. Cindy opened it to be rushed by her three boys like a tribe of small Indians. Terry walked into the house and admired the trappings of the home. She heard the playful roar from the children. A smile covered her face remembering growing up in the same surroundings. Rushing to greet her mom and dad from the day's work and telling them all the day's most interesting news that really wasn't interesting, but they listened anyway.

"Sorry about that" Cindy said and banished the boys to the back yard. "They're too much like their father. Sit down, care for a cup of coffee?" she asked.

"Yes, I could use some," Terry said and she sat down at the kitchen table.

"So, you're the famous Terry that has turned Tom inside out for the last two months," Cindy said with a girlish, *tell me all the dirty secrets*, grin. "You sure have got that boy tied and ready for market, if you know what I mean. From the look on your face, you're just as hooked as he is."

Terry sat at the table and blushed, realizing Cindy could read her and seemed to know a lot about her and Tom. "How much has Tom let slip?" Terry asked.

"Oh, Tom hasn't said anything. In fact, he won't tell Jerry any of the juicy stuff and it just drives him crazy. Your Tom can kiss and not tell," Cindy said. She sat down at the table with the cups of coffee and turned to Terry with a serious look. "Let's hear the good stuff, girl," Cindy said.

"Can I ask you something?" Terry said calmly. "Are you scared when Jerry's out there hunting killers all the time?"

"Yes, every minute. I thought all of this was over when he left the army. But I know Jerry. He's the best at what he does. If anyone can find them, Jerry can and he'll bring Tom home safe, too," she said placing her hand on Terry's offering a soft and comforting smile.

"So tell me about you and Tom?" she asked. Terry blushed.

# Chapter Thirty-Seven

"Why is he doing this to us?" Lacy cried looking again at Steve.

"He thinks we're the monsters in his nightmares. We have to keep talking to him long enough to be found or convince him we're on his side," Steve said.

"Do you think this will really work?" she asked.

"It's the only chance we have."

"You hear that?" Steve said as he heard the sound of a helicopter in the distance. "They're getting closer. It won't be long now, you have to hang on, Lacy," he told her.

Hearing the noise from the helicopter, the hunter emerged from his safe place. He ran to look out a window. He spotted the helicopter in the distance.

"So, they bring dragons to defeat me," Wallace said loud enough for Steve to hear.

"Your dragons have lost their way," Wallace told the two chained to the wall.

Steve heard what he had said in the other room. Steve looked at Lacy and nodded to make sure she was still okay and ready to continue their ploy to survive.

She nodded in return with a small smile before the hunter arrived back in the room.

"Your help has not arrived," he said. "I am a better hunter than the dragons you have called. You can't defeat me," he proclaimed.

"Why would we want to defeat you? We're here to join your fight," Steve said. "Don't you understand?"

"You are not a hunter. I do understand, I am not stupid," Wallace yelled.

"We're just trying to make you see we're with you. We'll follow you into battle to defeat them, if you will spare our lives," Lacy said softly holding back her fear. "I'm no longer afraid of death. I have hunted to find you to help in the battle against the horde. But, if I have to die to protect the hunter, then take my life. I'll add to your power and help you defeat the monsters," she said nobly.

"Could it be true?" Wallace spoke from the darkness. "I have found others like me, but how could this be? There is only one hunter. If you're lying to me you will suffer more than the others ever did," he warned her and looked into her eyes again for any sign of deception.

She jumped in fear when he grabbed her hair and looked into her eyes.

She opened them full and wide. "Look into my soul and tell me if I'm lying," she said not showing any signs of fear.

"No, it can't be true, I am the only one," Wallace said. "You must know your prey, they are clever and swift. Once you have them in your sight you must not falter, or you will have lost," he said.

Again, he retreated to the safety of his room.

"Nicely done, Lacy," Steve said.

"I hope they get here soon, I don't know how much longer I can do this," she said. The fear returned with a tear that ran down her forehead to her hair.

Steve heard the hunter enter the room where he and Lacy fought to stay awake. He felt the pain on the back of his head and hanging off the end of a table made it worse. Steve moaned with pain.

"Are you okay, Steve?" Lacy asked.

"Yes, my head hurts, I must have been hit from behind."

"You gave me no other option. A good hunter will change the hunt depending on the prey. You were surrounded by other monsters, but you still fell into my trap. I watched you for days make the same predictable moves, not knowing that I watched. I took the place of the guy in the coffee house and when you entered and turned your back to pour your coffee, I took you the same way I take other animals. Just one swift strike to the head." He hit the end of the table Steve was on, making a loud bang. "Your first strike must be vicious and true. If you can't take the prey in one strike, it could turn on you and you will be in for the fight of your life."

"I couldn't hunt you the way I did the others, you had monsters in the house and following you. You are not a hunter. You're a monster that tried to set a trap for me. But the true hunter watches, waits for as long as it takes to find the right second to attack. Once I had you, I loaded you up and the hunt was over. I was gone before the rest of your monsters knew I was there," Wallace said.

"But why me?" Lacy cried.

"You are the one that gives the commands. You stood back and screamed at the child and watched him carry out the torture," he said. His anger rose as he told the story of the child. "I would run and hide, but you would send him to find me and beat me, screaming and yelling into the night. No sleep or rest from days of you haunting my dreams. But you are the one that will feel the pain. No tricks can you do. I fear your threats no more. It is time," he said in the still cold tone. He emerged from the dark shadows of the corner of the room. "The hunter must change with the prey," he repeated and pulled the large hunting knife from the scabbard on his belt. "You will watch the tormentor die and you will see me take his power before I take yours." He moved over to Steve. He grabbed him by the hair and pulled his head out straight.

"I'm sorry, Lacy," Steve said.

# Chapter Thirty-Eight

"Cap, think I found something, two hundred yards south of you," one of the ranger's voices came from the radio. "On the way," Jerry said. "Everyone stay put," Jerry commanded. He made his way to the location the call came from. He spotted the ranger down on one knee looking through his rifle scope.

"What's out there?" Jerry asked as he came up behind the ranger.

"One hundred yards out and down at the base of the tree," he told Jerry.

Jerry pulled up his rifle and looked into the scope and studies what the ranger had called about. In the base of a large tree were drawings he recognized. "Everybody on me," Jerry ordered. "Good eyes," he told the ranger.

Within a minute the entire team had gathered around Jerry. "One hundred yards due north is a possible target, no sighting, but need eyes on it as I move in. Smoke, you take your group and head in from the west. Raider, you go in from the east. The rest spread out and follow me. No noise," he reminded them before they moved into the woods.

Silently, Jerry approached the tree and listened for any unnatural sounds. He reached the tree and found a hollowed out place in the base big enough for someone to have made a fort out of. He crawled inside and found more of the same childlike drawings they had found at the two previous wooded locations.

"Team one to base," Jerry said into the radio. "We need a fly over this location. Tree fort found in woods, same as before."

"Everyone hold their positions, dig in," he commanded while they waited for the helicopter. Looking at the drawings, he noticed one of the monsters seemed to be holding a microphone standing next to one holding a gun. Both of them had their heads removed, and standing over them was the hunter with his sword thrust in the air saying the words, *I am the hunter.* A cold chill ran through his body. "Smoke, Raider, on me" he called. "Smoke, five hundred yards to the south, Raider, five hundred yards to the east, I'll go five hundred yards to the west. Do not approach, watch and call if you have a sighting. The rest of you hold," he ordered and the three men moved out to their assigned locations.

Time went slowly as they moved out into the woods. Jerry moved quickly to the west. The helicopter flew overhead, heading west. He knew he was going in the right direction. He picked up the pace through the thinning woods. two hundred yards from the edge of the woods, he caught a glimpse of a group of buildings through the trees.

"Team leader, this is Helio 264. You have target, five hundred yards west from last position, no movement from up here, over," the pilot said through the radio.

"Thanks helio 264, we'll check it out, over," he answered and watched the helicopter fly away. "Rangers, five hundred yards west move fast we have target," he repeated into the radio. Jerry moved closer to the edge of the woods and squatted behind a tree with his rifle scope to his face. He looked over the buildings for any sign of movement.

"Smoke, cover the road entrance to the north, nothing gets out. Raider, move your team around to the west side of the building and spread out, we don't want this guy slipping out between us this time. Call when you're in position," Jerry ordered.

With the commands given, the team of army rangers

moved through the woods in all directions. This time on full alert. The team set up the perimeter and they called Jerry.

"Okay, advance on my go," Jerry said and moved through the opening in the trees.

They advanced on the first of the buildings and looked in the windows finding it empty. Jerry gave the sign to move on to the next. He came across tire ruts in the ground from repeated travel in and out of the building. He knelt down to feel the depth of the tracks. He directed his team to move around to all sides of the building. They approached cautiously, their weapons at the ready. With all the rangers in place, Jerry took a deep breath. He and another ranger grabbed the handles on the door.

"On three," Jerry whispered. "Slide the door slowly," the ranger replied with a nod. "One, two, three," Jerry whispered the count and the two pulled at the doors. Sliding the doors open just enough to move through, Jerry moved in slowly and five of the rangers followed. He entered the first room, it was empty. The tracks ended at the door and there were oil spots in the dirt. "Had to be where he parked," Jerry said.

"We're in," Jerry radioed Raider who was at the back of the building. "Enter slowly, no sound." Jerry moved into the next room where he found an almost spotless room, two stainless tables hung almost vertical in racks on the walls. The corner a stack of boxes. They spread out through the room and one of the rangers found a pile of cut up clothing. He moved closer and handed the items to Jerry. His cold look confirmed they were in the right place. The anger in his eyes was clear to everyone in the room.

"Let's move." He stealthily moved to the door to the next room. Softly, he opened the door and entered the adjoining room. He stood up from his crouched position. Raider and the other rangers entered through the back end of the room. Jerry pulled the radio from his pocket.

"Team one to base, Team one to base, over," Jerry said.

He waited for a response while the rangers spread out through the room.

"Dispatch to Team one, go ahead."

"Send the crime lab and tell the sheriff we found where he's been. No sign of Belcher or Lacy but there's been killings here," Jerry said.

Cleaning equipment in the corner sat buy a piece of equipment that gave Jerry a cold chill that ran through his bones.

"You might want to see this," Raider told Jerry.

He led him through the doors to another room and pointed at the dark entrance to another small room. Jerry turned on his flashlight and peered into the room. The walls were covered in the drawings of the hunter. The same as the ones they had found in the woods at every location they had been.

Jerry left the room and walked through the rooms back outdoors. He stood and looked into the woods with a stare of frustration.

"Where are you, you son of a bitch?" he asked.

Jerry watched as the other teams arrived on the location.

Tom walked up to Jerry and stood beside him and Herb.

"I have no clue what to do next," Tom told the men.

"Neither do we," Herb admitted. They stared into the woods, looking and hoping, for a sign to lead them. Jerry remained silent.

\*\*\*

"The place was sanitized, and another room full of drawings. Out in the woods there was another hiding place also full of the same drawings, but no sign of Steve or Lacy," Jerry explained to Lester when he got out of his car.

Lester put his hand on Jerry's shoulder and saw the defeat in his eyes. He looked around at all of the men who had searched through the night. They sat on the ground, exhausted from thirty six hours of climbing through the woods, searching empty buildings, and coming up empty handed.

He turned when the crime lab arrived along with five other officers the sheriff had called to the scene. "Take your teams and go get some rest. We'll get all this bagged and tagged and to the lab. We'll regroup in the morning after the docs go over all this to see if it can lead us anywhere. We'll find them," Sheriff Lester told him.

"You know they're already dead," Jerry said.

"Not until we find the bodies," Lester told him. "There are rooms ready at the motel in town, booked by the Sheriff's Department for the rest of you guys that need a place to sleep," he told the group of men.

\*\*\*

After loading up all the teams, Lester leaned over to Jerry and whispered into his ear bringing a small smile to his face.

"Hey, kid, you ride with me," Jerry told Tom and he climbed into the truck. "It was a good plan kid," he told Tom while he drove down the road making the hour trip back to town.

"They're dead already aren't they?" Tom asked. "Steve wouldn't give up trying to find us!"

"No kid, he wouldn't and neither are we. But even Steve would have to stop and regroup to find a new direction to look. We can't find him if we're so tired that we can't think straight. Steve knows how to play the game. He probably has this guy's mind in knots right now," Jerry said knowing in his heart that they were most likely dead, but he didn't want to admit it to Tom. "Why don't you come home with me? We'll get some food and some sleep." He picked up the phone to call Cindy to tell her they were on the way.

"No, I'll sleep better at home," Tom said. He laid his head back and closed his eyes. "Tell her not to make a fuss. I'll just go on home."

"Too late, she's already cooking, so if you don't stay, you'll piss her off," he told Tom with a grin.

Pulling up to the house, the two exhausted detective's emerged from the truck to the normal sound of the kids running and screaming as they streamed out of the front door and leaped into the waiting arms of their dad. Cindy stood on the front porch. Seeing Jerry with the boys brought a smile to her face.

"We didn't find him," Jerry said quietly.

"You will," she said.

"Tom, come on in, I have food ready, you must be starving." She grabbed his hand leading him into the house. Jerry led the pack inside.

"You know, you guys don't need me hanging around, I should just go on home so I can shower," Tom said stopping at the door.

"Are you sure you don't want to stay and have something to eat?" Terry's voice came from the kitchen.

He turned as Terry walked into the front room. A wave of emotions covered him and he ran to her. His eyes lit up as they had every time he'd seen her.

"What are you doing here?" he asked with excitement. He lifted her in his arms.

"I heard the news, and I couldn't get you on the phone, so I jumped on a plane," she said and they kissed.

"You are a sight for very tired eyes," he said and realized the stubble on his face must have been rough on her soft skin. "Sorry, I guess I need to clean up a bit." He rubbed his face.

"No, you look just fine," she said, her gaze never leaving his.

"Get a room you two, break it up, I'm hungry," Jerry said with a laugh. He grabbed Tom by the back of the neck and led him to the kitchen.

Sitting down at the table and eating, Tom hardly took his eyes off of Terry.

"So what did you find out there?" Cindy asked Jerry.

Quiet filled the room. Tom looked sadly into Terry's eyes and confessed, "I didn't get him."

"You mean we didn't get him, but we're not going to stop until we do," Jerry said.

Tom continued to look into Terry's soft hazel eyes, again feeling intense defeat.

"Someone will, I know he'll pay some day. I'm not here for revenge, I'm here for you," she said. She leaned over to touch his face with her soft gentle hands. "Now, eat so we can take you home and clean you up, you really smell," she said with a smirk.

Finished with the meal, Tom and Terry started to leave. In the front room Jerry's three little warriors watched cartoons.

Tom's attention was captured by the breaking news story that interrupted the show.

"We go live to the Sheriff's Department where we continue the story on the abduction of Sheriff's Detective, Steve Belcher, and our news anchor Lacy James. We take you to where Tony Winters is reporting live. Tony, what do you have for us?" Tom sat down on the couch by the boys.

"Jim, here at the Sheriff's Department, we have watched the teams returning from the search that has gone on for almost two days. None of the teams are giving us any information. The look on all of their faces tells a story of concern and frustration. As you know from the murders, the victims' bodies were found in their homes after the second day of their abduction. The Sheriff's Department has had both Lacy and Detective Belcher's homes under close guard since they were abducted. With no word from the search, it's feared that neither of them will be found alive," he said and the camera panned away from the reporter to Steve's car, sitting alone in the parking lot. "As you can see, Detective Belcher's car sits all alone, waiting for its owner to return," Jim said and the eerie sight of the car completed the sad report.

"Pause that," Tom said and he jumped from where he was seated on the couch.

"Jerry run that back to the shot of the car," Tom ordered.

Jerry grabbed the remote, surprised by Tom's reaction and paused the live broadcast on his DVR.

"What is it, kid?" Jerry asked as he worked the remote.

"Stop right there," Tom said with excitement. "Look at the house in front of the car." He pointed at the screen. "Do you see it?" he asked Jerry.

"Son of a bitch," Jerry said and hopped to his feet. "Let's go," he said.

"Where are you going?" both Terry and Cindy asked.

"Stay here, I'll be back in a while," Tom told Terry and he rushed out the door.

"Hurry up, kid, let's move," Jerry said. He revved the engine in his truck, inpatient to get moving.

Tom jumped in the truck and Jerry peeled rubber as they left the driveway.

***

"Well, it looks like just me and you, closest car is fifteen minutes out," Tom told Jerry after he ended his call with the Sheriff's Department.

"I'm not waiting that long," Jerry replied.

He sped to the station and pulled down the block to the end of the street. Jumping out of the truck, he pulled out his rifle.

"You go to the back of the house, and I'll go in the front. Sixty seconds from now we go in at the same time,"

Jerry said.

Just as they are about to make their way around the house, Herb pulled up behind Jerry's truck. He got out of the SUV.

"I saw you driving like you were going to a fire. What's up?" Herb said.

"You go with Tom around the back, the garages are all on the back of the houses in this neighborhood. I'll go through the front. Sixty seconds from now," Jerry repeated and they all checked their watches.

They separated and snuck around to their positions. Tense with excitement, Jerry approached the doors as the seconds counted down. With every tick of the second hand the adrenaline pumped heavily through him. The time expired and he lunged through the doors.

Jerry moved through the shadows inside the house, meeting Tom and Herb in the kitchen area, they stopped, in shock at the scene they found. Jerry and Herb moved to check the rest of the house. Returning from the upstairs, they found Tom still standing and staring at the gruesome sight of Steve and Lacy's naked bodies sitting at the kitchen table, bloody, with their heads switched and the dried blood pool covering almost the entire kitchen floor. With no one in the house, the three walked back outside to the front of the house as three patrol cars arrived.

"Seal the scene, no one goes in until the lab gets here," Jerry ordered the officers. He posted them around the house but didn't let them inside.

"How did you know?" Herb asked Jerry and Tom.

"Look up," Jerry said. They turned to face the front of the house and looked up at the windows of the second floor.

"Son of a bitch!" Herb said.

In the window of the upstairs bedroom was placed another drawing of the hunter standing on top of the pile of dead monsters with his sword lifted up in the air proclaiming his victory.

"He was right here all the time, right under our noses, and we spent our time screwing off in the woods," Jerry said. "And before you say or think anything, it's not your fault kid," Jerry told Tom whose face already showed that he felt at fault for the wild goose chase he'd suggested.

"You led us to find him, you had no idea he was moving around under our very noses within twenty yards of the police station," Jerry said.

Seeing all the commotion across the street, a news crew converged on the scene.

"Get these people back at least one hundred yards," Jerry ordered the officers guarding the scene. They strung up the police tape and sealed the off the scene for the crime lab. Jerry, Tom, and Herb watched Carol arrive.

"You sure you don't want someone else to do this?" Jerry asked her.

"No, they were both friends of mine, there's no one better to take care of them than me," Carol said and pushed past Jerry to enter the house.

Jerry followed her into the kitchen to see the horrific scene. She broke into tears at the sight of their mutilated bodies. She checked the bodies and returned outside. Tears streamed down her face when she and Jerry walked up to Tom, who comforted her while she sobbed.

"They've been dead for over twenty four hours," she told them and stood with Jerry and Tom.

The crime scene van arrived with Lester leading the way. Jerry let Lester lead the group into the house. Lester returned and walked up to Jerry, who still continued to stare into space, knowing the killer had bested him again.

"Right under our noses," Lester said. "How the hell did he pull this off with us, the State Police, the FBI and every resource we have in the area and he did it right here?" Lester asked

"A single silent warrior can kill every one of his

enemies in the dead of night with just his hunting knife," Jerry said reciting the words of one of his instructors. "He moved to this house when he took Steve and Lacy. He had to know we were watching for him. All of the others he killed in his slaughter house. He could clean there, no blood in or on the bodies." He turned and looked back into the kitchen. "He had no way to clean up here. He changed with the hunt, he adapted. He knew if he took Steve that we would be close behind. He had to get under cover fast. This is less than two minutes from where he took Steve. He had us beat the entire time."

"But how can he be that good?" Lester asked.

"Because he's a warrior hunter and he's still out there," Jerry said. He turned his attention back up to the window where the drawing hung facing out for all to see the child like written words of the killer.

*"NOW I HAVE THE POWER"*
\*\*\*

Somewhere in a deep thick section of woods, the hunter sat in hiding. Surrounded by his drawings to keep him safe, his arms wrapped around him to hold and comfort him. Sitting, rocking back and forth muttering to himself,

*"They can't find me here, they can't find me here, they can't find me here..."*

Made in the USA
Middletown, DE
10 October 2017